Hooked By You

Chicago Steel
Book 1

Jessica Buss

Hooked By You
Chicago Steel Book One
Jessica Buss

Published by: 907 Publishing, LLC.

First Edition July 2022
Second Edition July 2023

Developmental Edit by Emerald Edits

Copy Edited by Ink Machine Editing

Cover Photography by Eric D Battershell, O'Snap Media

Cover Model Carlus Tyler Reed

Cover Design & Internal Formatting by Feed Your Dreams Designs

Ebook ISBN: 979-8-9863903-6-9

Paperback ISBN: 979-8-9863903-7-6

Dedication

For Darren,
My love, my biggest cheerleader, my best friend, my real-life hockey romance.

Chapter 1

Samantha

Have you ever survived a tornado? I haven't, but in the last twenty-four hours, I've experienced an emotional one. The swirling chaos and confusion have completely overwhelmed me. I've been struck by the realization and truth of what I've endured. And it's left me utterly destroyed.

What triggered it all, you ask? A lifetime ago... okay, okay, hours ago, I was blissfully sitting in my fiancé Mitch's office in the heart of New York City, gazing out the window. The skyline was breathtaking, and I couldn't help being mesmerized by it while Mitch talked to a prospective client. Earlier in the day, I had flown in to see him, as it had been a few weeks since we'd been together. During the month prior, every time we talked, he'd complained about me and my lack of support for him and his job. So, there I was, doing just that, supporting him. He'd kept mentioning that he wanted me to be with him when he finalized a deal to represent an up-and-coming NBA player. And today was that day.

"Yes!" Mitch whooped as he hung up his phone. He lifted his fists high in the air in celebration.

"Deal done?" I asked, even though it was more than obvious. It was just another way to stroke his very sensitive ego. Being engaged to the Fox heiress, Mitch was always looking for ways to toot his own horn. I somewhat understood that. He was trying to make a name for himself.

"Yep. Marcus signed on. I'm representing the next NBA star." He flashed me a wide grin as he puffed out his chest.

"Well done, Mitch. I'm happy for you and glad I was here to witness it. It's too bad I have to get back to Chicago tonight and we can't fully celebrate."

Mitch shrugged his shoulders. "I'm used to it."

What? I was appalled at his response. Had I heard him wrong? "Excuse me? You're use to it?" Placing the papers I was holding down, I stepped toward his desk. "What are you saying?" It was impossible to hide the frustration in my voice.

"Whoa, Samantha. All I was saying was that you're usually in Chicago when I close a deal. Celebrating in person doesn't happen very often."

Hearing his words, I lessened my defensiveness, dropping my arms that I'd apparently crossed against my chest. "Then let's celebrate now," I offered while grabbing the bottle of Dom Pérignon I'd purchased to mark the occasion.

Pouring us each a glass, we toasted to his new client. As the bubbles trickled down my throat, I thought about what Mitch had said and why I'd been so reactive. Normally, his snide remarks about how I was never there for him weren't so blatant. He's passive aggressive at best and usually his words were wrapped in alternating layers of niceties and judgement. Today, though, they appeared distant, rude, and hurtful. Not caring to deal with it, I picked up the champagne to pour myself another glass when Mitch piped in. "Just one glass for me, Samantha. I still have some things I need to finish up here before calling it a night."

"Does that mean you aren't giving me a ride to the airport?" I asked, my confusion apparent. We hadn't talked about it, but I assumed that he'd want to spend a little time together outside of the office since I'd visited him. *My mistake.*

"We have drivers for that, Samantha. I'm sure one is still around and available to give you a ride. If you don't mind, I need to get back to a contract review before it gets too late."

Flabbergasted, I set down my glass and grabbed my coat and briefcase. Walking over to Mitch's desk, I assumed he'd at least stand and kiss me goodbye, but to my surprise, he remained seated, staring at some paperwork as if I wasn't even there. *What is happening?* His behavior completely baffled me as I walked past him.

"Bye, Mitch," I called over my shoulder. An unintelligible grunt was all I was given in reply.

Veronica, his eager assistant, called out something as I stumbled past, but it didn't register. All afternoon and evening, Mitch had been noticeably distant, and I'd shrugged it off. During our entire relationship, he'd never been overly affectionate. In fact, he'd barely hugged me when I arrived earlier. I got the feeling he was more excited to show off his accomplishment than see me. His cold and distant behavior was upsetting, but instead of turning back to his office to demand answers, I reminded myself it was because he was busy and distracted. Nothing more. I didn't have anything to worry about.

When I reached the lobby, I saw Frank, my dad's driver.

"Good evening, Miss Fox. Need a ride anywhere?"

"Hi, Frank. I was just about to order an Uber to take me back to the airport."

Stepping toward me, he offered, "If you'd prefer, I can take you."

Smiling, I replied, "That'd be great. Thank you."

We walked out to the company's Cadillac, and he opened the door. Just as I was climbing in, I stopped.

"Frank, I forgot something in Mitch's office."

"Go ahead and grab it. We have time."

Heading back up, I reminded myself where I'd set it down after Mitch had hollered. Stepping off onto the floor, I heard noises that weren't commonplace in the office. I stilled my Louboutins and took a moment to place what I was hearing. Instead of normal office sounds, I heard something more natural. Primal, if you will. The noises were loud, intense, and unsettling.

Since being raised at the office, I was definitely familiar with normal office noises like the hum of the copy machine, phones ringing, or the ding of the arriving elevator. But this wasn't that. Standing just outside the elevator, I remained frozen in place.

Intense sounds of deep-throated moaning and grunting filled the open space. I looked around to see if maybe I exited on the wrong floor, but everything around me screamed familiarity. Acknowledging I was on the correct floor, I quickly needed to figure out what was happening. Focusing on the rushed and frantic sounds that were only getting louder, I moved closer. Even though I wanted to cover my ears, my brain propelled me forward.

A small memory tickled my brain. The one and only time I'd heard anything resembling these noises was when I'd accidentally seen a porno in college. During my freshman year, I'd gone to a party at one of the off-campus houses, and when I'd gone looking for the bathroom, I'd unfortunately opened the wrong door.

"Mmmm, yeah," a deep voice called out as I pushed

the door open. Before me was a co-ed lounging on his bed, naked. In front of him sat his laptop. Shocked, I stood there, frozen. Is he doing what I think he is?

"I've been a bad girl, Daddy. Are you going to punish me?" a whiny voice called from in-between his legs.

"Yes, I am," he answered, still unaware of my presence.

"What the hell?" I cringed.

Hearing me, his head popped up, surprised.

Then he smiled and asked, "Hey, sweetheart. Want to join me?"

Even in my quasi-drunken state, I knew I wanted no part in what he was offering. "A-as if," I stuttered before I stormed away, disgusted.

"Baby, don't go. I'm just getting started," he shouted as I continued to stomp down the hallway.

Drawing on that memory now, I recognized the sounds I heard that night were eerily similar to the ones I heard now. I remembered hearing slapping skin, moaning, grunting, and panting. I knew I hadn't stood in that doorframe long, but even then, I knew I'd never forget them. Until that night, those sounds were completely foreign to my naïve self. Did sex really sound like that?

My brain scrambled to come up with plausible

explanations for what I was hearing. The glaringly obvious explanation was gut-wrenchingly painful, and I refused to believe it unless I saw undisputable proof.

Nervous, I quietly inched forward, trying to remain undetected. I grabbed my cell phone, ready to call for help if something was wrong. *Ever the Girl Scout.* Who was I kidding? I hadn't made it past Brownies. I wouldn't have been prepared for shit if it hit the fan. And if what I suspected was happening, the Girl Scouts definitely didn't have a section in their manual instructing you on the appropriate way to handle it. As far as I knew, you couldn't earn a merit badge for creative positioning or sex noises. Wouldn't that be a kick? Maybe it could be called Madame Scouts?

"Ahhhh." An unmistakable scream of ecstasy tore through the empty office space, halting me from my tangent. After hearing that, there was no way my mind could deny the truth anymore. I couldn't justify that what I just heard was innocent. *No!* Whatever was happening was scandalous. That realization knocked the wind out of me. Reaching out, I placed my arm on the nearest desk to keep myself upright. Deep down, I knew it. Behind that door were my worst fears come true.

The truth slapped me hard, and I was stunned. *Mitch?* Was Mitch having sex... *without me*. It sounded nothing like when we had sex. Rather, it sounded hot and dirty. And did she scream? Really? He never made me scream. Nope, not once. Not only was I appalled at what was happening, I also felt cheated.

I was horrified and disgusted. But then I heard something that made my stomach churn and my skin crawl. In an unmistakably nasally tone, the mystery woman's words came out crystal clear.

"Right there. Harder, baby! Yes! Just like I like it."

My stomach heaved violently, and I forced myself to swallow down the champagne that was threatening to reappear. *Brrrp.* Blech.

As I edged closer to the door, slapping skin and labored breathing echoed off the office walls. A full-body shudder overtook me. Just then a jarring sound rang out, resonating like a mallet striking a gong. It was a deep and primal growl. Even feet away, I felt it register deep in my bones. The growl was authoritative and commanding. *Mitch?*

Looking around the office space again, I confirmed his nameplate. In shock, a cold sweat and shivers broke out all over my body. My stomach became a war zone. It rolled as if it couldn't contain the monstrous storm within its borders. I grabbed at it, resting my shaky hand over top. I felt like I was about to hurl. What the ever-loving fuck was going on? I had to know. Had to see it with my own two eyes.

It was Mitch, and he was in there. But with who? The only conclusion I could conjure up was Veronica, his oh-so-friendly assistant. At that thought, I became enraged. Anger flooded through me, pulsating hard throughout my body. I could feel my heart pounding in my chest. My fists clenched and I ground my back teeth.

Just as I was about to storm through the door to catch them in the act, another thought struck me: Mitch had growled. He never growled during sex with me. Actually, the only noises I could ever remember him making were short, stunted grunts when he came after only a few shallow, pathetic thrusts. Quickly, my anger changed to curiosity. What was making Mitch react that way? Inching forward, I had to know exactly what was happening, what she was doing to him.

Silently, I cracked the dark-stained maple door open wide enough for me to peer in unnoticed. Doing this embarrassed me. I felt like such a voyeur. But that feeling quickly subsided when my eyes landed on them. And what I saw sucked the breath from my lungs. Clutching at my chest in shock, I held my breath. Mitch had Veronica bent over his desk. He thrust into her with a force that I wasn't sure was even possible. I'd never seen him like that. He had never been that forceful or aggressive with me.

From my position, hidden in the doorway, I could see that his standard, well-put-together look had become rather tousled. His hair, normally styled perfectly, was in complete disarray. Sweat dripped down his temple, and his eyes appeared wild and crazed. Even through his dress shirt, I noticed his muscles flex and strain. My eyes traced down to his hands and saw they were gripping her curvy hips hard; he was probably leaving bruises. But right now, I didn't think either of them were concerned about that. It was more than obvious in that moment Mitch was definitely physically exerting himself.

In all our years together, I had never seen him this out of control. I couldn't help but notice the tidiness of his white button-up shirt and tie. It baffled me that his entire outfit was untouched by the frantic movements he was making. It looked like all he had done was remove his mediocre dick from his pants before he shoved it into his slutty assistant.

Veronica, his young, mostly plastic assistant, was laid out across the uber-expensive, dark-stained desk I'd picked out and bought for him when he'd decorated his office a year ago. Her shapely hips, stomach, and fake breasts pushed hard into his keyboard. I couldn't help but wince. Bet that's painful. *Serves her right.* It was tough having compassion for the woman screwing my fiancé.

Mitch had her head pulled back toward him with his fist that was wrapped with her long red hair. Her glistening, Botox-plumped lips, frozen in the shape of an O, disgusted me. From my initial glance over her clothes, I noticed that Veronica's A-line skirt had been shoved up past her waist. Otherwise, she was fully dressed. I made note that she was sans panties. This I confirmed with a glance down her long legs. Nothing was around her ankles where I'd assumed they'd otherwise be.

As I took in the scene in front of me, I froze, bearing witness to my fiancé screwing his assistant. A myriad of thoughts crashed into me. *How long had this been going on? How did it start? Did they even wait for me to exit the floor before they jumped each other? Who doesn't wear panties to work?* Two realizations came quickly, and I was instantly disgusted, embarrassed, and angry all at the same time. First, this was definitely not a onetime occurrence between them. Neither seemed concerned with being caught, so they must have gotten away with it multiple times before. Second, Veronica must've known from experience that panties would only impede a quick office fuck. So, I guess by her not wearing them at all she was being practical, right? Was I really giving props to the woman who had been screwing my fiancé? Yep, it seemed I was. How messed up was that?

Before I allowed myself to dive down that particular rabbit hole, I knew I had a choice to make. I could interrupt what was happening and confront them, or I could document it and use it to my advantage. I opened the camera on my phone and snapped a few pictures of Mitch and Veronica in the throes of passion. I made sure that each photo showed both parties clearly. That way, there was no deniability factor later. Having seen more than enough, I slowly backed away, making sure not to alert them to my presence. Walking back to the elevator, my emotions felt scattered and chaotic. It was hard to identify them.

Reaching the lobby, I stumbled out of the elevator, through the lobby, and to the car. “Miss Fox, are you okay? Did you get everything that you needed?” Frank asked, concerned.

Shrugging my shoulders, I climbed into the car.

Crumpled, well-used tissues lie scattered around my bare legs. They sprinkle the plush gray carpet of my walk-in closet like snowflakes on a quiet pond in the middle of winter. Tear-stained cheeks and red, swollen, puffy eyes adorn my near-average-looking face. Just because I come from money doesn’t mean I look like a cover model—pristine and perfect. In fact, right now I look exactly how I feel—utterly destroyed. What you’d see if you came close is the epitome of brokenness. Or maybe it’s just the accurate depiction of my current state.

Truthfully, if you saw me, you’d say I looked pathetic, and you wouldn’t be wrong. In fact, I wouldn’t argue with you one bit. I know my truth. Normally, when looking at me, you’d see an independent, focused, well-put-together, confident woman. Currently, a rumpled, sobbing, snot-covered heap is all you get. Truthfully, that is all that remains of me—a mess. I’m wrecked with a capital W. What makes it worse is that I'm currently hiding out in my closet, in the luxurious penthouse I purchased six months ago when I moved to Chicago. I'd moved here to open a satellite office for my family's business, Fox Sporting.

Leaving New York, flying home, even arriving at the penthouse, is all a blur to me. I'd held it all together until I crossed into my domain, where I was finally free to let go. And that's exactly what I had done. My brain is in chaos and I'm massively overthinking. And unfortunately, that has led to questioning.

In the past hour, I've questioned absolutely everything. When I say everything, I mean just that. Not those simple things like whether I scheduled my next dental cleaning or gyno visit, but all the big things. You know what I'm talking about. Huge life choices like career, self, love. And the lack of clarity regarding those choices is bone-chillingly terrifying. Honestly, I can't believe how much my life has imploded in the last twenty-four hours.

Shortly after returning home to Chicago, my immediate answer was obvious. I would allow myself to cry, hide, and wallow for the next few days while I decided on my next move.

So, here I am, doing just that. From the seated position in my closet, I reach up and pull my pink, fluffy chenille robe off the wooden hanger and down to me. I form it into a pillow and curl myself into a ball. Tears stream down my cheeks and I fluctuate between feeling sad, angry, and embarrassed.

Ding. Ding

My phone alerts me to a text. It's been hours since I arrived home and relegated to hiding in my closet. But the phone is too far away to reach, so I ignore it. In the haste to enter my apartment, I must've dropped it somewhere in my bedroom. Right now, though, I don't want to deal with anyone. I bury my head farther into the robe-pillow I've made and try to ignore everything.

Ding. Ding.

The blessed silence lasts only minutes before another text alert sounds. The idea of moving still sounds improbable, so again, I choose to ignore it.

Ring. Ring.

Ring. Ring.

Ring. Ring.

Before too long, the phone rings. Repeatedly. However, I just lie there, willing it to shut the fuck up. The only person who has ever been that persistent is Mitch, and I certainly do not want to talk to that fuck-faced cheating bastard.

Ring. Ring.

Ding, Ding.

Ring. Ring.

Ding. Ding.

Ring. Ring.

"Shut the fuck up!" I finally muffle-yell into the robe.

The continued incessant noise of my phone shifts my feelings of grief and embarrassment into a blinding rage in a nanosecond. Angrily, I throw my robe away from me and stand up. Once upright, I stalk toward my discarded items, which are lying in a pile on the floor next to the king-size bed. Digging out my still ringing cell phone, my suspicions are confirmed. Mitch has been calling and texting repeatedly. As I hold the phone in my hand, another call from him comes through. He seems desperate to get ahold of me. *Why?* Silencing the call feels victorious. I want to hop up and down, pumping my fists, but instead I open my phone's photo album. There, in living color, is the proof I'd captured confirming that Mitch is, in fact, a grade-A douche. Pain rips through my chest. I hadn't imagined it.

Hurt, embarrassed, and angered, I send a text to my dad, the CEO and founder of Fox Sporting.

ME

Hey, Dad. Just wanted to let you know I will be taking the next few days for personal leave. Please see the attached pictures if you need any further explanation. P.S. I am no longer engaged.

Then I send a text to Mitch.

ME

Hope you got your deal wrapped up and you got EVERYTHING you wanted.

Mitch instantly responds.

MITCH

You finally answered. To answer your question, I did. It worked out perfectly. I'm totally satisfied.

My stomach rolls and bile crawls up my throat. Anger pulses through my veins. If I were the Hulk, I would snap my phone in half because I'm gripping it so hard. Taking a moment, I pull in a cleansing breath before I type out the last message I'll ever send him.

ME

Looks like!

I attach the pictures I'd taken and hit send.

Hitting the blue arrow, sending the text to Mitch, feels downright divine. Instantly, a weight lifts off my shoulders. Instead of feeling heartbroken, I'm relieved. Before anyone else can contact me, I turn off my phone. I strip out of my clothes, dropping them at my feet. Around my pile of clothes, I notice my red painted toenails and let out a weak laugh. The pedicurist told me the name of the color is *Can't Be Beet*. Because, no! I can't be beat. And tomorrow... tomorrow, I'll show them all. But right now? Now, I'm going to take a moment to mourn all that has happened.

I climb, naked as the day I was born, into my ivory jersey sheets. As I lie there, ready to succumb to the extreme fatigue I feel in every cell of my body, I realize my only set plans for the near future are to pack Mitch's few items from up around my penthouse and get him out of my life for good. Drifting off to sleep, my thoughts are consumed with my future and the uncertainty of it. One thing I know for sure is that I won't miss Mitch. I am unequivocally free. My future is limitless.

Chapter 2

Samantha

Two days later, I'm forced to face reality when my brother Christian pounds forcefully on my front door. I've been unwilling to turn my phone back on, and because no one has been able to reach me, he's come to hunt me down. Looking through the peephole, I see a man I barely recognize. Christian's appearance is unkept. His nostrils are flared and worry lines fan out around his eyes. Feeling horrible that I've worried him, I fling open the door, and he rushes in, muttering under his breath.

Why is he so worried? It's only been a day or two since I returned from New York, right? I mentally track all the time that has passed, and then I realize. Christian's dressed in a rumpled suit and my cleaner came earlier in the day, so it has to be Monday. Looking at my brother, he's grumbling and looks pissed. *Is he mad at me?* "Mitch, that cock-sucking asshole." His murmur causes a boisterous laugh within me. Whipping his head around, his smirk speaks volumes. *What? Did I say something?* His reaction makes me smile. It's the first one I've had in days. With my unrecognizable laugh, I feel some of the pressure wrapped around my chest loosen.

"You look tense, Sam," he sputters while pulling his hand through his hair. *You don't look so good yourself, big brother.*

"I'm better now that you are here." It's true. His grumpiness toward Mitch has lightened my mood considerably. It is almost like magic.

"Good. Come here." Across the room, Christian forces a smile, opens his arms, and beckons me. Walking into them, he wraps me in the biggest, warmest hug. "I promise you, I am going to destroy him." At his promise, I shake my head, and Christian pulls back, confused.

"Sam, he needs to go down. Mitch is and has always been, completely useless. The only reason he's still at Fox is because you were engaged. Now that you've ended things, we can get rid of him. Right?" His tone is stern.

"Christian, we need grounds for firing him, not just thinking he's an asshole. I'm assuming Dad told you he cheated, and that's why you're so angry?" I break eye contact with him because I'm embarrassed. "I caught him with his assistant, Veronica, in his office, just minutes after I'd left. Instead of confronting them, I took pictures for proof. Dad can use those as documentation to get rid of both of them." It's impossible to miss the acidic tone of bitterness in my voice.

"Genius, baby sis," Christian compliments. The wrinkles near his eyes soften. He smiles wide and pulls me back into his chest, tucking my head under his chin. He's always hugged me like this, and it's my favorite. I always feel so safe and protected. I know he has my back, especially now.

After a few minutes, he squeezes me tightly, lowers his voice, and asks, "But, really, how are you doing?"

I rotate my head, resting my forehead against his hard chest, shrug my shoulders, and mumble, "I'm doing okay. I just want this over and I never want to see him again."

Christian squeezes my shoulders. Then, like a big brother, he breaks the seriousness of the moment with an attempt at humor. Making exaggerated sniffing noises, he pinches his nose. "When was the last time you showered? Sam, you stink! And when was the last time you ate?" Annoyed, I scowl at him.

Perturbed, I hiss, "I do not stink!" As subtly as possible, I lift my arms and covertly sniff my armpits. He smirks again, and all I can do is roll my eyes at him. "Regarding your eating question, does Ben & Jerry's count?" I snort, amused by my snarky reply. Yes, my answer is ridiculous, but they say that ice cream is the known cure for a breakup. Doesn't everyone know this?

He laughs, shakes his head, points toward the hallway, and instructs, "Go, take a shower. Then I'll take you out to dinner. I got some fantastic news today and I want to share it with you." He grabs my shoulders, turns me around, and gives me a gentle push toward my bedroom. Receiving my marching orders, I whisper, "Yes, sir."

"I'll make myself comfortable. Take your time," Christian hollers from my living room as I'm walking away.

When I reach my bedroom, I enter it slowly. *What an absolute mess.* I look around and see the discarded pile of clothes and work items scattered across the floor. Ugh! Somewhere, beneath it all, lies my beloved Burberry leather crossbody briefcase. I bought it for myself when I moved to Chicago. Right now, though, it's tossed somewhere on the floor. I know I need to dig it out, as it's filled with paperwork that needs my attention. But as I stand there, considering the last seventy-two hours, I decide I can deal with it all later. Maybe after my shower and dinner with my brother, I'll be ready to tackle all the work I've ignored.

Reaching down, my stiff body groans as I grab the dirty clothes and throw them in the hamper. When I enter my bathroom, I slowly strip off the old, holey t-shirt and cotton shorts I pulled on earlier today when I heard my house cleaner. When I finally step into the warm shower spray, my body relaxes and my thoughts escape into the mental loop I've been stuck on the past few days. Each time I rehash my failed relationship, I come to the same undeniable conclusion: I never loved Mitch. Yes, we were compatible. But he'd never cared enough about me. To him, I was just the Fox heiress. A place filler, a status booster. When I look back, I can't fault him entirely. I treated him the same. The only reason I considered dating him was because he checked all the boxes of what I'd always been encouraged to find. Honestly, even after all these years, I don't know who he really is. What I knew was that we looked good on paper. We had all the components for a successful couple. It didn't matter if we weren't in love or even attracted to each other. Over the past days, I figured out that in our relationship, he needed me more than I did him. We were just using each other. For him, it was to get a leg up. For me, it was to fill a slot. We were just playing a game. A game that is finally over.

During all the reflecting over the past few days, the same unnerving thought has been triggering me. When I think about Mitch's cheating, I don't just get angry, I get enraged. The baffling thing about that isn't that he broke my heart; he embarrassed and humiliated me. And now, I have to deal with the fallout.

How am I supposed to face the clients, investors, and staff once everyone finds out what he did? He didn't just cheat on me; he screwed his slutty assistant at the fucking office. My family's company. What a slap in the face!

I'm grieving over all the years I've lost. Mitch and I started dating freshman year in college while attending

NYU. Following college, we both began our careers with Fox Sporting. He was interning under my father, George, and busy learning the ins and outs of the industry. I, however, was using my business degree to become familiar with the entire financial side of the company. My dad planned to hand the business over to Christian and me when he retires in another five to ten years.

Mitch, too, fit into that plan. Or so he thought he did. Shortly after we started dating, it became serious fairly quickly, and I didn't question why. Christian and my best friend, Monica, did and voiced their concerns. But I didn't listen. I thought they were just jealous. Besides, my parents loved him. Mitch had aspirations to become a sports agent, just like my dad. My mom was impressed because he came from an excellent family. If I had to admit it, those things also impressed me. Or at least they did at first. Our coupling seemed easy and destined, so I never questioned it. Why would I? Almost everyone around me told me that what we had was perfect. They told me I was so lucky. Only now, I feel the opposite. Thankfully, I dodged a bullet by discovering the cheating before we got married.

Not long after we'd started working at Fox, an opportunity to expand our offices to Chicago arose and my dad sent Christian and me to check it out. Christian was the agent and I was the finances, a perfect balance for the new office. The Fox board of directors sent us with orders to find a suitable location, establish the new office, and expand our company. It was an exciting time. I didn't think twice about going. The opportunity was one I couldn't turn down, no matter what.

Being away from Mitch would be difficult, but I didn't doubt we would survive. We both agreed this move was fantastic for me. I was finally going to get my feet wet with all the financial responsibilities at Fox. In fact, Mitch seemed thrilled about Chicago and my moving there. Already, he seemed to make quite a name for himself within the company. I knew little about that side of the business, but I knew he had been signing and representing more notable athletes the longer he was with Fox. He even had his very own assistant, which he seemed really excited about. He told me he was embracing every experience he could. In hindsight, all I can now think is... *I bet he was!*

I rest my head on the tiled wall of my shower and ask myself for the thousandth time, *how did I not suspect anything was going on?* The heat of the water and the thoughts of Mitch make me sick. My stomach heaves and rolls, and the carton of Ben & Jerry's Chocolate Fudge Brownie I'd hoovered before my brother beat down my door threatens to reappear. Mitch disgusts me. How did I not see the real him? Apparently, I only saw what I wanted. I should have listened to Monica and Christian the entire time.

Maybe then I wouldn't be here, standing in my shower, trying to piece it all together and discover what

I missed. Sorting pieces, I remember that shortly after I moved to Chicago, we traveled often to visit each other. Initially, almost every weekend, one of us had made the journey to the other. But that didn't last long. About six months ago, Mitch suddenly had less time and flexibility. His visits to Chicago stopped, and he had stopped asking me to come to New York. Feeling insecure, I expressed my concerns about that. Instead of acknowledging my worries, he dismissed me quickly, his words condescending and sharp-tongued. It was as if he wanted me to shut up and stop asking. Not wanting to upset him, I did just that. Stuffing my feelings down deep felt wrong, but who was I going to talk to about it? Everyone thought he was perfect, and I didn't want to hear *I told you so* from Christian or Monica. Apparently, guarding my ego took precedence over that of my heart.

While washing my hair, my engagement ring snags, and it instantly transports me to last Christmas.

Months earlier, when I'd traveled to New York for the holidays, I stayed with Mitch, even though he planned to work the entire time I was there.

On Christmas morning, before we headed to my parents' house, Mitch shocked me with a surprise proposal. If I'm honest, it was absolutely awful. After boring sex, where only he'd orgasmed. *Asshole.* He retrieved a box, and I instantly panicked. He'd said something that was far from memorable as I sat there, stunned. When he slipped the ring on my finger, assuming I'd, of course, accepted, I froze. I hadn't even given him an answer. Then he headed to the bathroom to take a shower, completely oblivious.

Even now, months later, I'm still confused. Looking at my hand, I scowl at the offending piece of jewelry. Finished with my shower, I turn off the water. Once I'm dried off, I do my best to make myself look presentable. First order of business is hiding the awful ring far in the back of a drawer, never to be seen again. No matter how angry I am, I can't make myself get rid of it yet. Maybe someday. Next, I pull on the softest bra and panty set I have. Adding my favorite jeans and a simple black tank top, I'm beyond comfortable. Needing a little bling, I add my trusty silver bangles that jingle when I move. Throwing my hair into a messy bun, I add minimal makeup before I head out to find my brother.

When I enter my living room, I see my brother has, in fact, made himself comfortable. He's slouching on my couch with his feet kicked up on my coffee table. Despite his lazy posture, you can't miss the excited looks and excess energy pouring from his body. Christian's also sporting a killer smile. He is the epitome of confidence. Over the years, I've heard how gorgeous my brother is. Woman fall at his feet, raving about his looks, but all I can see is my brother, so... eww, gross.

When he sees me, Christian shoots up from his seat. "Ready for my good news?" He has the energy of a puppy.

"Yes, Christian. What have you done?" I say on a laugh.

"I finally worked out all the details of the new contract with Lucas Bouchard."

"Who?" I ask. Often, I don't recognize the athletes our company is trying to sign with. Sports aren't my thing, unless you're talking about yoga. I'm a numbers girl who can lose herself completely in a spreadsheet as easily as a good book.

Christian throws his hands up in mock horror. "You're kidding, right, Sam? How do you not know who he is?"

"Is he an athlete?" I guess. Christian nods, unimpressed. "Well then, there's your answer."

"Yes, Sam. He is a professional hockey player in the NHL. He was the one I was scouting over Christmas."

I hug him. "That's terrific. Congratulations." My stomach growls. "Now, can we go eat?"

Christian just laughs at me as we walk to my front door. I'm proud of my brother. He's an outstanding agent, always going the extra mile.

Chapter 3

Samantha

After sharing his good news, my brother and I head over to Mateo's Italian restaurant. It's a hole-in-the-wall restaurant that serves the absolute best Italian food, family style. We share bruschetta, chopped antipasti salad, garlic bread sticks, lasagna, and tiramisu. I gorge, hoping if I overeat, I will finally feel something other than numbness or anger. While mindlessly forking my salad, my brother talks. "You know Dad will expect us both to come to New York to be part of Lucas's signing."

Nodding while rubbing my temple, I mumble, "I know." The beginnings of a migraine are taking hold of me, and I know it's only the beginning.

I look at my now bare ring finger and wince. My brother, always observant, notices and places his hand over mine. Our eyes connect and he asks one simple yet heart-wrenching question. "Sam, do you want to talk about it?"

A lone tear slips down my cheek and Christian wipes it away. Concern is stretched across his face; his furrowed brows and tight lips are dead giveaways. "I don't even know where to start," I whisper while blinking back crocodile tears.

He squeezes my hand and suggests, "How about at the beginning?"

"How much time do you have?" I joke.

He looks deep into my eyes and answers, "As much as you need."

Christian listens as I recount the past months and years with Mitch. He remains calm and quiet until I get to the part where I caught Mitch cheating with his assistant. Then, as if I flipped a switch, his body starts radiating with anger. A feeling I know too well.

"That fucker," he growls.

A surprised laugh rattles my chest and I smile. Christian catches it, quirks his head, and asks, "What did I say?"

"You said something?" I sarcastically question.

Through everything, my emotions have been in constant freefall, hard to identify from one moment to the next. But right now, sitting here across from my brother, I realize I feel happier than I've felt in a long while.

In my next breath, I confess something that's been

on my heart for far too long. "I never should have gotten engaged to him."

Christian nods. "You're right, Samantha. He's always been an asshole, and I'm glad you finally saw it before you married him. I'm not sure how I would have handled that."

"What do you mean?" I know Christian didn't like Mitch, but I didn't realize he actually hated him. *What would he have done?*

Shrugging his shoulders, he doesn't answer my question, instead shifting the conversation. "You know Dad told me about Mitch's cheating?"

I didn't, but it doesn't surprise me. My dad and brother are extremely close. Dad was probably venting about it to Mom, and Christian probably walked right into the middle of it. My parents wouldn't care that he heard. They knew he didn't like Mitch. "Mitch the Dick," I mutter to no one.

Christian hears it and laughs. "That's perfect, Sam."

After we finish dinner, while we're enjoying our espresso and dessert, Christian reminds me that when we head back to New York, I need to appear strong and confident. Show everyone Mitch didn't break my heart and I'm better off without him.

"Ugh," I mutter, placing my hand on my full stomach. Just the thought I might run into Mitch makes me feel nauseous. "I can't see him," I inform Christian, knowing that any Fox engagement will probably have many of the people who, only months ago, surrounded Mitch and me with congratulations on our engagement. Now I wondered if taking out a billboard in the middle of Times Square, calling him out on his cheating ways, would be too drastic.

A few weeks later, Christian and I take the Fox private jet to New York City for the signing. After a brief stop in the office, where I avoid any run-ins with Mitch—hallelujah!—Christian and I head out to our parents' estate. Once I'm dressed in my chosen armor for the evening—a new black Dior dress—I head downstairs to join my mom and Christian. Along with my dress, I'm wearing Christian Louboutin peep-toe platforms, which I know make my ass look phenomenal.

"Stunning, Samantha," my mom coos when I reach the entryway.

Emotionally, I'm still in a massive funk. It's not just the dissolution of my relationship with Mitch, it's because of everything I've been through in the past few weeks. I'm still so angry. Unfortunately, I'm not just angry at Mitch. I am angry and disappointed with myself. I've been so stupid. I allowed myself to sidestep my wants, needs, and dreams in order to settle for a less-than mediocre man. All the pain I'm experiencing is my fault.

As we drive into the city, my anxiety is at an all-time high, and I cannot stop fidgeting. Reaching over, my brother grabs my hand. "You got this, Sam. Show them the badass I know."

When we arrive, a marketing executive for Fox whisks us to Dad's office. Walking into the conference room minutes later, my family is a united front. "Looks fancy," I whisper to my mom as I notice all that marketing has set up for the press conference. The signature Fox logo, an artistically hand-drawn fox, is proudly displayed across the wall. Next to it is a large table where Lucas will sign in front of the larger news syndicates in attendance. They also set a promotional banner up for pictures. *I hope I'm not in any of those.*

Like the rest of the room, I'm waiting for the guest of honor to arrive. When the most handsome man I have ever seen walks into the room, it sucks the air from my lungs. *Holy shit.* Reaching over, I place my hand on my mom's arm to stabilize myself. Being in his presence makes me feel off balance. There's an electricity in the air and it's commanding. Suddenly, I'm restless and amped up. It feels like I've downed twenty cups of coffee, like I'm expecting something exciting to happen any moment. Around me, the sound of rapidly clicking cameras is deafening. Suspicions confirmed, Lucas Bouchard has arrived.

Over the last week, I have read more than a few articles on this mysterious man. Trying to familiarize myself with our newest client has been enlightening. Most of the articles I read mentioned his phenomenal hockey skills but also that he is incredibly giving in his time, service, and resources. Thinking back, I can't seem to recall any of the articles having headshots of Lucas. This, right now, is my first time seeing him. And, wow, I really like what I see. The pictures I've seen when he's dressed fully in gear and playing hockey do not do him justice. Not. At. All. They don't allow you to fully appreciate that, in fact, he is a certifiable god. Lucas is tall and in amazing shape, which you can tell by the fit of his tailored suit. His dirty-blonde hair is styled with an effortless look. Cheekbones that look as if well-known artist Antonio Canova chiseled them beg to be traced. A day's worth of scruff covers his face and makes him look rugged and sexy. His crystal blue eyes, ablaze with so much emotion, draw me in. It's a weird reaction I can't explain. It feels like I could get lost in the mystery of his eyes for days. I wonder if they're like Shakespeare, da Vinci, Cicero, and the Bible suggest: windows to his soul.

Basically, Lucas is the incarnation of all my dirtiest thoughts. Now, seeing all of him, I can tell you one thing: I want more. *What am I saying?* Obviously, my hormones are responding to whatever pheromones he's emitting, and it's scrambling my brain. Any woman would want to sleep with him, right? So then, why not me? Before I even consider that, I remind myself it's never going to happen. Grinding my teeth together, I chastise myself. "It's never going to happen, Samantha. He's a client and completely off-limits."

Lucas glances around the conference room and our eyes meet. Instantly, my knees turn to jelly. He tips his head and lifts one corner of his lips, shyly smiling at me. And my heart flutters. *Why is he having such an impact on me?* Then he steps toward the podium and shakes my dad and brother's hands before finally sitting down at the table. Christian joins him while my mom and I step to the side. My dad confidently strolls up to the podium. After briefly mentioning Fox's history and mission, he reads Lucas's prepared bio.

"Lucas Bouchard was drafted to the New York Chargers from the Ontario Hockey Junior League when he was only eighteen. In his first year in the league, he was awarded the impressive Calder Trophy, joining other hockey greats like Bobby Orr, Mario Lemieux, and Scott Gomez. He is an exceptional part of the hockey community. But what you might not know, something that also makes him exceptional, is what he does off the ice. Lucas volunteers many hours working for his own non-profit. He started it to benefit those in the community seeking to escape domestic violence. Standing here today, I am proud to announce that Fox Sporting is thrilled to be representing not only a dynamite professional hockey player but an outstanding man."

When Dad finishes his prepared comments, he invites Lucas to the podium. Before he even speaks, I'm already in awe of this man. I'm not sure I'll be able to handle it if he has a deep, sexy voice too. Shifting on my heels, I wait on pins and needles for him to say something. But before he does, he smiles. *Sigh.* Lucas has perfect white teeth and plush pink lips that I want to nibble. My heart stalls. *Seriously?* He has to have a girlfriend or a wife. I quickly glance at his ring finger and it's noticeably bare. I'm not sure how to feel about that, but I definitely feel something.

Lucas talks about his career in hockey. He mentions how grateful he is to have had so many memorable opportunities. You can see how passionate he is about his volunteering and non-profit work because he lights up like when he talks about them.

"Starting my non-profit was a simple decision for me. The community had a need, one which I was familiar with, and I had the resources to help. It hasn't been a straightforward process. There's no how-to manual, but it's been beyond rewarding."

Once done with his speech, he fields questions from the press about why he's switching representation and his future plans. Lucas shares with them he's switching firms because he feels like he needs one that holds the same vision as he does for his future. One reporter mentions retirement, and Lucas lets out a deep, throaty laugh that registers in my core before he answers honestly.

"You know as well as I do, hockey can be brutal. As professional athletes, we train at a higher caliber, hoping that the work we put in will be enough to protect us from injuries. However, sometimes, it doesn't matter what we do, injuries happen and sometimes those are career ending. My plan... is to keep playing until either my body or heart isn't in it anymore."

His comments make me wonder about several things. How long do careers usually last in the NHL? And what will he do after he retires? Lucas answers a few other general questions about the upcoming season and his opinion on whether New York will be in the Stanley Cup.

"Thank you all for coming. We are very pleased to welcome Lucas to the Fox family," my dad says as he steps back up to the podium. Everyone watches as he, Christian, and Lucas sign the contract in front of the press. Then they move over to the Fox banner for some photos. My mom reaches over, takes my hand, and squeezes it. I squeeze back, and a voice I never wanted to hear again calls out to me. "Samantha."

I hesitantly turn toward the voice that makes my skin crawl. Grinding my molars together, holding back the snarl that wants to escape, I offer an indifferent, blank stare. This is not the time or place for a run-in with Mitch, and I am keenly aware of that. Unfortunately, he is too, and he has me cornered like a trapped animal. Mitch knows how important this signing is to

Fox Sporting, and he knows that because of that, my behavior will remain controlled and civil. He's counting on it. Smugly standing there, challenging me. He's wearing a slimy smirk across his face. *What did I ever see in him? He looks like a rabid weasel.*

"Mitch, this is not the time. Please leave now," I murmur in a hushed tone. He freezes when he hears the coolness in my voice. *Was he expecting more? I won't give it to him. He's not worth it.*

No words are necessary for me. But needing to get out of there is. I don't want to ruin the signing and cocktail celebration, so I look for the nearest exit. Anger crashes through me, making me twitchy, but I refuse to show it. My mom, silently standing next to me, squeezes my hand and then leans into my ear. She whispers, "Go to your dad's office and I'll get rid of him. Join us at the cocktail reception when you feel up for it. I know your dad and Christian would love to introduce you to Lucas."

Relieved, I nod my understanding and brush past Mitch. When he goes to grab my arm to pull me in, I watch my mom step toward him. In her scary, warning tone that makes me shiver, I hear her say, "Mitch, darling, I don't think it would be very fitting for you to create a scene at this lovely Fox event, do you?"

As I walk away, goose bumps break out over my entire body. Thankfully, I'm not the one in trouble. My mom is incredible, but she can be terrifying when she wants to be. Mitch is now in her sights. I would like to say I feel sorry for him, but I don't. I glance over at Lucas and catch his eye; he gives me a sexy smile that ignites something within me, leaving me feeling warm and tingly as I make my escape. The feelings coursing through my body make me almost forget the interaction I just had with my ex-fiancé. *Holy hell!*

I head to my dad's office and decide to raid his secret candy stash. A little dark chocolate always makes me feel better. I find a dark chocolate and sea salt candy bar and I snap off a square. "So good." I moan to myself. I nibble on it, hoping to get myself back under control. Before I head into the cocktail reception, I need to shake the desire to harm something or someone. As I sit here, I wonder why Mitch is even at the event. He isn't senior management and doesn't need to be at the signing. All I can guess is that he came because he knew I'd be here. Will this be the first of many showdowns I have to expect? Right now, I'm thankful I work in our Chicago office.

Tonight, though, I wish he weren't here. I wanted to avoid any confrontation that would draw unwanted attention to Fox Sporting.

Knock, knock

Christian strolls into the office, looking as cool as a cucumber. "Sam, you in here?"

"Yep," I answer, popping the p with extra flair as he steps up to the couch I'm currently relaxing on.

"Let's get going. The cocktail reception has started,

and I promised Lucas I'd get introductions over quickly."

Sliding my heels back on, I look up at my brother. "Is *he* going to be there?" It's obvious we both know who I'm talking about.

Christian shrugs his shoulders. "He might be. Dad hasn't fired him yet," he quietly, yet hesitantly, answers.

"What?" I scoff.

"All I know is that Dad has been documenting Mitch's work lately. He has some concerns, and he wants to make sure Mitch's firing is based on his inability to meet the company's goals and objectives. Dad doesn't want Mitch to retaliate and say the termination is because of you," Christian confesses.

Even though I'm annoyed with my dad, I understand. "That's smart, I guess. But I still don't want to see him. My plan is to avoid him like the plague."

Christian pulls me to my feet and wraps his arm around my shoulders. "Let's go do this. I want to introduce you to Lucas."

After he escorts me to the reception, he's pulled away by some lingering reporters. Glancing around the room, I notice how elegant it all is. Silver and white cover every surface in subtle, stylish ways. The decorator must have worked hard not to make it look gaudy. "It's a winter wonderland," I whisper to myself as my eyes trace around the room, noting who's in attendance. When I realize I don't see Mitch, my shoulders relax and I take a cleansing breath. Glancing around the room again, I make note of who I'd like to see.

Just in case of another run-in with Mitch, I need a drink. I spot an off-set bar hidden in the room's corner. Approaching, I note the man already there. He's faced away from me, but it's impossible not to notice his strong, well-defined build that has me desperately lusting after a complete stranger. *What is going on with my hormones?* When I finally arrive at the bar, the bartender shifts his focus to me, ready to take my order. "Grey Goose martini, dry and dirty with extra olives, please."

The mysterious man, whose face is turned away from me, snickers and then mutters to himself, "Dirty."

Clearing my throat, I say, "Excuse me?"

He turns fully toward me and my breath catches. It's Lucas. Suddenly, the room feels overheated. I fight the urge to cool myself by using my hand as a fan. When he speaks again, catching me off guard, his words are clear and concise. He waggles his eyebrows playfully as he says, "You said dirty. Is that how you like it?" The serious note to his question lets me know he isn't just teasing. A devilish smirk dances across his incredibly handsome face and my stomach cartwheels. *Lord, help me.*

Unsure of what to say, I take a moment. *Is he flirting with me? Why?* He's like a fifteen and I'm maybe a seven. *Confused much? Yeah. Me too.* There is no way he's attracted to me.

If he is flirting, I'm in real trouble. Flirting is so far out of my wheelhouse. I've never been skilled at it and now when I need the skills of a master, I've got nothing. The most attractive man on the planet is face-to-face with me and I've gone mute. *Say something, Sam!* Otherwise, in a few minutes, he'll high-tail it out of here because I can't even manage a decent conversation.

Looking back over at him, I see he's waiting for me. I don't know how to respond. Instead, I just stand there mute, channeling a mime, secretly hoping a divine intervention will provide me with the right words.

Before I manage an actual answer, the bartender returns with my drink.

"Thank you," I say, plastering on a smile.

Taking a sip, I close my eyes and savor the way the refreshing drink travels down my parched throat. Maybe it will be the liquid courage I need to have this conversation. After another sip, the crisp, cool drink extracts a moan from me. It's delicious, and it's making me feel stimulated in all sorts of ways.

Before I open my eyes, I feel Lucas's stare focused intently on me, heating my body. When our gazes finally lock, I notice his azure blues are bright and expressive. They're full of heat and desire. I stand there as he peruses my body, starting with my hair, then on to my lips, breasts, hips, and down my legs. I've never had a man's eyes rove over my body like this. It's almost like a physical touch. Goose bumps erupt across my body under his pointed perusal. My stomach clenches, my nipples tighten, and I feel a deep pull on my sex. When his focus finally returns to my face, I notice him swallow hard. I lick my lips and smile at him. He mirrors it, and shivers roll down my spine.

"So. Do you like it dirty?" he asks again in a throaty, gravelly voice that makes my knees go weak. I place my hand on the bar, steadying myself.

"I do," an unfamiliar voice answers. And I'm surprised that the rich, sultry, desire-soaked voice is coming from me. *I sound sexy.* The smile stretched across Lucas's face stirs up butterflies in my stomach. Stepping closer to me, he places his large hand on my hip, pulling me closer. My body goes willingly to him. Still touching me, he traces circles over my hip bone in a slow, seductive, claiming way. My heart pounds in my chest and I feel lightheaded. *Am I going to pass out? No, I can't.*

Lucas's touch is incredibly intimate and sets my body on fire. "Let's go over there," he says as he steers me away from the bar with the suggestive grip he still has on my hip.

Where he leads, I will follow.

Even though I recognize this man has full control of me, I find I don't mind it one bit. My body is craving him and what he's making me feel. He's electric. The pull he has is both alluring and baffling.

After finding somewhere less crowded, we easily slip into conversation. The introduction my dad gave during the press conference gives me a bit of an advantage. Lucas tells me he was born and raised in Ontario, Canada, by his mother.

"The work you've done with charities sounds amazing. Can you tell me more about it?"

"I started a non-profit that oversees the needs and services for women trying to escape domestic abuse situations. We built a hidden shelter that provides housing and care for about ten women and their children. Our mission is to get them into either a job or an educational opportunity. We supply help in getting them healthcare and social services. We have legal aid that is on call for advice on anything they might need from child custody, divorce, protection orders, etcetera." He speaks confidently as he answers me. Passion, honesty, and determination infuse his words. I'm impressed with all he's doing to help these women who are trying to escape horrible situations.

"That sounds both impressive and comprehensive," I gush.

"I want to ensure that the women we help have access to anything they need to help them succeed in their new life. I want them to feel confident and strong as they rebuild themselves." He beams as he explains more about the shelter, even telling me he named it Hidden Angel.

"It's a beautiful name, but why call it Hidden Angel?"

"When I was a toddler, my mom, Amelia, left my

abusive dad and found her way to a hidden shelter for women of domestic abuse in the next town. My dad came from a rich family. He was influential and well-connected in our area, so no one would have believed my mom if she called the authorities. My mom told me when I was much older that the director of the shelter was afraid that because of this, my mom would find it hard to escape him.

"In the shelter, my mom had access to services that assisted her in finding a job, filing for divorce and custody, and finding housing. I was too young and don't recall any of it. My mom remained close to Patty, the director of the shelter. Patty has become like an aunt to me and has always bragged about all my mom has endured and overcome. Patty and her staff became our hidden angels, and so I named my non-profit as a tribute to them."

Chapter 4

Lucas

Tonight is going to suck! I mutter to myself while pulling on my Tom Ford suit in my spacious New York penthouse. Just another night filled with all the fake smiles, firm handshakes, and ass kissing I could handle.

Mentally pumping myself up as I walk into the conference room, I hardly notice the constant clicking of the camera when my eyes take in the most breathtaking woman I've ever seen, rendering me dumbstruck. *Goddess. Gorgeous. Decadent. Majestic. Bewitching. Mesmerizing.* My mind fills with adjectives to describe her as my eyes trace every curve. Standing next to Mr. and Mrs. Fox, I wonder if this is Christian's sister. The one he'd mentioned. The one who was engaged to a shmuck. His words.

Strutting up to the front of the room, I love that her eyes remain on me. *Captivating*. This woman is perfection. Her long, shapely legs, which I desperately want to wrap around my waist, make her a little over average height for a woman. She has shoulder-length chocolate brown hair with light caramel-covered highlights that give me a Pavlovian response. Licking my lips, I whisper to myself, "Divine." Years before, I had the pleasure of tasting a caramel turtle cake that my teammate, Josh Gibson, had hand carried back from visiting his family in St. Paul. The dessert had been delicious and sinful, unbelievable and life changing, just as I knew this woman would be.

Noise fills the room as Mr. Fox introduces me and again, my eyes find the goddess. My fingers flex, wanting to reach out and touch her. Visions of her naked in my bed with her sated body splayed across my sheets, fly in hyper speed through my mind. *Down, boy.* I swear at myself while shifting in my seat. Pitching a tent at my signing party is not the press I am going for. During my rookie year, I might not have cared, but the much older and wiser Lucas does.

Forcing my eyes away from the stunner I suspect is Samantha Fox is harder than I thought. I tell myself that if I look away long enough, my boner will deflate. And I swear to myself that I'll do whatever is necessary to meet her at the cocktail party later. She's like a flame and I'm a moth, completely drawn to her.

After the signing and various photo ops, we make our way over to a cocktail reception that is being held to celebrate my joining the Fox family. I hate being the center of attention, but it comes with the job of being one of the highest paid wingers in the NHL. Between that and my endorsement deals with Nike and CCM, I spend a lot of my time in front of the cameras.

After a few handshakes, I find a quiet bar off to the side, ordering something. Then, ten words spoken in the sexiest voice I've ever heard change my life. *Grey Goose martini, dry and dirty with extra olives, please.* My brain snags on the word dirty and spirals. "Dirty," I huff to myself. If she's as sexy as her voice suggests, I'd like to do some dirty things to her. Turning around and taking in the body that goes along with the sultry voice next to me, I almost swallow my tongue. It's Samantha. Looks like I don't need to hunt her down. She found me.

Not only is this siren gorgeous, but her voice is orgasmic. I'm sure she could get me to full mast in seconds by just reading a grocery list. If she ever got near my ear and whispered anything dirty, I wouldn't survive. I'm sure I'd spontaneously combust. *Was that even possible?*

She reaches for her martini, closes her eyes, and takes a sip. Watching her throat bob forces my mind to go blank. After she takes another sip, releasing a breathy moan, my barely there resolve almost shatters. If this wasn't a party to acknowledge my transfer of representation, I'd go full-on caveman. Pound my chest, throw her over my shoulder, and drag her to a dark corner to ravage her thoroughly. Thoughts of doing that race through my mind. I lackadaisically trace my eyes up and then down her body. Taking a moment to linger longer on her lips, breasts, hips, and legs. I notice a visible reaction in her during my open perusal. Her breath quickens, and she licks her lips. She enjoys watching me appreciate her body. I question how far I can take that.

Fuck me. Needing to cool down before I do something regrettable, I take a large drink of my ginger ale. The crisp bubbly drink dances on my tongue and leaves me both buzzing and very sober. Clear to make good decisions. Early in my career, after I'd made far too many bad ones, a senior teammate had pulled me aside and showed me the whiskey ginger ale switch. And I've been using it ever since.

When I'd checked her out earlier, I'd noticed Samantha wasn't wearing an engagement ring, and it's hard to describe the giddiness coursing through my body. Shortly after we began our conversation, I knew I wanted to get her to myself. For the first time, I feel an uncontrollable, possessive nature for a woman, and I don't want to share her. *Mine.*

My desire for her grows the longer we talk. She's not interested in shallow things but asks me about the non-profit I started. And for once, I find myself excited to be having a conversation with a woman, anticipating what she'll say next.

"So, what do you do for fun? You know, during the weekends or after work." I'm hoping we have common interests. Maybe we can spend more time together. *Where'd that come from? I don't spend time with women doing anything other than fucking.*

"To be honest, Lucas, I don't go out much. I'm more of a homebody. Other than yoga weekly, spa trips occasionally, or brunch with my best friend, I love to spend my free time reading."

"Oh, okay. Well, what are your favorite restaurants?" *For date ideas. Again with these thoughts. Has my mind been hijacked? I don't go out to eat with women, I go out with my boys.*

Samantha smiles at me, and it feels like my heart skips a beat. "My favorite restaurant in Mateo's. Their food is divine."

Scratching my head, it doesn't sound familiar. "Haven't been there. Where is it? Maybe we can go together and you can tell me what to order."

From the questioning look on Samantha's face, I'm confused. "Do you not want to go together?" I ask, feeling slightly dejected.

Samantha shakes her head. "No, I'd like to go together, but it's in Chicago, where I live. And you live here."

Knock me over with a feather. Learning Samantha lives in Chicago is disheartening. After tonight, I'll likely never see her again. Thinking about that hits hard, like I've been slammed hard against the boards. "Pfft." I let out a deep exhale.

Samantha notices and reaches out to me. "Lucas, are you okay?"

I nod as Christian walks up, effectively ending our conversation.

"Lucas. Man. Isn't this party great? I told you it'd be great." Guess he hadn't noticed I've spent most of my time here, flirting with his sister.

"Yeah, man. It's been amazing," I answer, locking eyes with Samantha, who gives me a soft smile.

The bartender approaches. "Excuse me for interrupting. I'm about to close out the bar for the evening. Is there anything else I can get you?" Then he winks at Samantha. Before I know it, I release an almost indiscernible growl, telling him to back off.

I'm jealous of the bartender. It's not like she's mine. What the fuck is wrong with me?

Christian side eyes me. Quickly, I look away like the guilty fucker I am. Unable to explain it, there's just something about Samantha. She's special.

Being around her is making me feel like a desperate man. And that never happens. With women, I am always in control. With her, however, I'm grasping at straws, trying to remember which way is up. She's got me totally off-kilter.

Chapter 5

Samantha

When Christian approached Lucas and me minutes ago, all I could think was, *here we go. Big brother mode activated.* We are all distracted when the bartender sneaks up, asking if we need anything else. His wink is cute, but my attention is stuck on someone else tonight, so I just politely smile at him.

"The reception's wrapping up. Do you want to head to a club with me? You know, drinks and hot ladies." I roll my eyes as Christian waggles his eyebrows suggestively. There's no way Lucas won't join him.

Begin let down in three, two, one.

"Actually, Christian, I was having a great time with Samantha." Looking at me, he shifts nervously. "I was wondering if you aren't busy, maybe you'd like to go grab coffee or something?" His eyes twinkle as he awaits my response.

Surprised, I gush out, "I'd love to. If you're sure?"

Lucas's deep laugh makes my body turn to mush. "I'm definitely sure."

What the hell is happening? Looking at my brother, I shrug my shoulders. He looks as confused as me.

"Okay. You guys have fun. I'm going to say goodbye to a few board members, then head out. Have a good night."

"Sure, man. Hey, next time you're in town, we can hang out?"

Christian nods before walking away.

"Let's get out of here, yeah?" Lucas commands while dragging me to the exit.

"Okay," I titter as my heart pounds in my chest. I'm both excited and nervous. The energy circling in my body is making me feel flustered. But in a good way.

Lowering his voice, he directs, "This way." My curiosity piques. Would he be like this in the bedroom? Demanding, controlling, dominant? Would I like it? At the thought of that and how I'm intrigued, a nervous giggle escapes, causing Lucas's attention to shift to me. He gives me a sly smirk, as if he knows what I'm thinking. And he'd be happy to deliver.

Since I lost my virginity during my freshman year in college, I have only been with one guy. With me, Mitch was a clean-cut, sensible, boring guy in every way imaginable. Veronica, however, may feel differently. *Good riddance.*

However, from my lack of experience and exposure, I'd just assumed all guys were that way. But every time I read an issue of *Cosmopolitan* or overheard some woman talk about guys she's been with, I'd questioned if something different existed. Those women had always mentioned being with guys who were crazy, wild, and deviant. Like unicorns of the bedroom. So I wondered, are these guys real? If so, I rationalized they had to be rare. I had never encountered one, not that I'd been seeking them.

Those women had always said the guys they were with were extremely confident and knowledgeable about their skills in the bedroom. That they could deliver multiple orgasms in one night. That couldn't happen, right? Over all the years, I could probably count on one hand the number of orgasms I'd received from Mitch. My BOB, however, was quite proficient at getting the job done. And the longer I'd dated Mitch, the more often I'd realized it would be the only thing delivering an O to me.

But as Lucas leads me away, I wonder if I am holding on to my very own unicorn. Is he like them? Like all those guys I'd heard about? Suddenly, frenzied feelings surge through me, lighting my entire body up. I can't wait to find out.

I love the feeling of Lucas's hand on my back,

expertly guiding me through the building, into the parking garage, and to his matte black Audi R8. "Let me get that for you." *What a gentleman.* After I settle in, he reaches over my lap, buckling me in tight and secure. I feel a stirring low within me. I press my thighs together, trying to ease it. Before he pulls back completely, he nuzzles his nose into my hair and whispers into my ear, "You smell divine." Shivers break out across my body and I thrust my chest forward, presenting myself to him. He steps back and gives me a panty-melting grin that promises so much more. *Eek.*

Once he's in the car, the air around us shifts. We inch closer together, mirroring each other. Lucas reaches out and pushes my hair behind my ear. When moving his hand back, he skims his finger down my jawline. His touch is heavy and controlled, but it feels sensual and decadent. *What would it feel like all over my body?* The temperature in the car is rising and I feel my breath becoming labored, as if I'm panting. Looking at me, his eyes focus on my lips and he licks his own. Watching the pink of his tongue dart out makes shivers spread across my skin. Suddenly, I'm desperate to have his sexy lips kiss all over me. *What is he doing to me?* Around him, I feel strong, sexually confident, and empowered.

Harnessing those feelings and throwing caution to the wind, I slowly lean into him. He reaches for my chin, tugging me closer. Our mouths collide. At first, his lips move tentatively against mine, but before long, things change and he pushes his tongue forward, parting my lips. Our tongues wrap around each other and he sucks on mine. "Ohhhh." A moan comes from my throat and Lucas responds by taking his hands and cradling my face in them, as if he's holding something precious.

Wanting more and figuring I'll need to instigate it, I reach down and unbuckle myself. Climbing onto him, I straddle his lap. "Tight," I mumble, with the steering wheel pushed against my back. Lucas lets out a laugh, then hits a button to adjust his seat. Changing to our new position forces me to grind into his lap. *Damn. That feels so good.*

Lucas growls into my mouth and sucks hard on my tongue. He then drops his hands from my face to my hips, holding them steady.

Effectively locked in place, I rock back and forth, chasing the high I'd gotten from rubbing my clit against his hard cock. The feeling is delicious and I pull back from our kiss to nip and bite him. Sucking his lip into my mouth, I run my fingers down his chest, taking in every peak and valley. Lucas's body is insane. He's like my personal Calvin Klein underwear model.

Feeling brave and wanting to take it further, I walk my fingers down to his belt buckle. Before trying to undo it, I slip my fingers behind the material along his waistline. With each pass, I let myself dip lower, and he sucks in, allowing me more room. It's like it's his subconscious giving me permission.

Just as I go to the buckle to undo it, his hands come up to stop me. Feeling like I did something wrong, I freeze, unsure of what to do next.

He says nothing. After a few moments of silence, he kisses me again. As we kiss, I notice his hands remain locked on my wrists. I try to move them again, reaching for his belt, and his hold on me tightens. He pulls his lips away from mine. Panting, we silently stare at each other. "Samantha..." he finally rasps. His voice sounds breathy, but I hear a hint of what sounds like sadness and regret.

As if I'm doused in ice-cold water, the realization hits me. In an instant, I understand completely why he's stopped me: he doesn't want me. I stupidly assumed that he was into this, but I was horribly wrong. After I tug my wrists from his grasp, I climb back into my seat and right my clothes. I grab my wristlet from the floorboards where I'd abandoned it and reach for the door handle. Just as I swing my door open, he leans over and tries to stop me. "Where are you going? I thought we were going to go somewhere and talk."

Mortified, I can't think of a suitable response. I look at the open door, then back at Lucas. Regret blazes hot across his face. And I need to get out of there now. "I think I'm going to go home. Tonight... tonight has been one that I won't forget for so many reasons. And because of that, I think it would be best if I left now."

Before he can even respond, I climb out of his car. Turning back to the open door, I spit out, "I hope you'll be really happy at Fox Sporting. Best of luck, Lucas."

I shut the door harder than necessary and try to hold my head high as I step away from his car. Heading back into the building that Fox Sporting calls home is upsetting. This is not how my night should've ended. As I stew, I order an Uber. While I wait for notification that my ride has arrived, I slip off to the restroom to hide. The last thing I need is to run into Christian, my parents, or anyone else I know. Heaven forbid if Mitch is still circling, waiting for another shot at me. He'll be sorry. There is no way I'd be able to hold back with all the emotion coursing through my body.

When I'm notified my ride is here, I scoot out of the building, lightning fast, and hop into the waiting car with Daniel, my Uber driver. The ride to my parents' estate is quiet. I try to focus on the music playing on the radio instead of my own chaotic thoughts. "This is what you came for" by Calvin Harris comes on and, in an instant, I'm sucked into the sultry song. Listening to the words, I can't help but wonder what it would be like to garner some man's undeniable attention.

The drive to my parents' house has always been peaceful and rejuvenating for me, but tonight, with my mind restless and the plethora of confused thoughts made worse by the song, I find it unbearable.

Before I know it, Daniel pulls into my parents' estate and everything is quiet. Either my parents aren't home yet or they're already in bed. Thankful I can avoid any more interactions for the evening, I let myself in and trudge upstairs to my old bedroom. Shutting the door, I kick off my heels, unzip my dress, and remove my thigh highs. Then, after I clean my face and brush my teeth, I climb under the covers in just my matching black lace Victoria's Secret bra and panties. Because of the emotional toll of the night, I pass out quickly.

The next morning, I wake up at ten o'clock and drag myself into the shower. Christian and I plan to fly back to Chicago on the Fox Sporting jet at two this afternoon, so I know I need to get moving. While the shower warms, I pick my discarded items up off the floor and repack my small carry-on. Once I'm in the shower, I stay longer than normal, allowing the hot water to work on the knots that plague my shoulders. I tell myself that I need to schedule a massage for the following week. Maybe my bestie Monica will come with me. We can turn it into brunch and beautification; my treat. Since she's a teacher, on her feet all day long, working hard, she's probably needing it too. Even though she doesn't make much money and she'll probably say no. But it's my idea, so hopefully she will agree to letting me treat us both to some pampering.

After drying off, I throw on some butter-soft leggings and an oversized organic cotton shirt I'd packed to travel home in. Pulling my wet hair into a messy bun on the top of my head, I brush my teeth and swipe some Chapstick along my lips.

Tossing the last items into my bag, I zip it shut. Heading down the stairs with my arms loaded, I hear the familiar voices of my parents and brother, and I stop in place. Preparing myself, I know I need to walk into the kitchen with my game face on. Even though I'm far from fine, I need to show them I am just that.

When I finally step into the kitchen, their jovial conversation halts immediately, and my pre-planned "good morning" dies on my lips. Looking at them, I wonder what's happening. My mom approaches slowly and hugs me. I freeze. *What does she know? Had she seen what happened with Lucas? Did she see me run away with my tail between my legs?* And I'm mortified all over again.

"Oh, honey, are you okay?" she croons.

Pausing, I look at the three of them and answer in a sharp tone. "I'm fine."

Christian steps forward and says, "Sam, we're just talking about Mitch and last night. Mom and Dad didn't realize he was going to come to the signing, let alone approach you. They feel terrible about what happened. Are you okay?"

Moving my hands to my hips, I'm relieved they aren't asking about Lucas. When I answer them, I make sure I'm calm. "I'm fine, really. Did he hurt me? Yes, he did. But I am not letting him win. I am over him. Okay?" I relax my stance, hoping they'll let it go. Plus, I don't need them to realize I'm still on edge after last night. Any further interrogation from them would be torture.

They nod at my reply, and I notice a look exchange between my parents. I know they want to make the situation better for me, but they can't. My dad speaks up next and confesses, "Samantha, I have been working with HR to ensure that I follow all the steps in order to get rid of both Mitch and Veronica. Honestly, I didn't think he would even show up to the signing. He knew you would be there, so I'm baffled why he even came. If I ever thought he would've been that ballsy, I would have attempted to shut him down before he even had the chance to approach you. I'm really sorry." I nod my understanding but keep my thoughts to myself.

Christian comes up to me and pulls me into his side protectively. He wraps his arm around my shoulders and hugs me tightly while confessing, "You know, Sam, we are going to take him down. We just want to protect Fox and do it all legally."

"I get it. Really, I do. I was just unprepared to see him. Right now, I am beyond ready to get back to Chicago and far away from any potential run-ins with him," I confide. That's only a half-truth. I want to get as far away from New York and all its male inhabitants who aren't related to me.

Christian again hugs my shoulders and suggests, "Then let's do just that." He pulls his phone from his pocket and dials the private airport to see if the jet is ready. After confirming that the flight crew is ready, we hug our parents, and Dad's driver takes us to the airfield.

Chapter 6

Lucas

After Samantha climbs out of my car and wishes me luck, I sit there, feeling unsettled and dismissed. "Fuck!" I shout loudly to no one. What just happened? It had been going so well. Our conversation had been engaging and entertaining. Kissing her had been incredibly hot. She was amazing in every way. I knew Samantha was more special than a car fuck, and so I had stopped us from doing just that.

Really, I had wanted to go somewhere and continue the conversation we'd been having at the cocktail reception, but when she climbed into my lap while we were kissing, plans got derailed and my brain short-circuited. Before I knew it, my cock was steering the ship and encouraging me onward. The heat coming off her as she ground into me was insane. Never had I wanted someone so badly. My body was in full agreement, as I had never been that hard and ready to blow.

She was the entire package. I already knew I would thank my lucky stars if she ever ended up between my sheets.

I lucked out that she was no longer engaged. But despite her availability, I knew I didn't want to be a rebound or regret for her. And because of that, it was only right to stop things between us.

Unfortunately, now, as I sulk in my car, alone, with a serious case of blue balls, I question if she and I would be anything at all. Her good luck speech had been full of hurt and spite. She had slashed me deep with her words, destroying me, and it fucking hurt. Apparently, all she wanted from me was a quick fuck. She had just wanted my body, nothing more. And because my dumb brain had forced me to be a gentleman and stop things, I was now even without that. What a fucked-up situation. I was a loser on all fronts.

While sitting there in my car, with my eyes closed and my head leaning back on the seat, a song I had never heard came on the radio. Its words struck a chord. The song, "This Is What You Came For" by Calvin Harris, made me instantly think of Samantha. I had watched her at the signing and longed to meet her at the cocktail reception. And when I finally did, my expectations were blown out of the water. She was even better than I'd imagined.

Seeing now that I screwed things up between us, I had a decision to make. Let her go or try to fix things?

What was I going to do? Our interactions over the evening had been electrically charged and unforgettable. Even though I was forever single, I still recognized how uncommon our interaction was.

Had I screwed things up by not screwing her in my car? No matter how many times I asked myself that question, I came to the same conclusion: No, I didn't. Even knowing that she would walk away in the end, I still would have stopped us. Samantha was more than a hookup. She deserved more. No matter how badly I want her, I would not allow myself to be that guy this time. If I were honest, I usually am that guy. You know, the one who did or said just about anything for a quick no-strings-attached fuck.

Over the years, I've had my share of one-night stands. But I'd always been clear about my intentions with the women. I had never asked for anything other than one night. Afterward, I didn't stay, and I didn't do repeats. And I was extremely selective about who I approached. If they approached me, it was always an automatic no. I didn't want desperate; I wanted available for the moment. Because of my status as a professional athlete, I get more attention and offers than I prefer. And because of that, most believe I'm a manwhore. It isn't the truth, though.

Over the last few years, I've let the rumors fly because it's easier than addressing them. I'd screwed up my rookie year. I'd partied too hard, and that came back and bit me in the butt in an almost career-ending way. After facing the realization of that, I've led a pretty tame life. I've learned I don't have to explain myself to anyone and not to care what people say about me. Those who matter to me knew the truth; those who don't could believe whatever they want to.

I drop my hands from the steering wheel, still shocked by what transpired between Samantha and me. The thought of being with her is mind-altering. I need to get her out of my system because we will never be together.

Needing something to do to get tonight off my brain, I pull out my phone, ready to call my teammate, Miles, and see if he's out, but the idea of actually doing that makes my stomach clench. What had she done to me? Just thinking about another woman makes me feel guilty. Why is that? I don't understand. I'm not committed to her. We just met. Yes, she is undeniably the most attractive, smart, funny, and real woman I have ever come in contact with, but I don't do relationships, so we'd never be in one. Even though I just met her, I know Samantha isn't someone I'm going to walk away from or forget easily. The scariest thing about that is that I don't want to do either of those things.

"Get your shit together," I growl out loud.

I start the engine, realizing that I've been sitting in my car by myself in this empty parking garage for quite a while. Not wanting unwanted attention for appearing creepy, I head home. I also want to avoid Christian, because he would definitely ask where his sister is. After the last hour, I'm not looking for a confrontation with him or having to explain what happened between Samantha and me. It's not like I could, anyway. I didn't understand what happened, so trying to explain it to her brother sounds like a guaranteed way to get my ass kicked.

Speaking of Christian, maybe in a few days I'll call him and ask for Samantha's number so I can apologize for the way things transpired between us. I feel like I need to explain myself to her. But I'm not sure how I would do that. The whole last part of the evening had been a clusterfuck. The only thing I understand about our last moments together is we filled them with misunderstandings and miscommunications. I need to explain why I stopped things from progressing any further between us. She had to know from my body's extremely obvious reaction to her I wanted more. But I never got the chance to explain my actions before she ran from me.

I drive home to my empty penthouse, promising myself that I will figure it out. I'll fix things between us. Once I figure out how.

Chapter 7

Samantha

Getting back to Chicago is just what I needed. I buried myself in contracts and other business obligations. I hoped if enough time passed, my anger toward Mitch and my embarrassment surrounding Lucas would dissipate. I visited my yoga classes religiously, knowing that if I kept my stress under control, I'd survive this. There was one thing that plagued me that I couldn't explain, though. It appeared the morning after Lucas's dismissal and was a persistent ache in my chest. It was baffling.

When I discovered Mitch cheating on me, I hadn't experienced anything like this. Over the previous weeks, I'd become introspective, and in re-analyzing my relationship with Mitch, I'd concluded all the same things as before. He wasn't *the one*, not the one I wanted for my forever. As I thought about it all, my feelings shifted. Regarding him, most of my feelings of anger had subsided. When I thought of him now, I felt only relief. Relief that I wasn't engaged to him any longer and that he wasn't in my life.

So then, why am I experiencing this discomfort in my chest, week after week? Do I have heartburn? Maybe acid reflux? There has to be an obvious answer, right? Besides yoga, I reworked my diet and visited my internist to have an STD panel and a standard blood-work panel run. The STD panel was necessary because I wanted to make sure Mitch hadn't left me with an unwanted gift from his philandering. According to my doctor, everything appeared normal, and I'm grateful for that, but I want an explanation for the incessant discomfort. As more weeks pass by, I notice the ache lessen. But it never completely goes away. I mostly notice it at night when I'm alone with my thoughts and not distracted by the business of work.

A few weeks after the cocktail reception, Monica and I finally meet for brunch. As we sip mimosas, we catch up on the past few months. She knew I'd broken off the engagement, but we'd both been busy with work and unable to meet.

Monica hasn't heard the full story yet. Like Christian, she'd never liked Mitch. While in college, one night after drinking too much, she confessed she thought he was slimy, shady, and only after me because of who I am. Over the years, she made comments about how she thought I could do better. Usually, those comments coincided with when he did something dumb. As soon as we got engaged, she held her tongue.

Truthfully, when Monica confessed her unease with Mitch years before, I had agreed with her. But at the time, I couldn't just admit that. I mean, if I thought so poorly of this "perfect" man, what did that mean about me? I hadn't been able to confront it, so I just ignored my feelings and continued dating him. Before I knew it, months together morphed into years and our dating turned into an engagement. Hindsight is 20/20, right? Because looking back now, I recognize my refusal to deal with it was just avoidance.

"So... what really happened with Mitch?"

Letting out a sigh, I give her the story. "I had gone to New York to help him celebrate a noteworthy signing, and minutes after we toasted it, he ushered me out of his office with the excuse of too much work to give me a ride to the airport. I'd forgotten some papers in his office during the rush of it all, and when I returned to collect them, he was having sex with his assistant in his office, on his desk."

Monica gasps. "Wait! What? The desk you picked out?" Enraged on my behalf, her face turns red and she sputters. "That no-good asshole. He's such a cliché."

She's right. Mitch is both an asshole and a cliché. And no longer my problem.

"Hold on... still catching up here. You caught them... having sex? What did you do?"

Nodding, I confess, "I didn't do anything but snap a few pictures for proof and hightail it out of there with my tail between my legs. I didn't want to see what they were doing. And the noises they were making? Monica, he never made those noises with me."

Looking at my best friend, I see her eyes grow wide. Then she leans toward me and whispers, "Do we need to kill him? Or maybe just maim him a little? I grew up on a farm. I've seen castration and I know we have the tools for it."

A laugh bursts from my lips and she looks at me quizzically. *Oh, shit. She's serious.* "No, Monica. I don't think we need to hurt him. I sent the pictures to my dad, so he's working with HR on how to take care of Mitch and his use of the office for his extracurricular activities."

As our conversation continues, she stops me and mentions she noticed something strange. "Sam, why do you keep rubbing your sternum? Did your breakfast give you heartburn?"

I look down, and, sure enough, I'm using the heel of my palm to rub my sternum. How long had I been doing that? I realize immediately that I've been trying to massage that nagging ache I've been feeling for weeks. Is it helping? I noticed the ache hasn't been as strong for the past few days, so maybe? When had it lessened? Was it after the unhelpful and inconclusive doctor's appointment? When I changed my diet? Or when I began doing daily yoga classes?

But the ache has a familiarity with it. A distant memory floats to the surface of my mind. Throughout my twenties, I read plenty of romance books, and I remember one specifically that shredded me emotionally. That novella gave me the same ache I now feel. During the climax of the story, when the heroine's heart shattered into a million pieces, it felt like mine had done the same. *No.* My ache isn't because of heartache. I know I'm definitely not heartbroken over Mitch. So then, what is it? The only person I'd recently had potent feelings for is... Lucas.

With Lucas, I still feel incredibly sad and disappointed that nothing came of our intense attraction and connection to each other. Despite that, I still wouldn't say I'm heartbroken over him. *That wouldn't make sense.*

Lost in my thoughts, I don't realize Monica asked me something. When she places her hand on my arm and squeezes, I come back to the present, feeling both confused and conflicted.

"Hey, Sam, where did you go? You looked like you were having a whole mental battle inside that pretty head of yours. Care to share it with the class?" Phrasing her questions like that always makes me laugh. It's Monica's standard, being a teacher and all.

I laugh and then apologize for getting lost in my thoughts. "Sorry, I was trying to figure out when I started rubbing my chest. I started feeling the ache while in New York a few weeks ago. It was the morning after the cocktail reception Fox hosted celebrating the signing of Lucas Bouchard."

"Wait! Your company signed Lucious Lucas?" she squeals.

My mouth drops open at her reply. "We... did. But I didn't realize he was so well known. Did you really just call him Lucious Lucas?" I ask hesitantly.

She nods quickly before she gushes, "Have you seen him? He is delicious, and I would do anything for a night with him!"

"Ugh." I groan at her response. I could have had a night with him, but that's far from what happened. Monica notices my reaction and looks at me with concern. Gone is the overzealous fangirl from moments ago. Before me now sits a fiercely loyal and protective best friend, sporting an intense scowl.

"Sam, what happened with him?" she demands.

Still embarrassed, I'm slow to admit what transpired that night two weeks ago. "We... uh... we kind of met."

"Okay, so you met him? Is that all that happened?" she asks, unsure of how to proceed.

"Not exactly," I admit shyly, and I feel my cheeks warm. I look down at the table, flustered. When she makes a disapproving noise, I look up at her through my eyelashes.

"What do you mean, 'not exactly'?" She parrots my response in her strict, no-holds-barred teacher's tone. The question gives me shivers; the bad kind. I feel like

I'm in trouble and being called into the principal's office.

"You could say we hit it off," I admit.

Monica gapes at me, then leans into the table and whispers, "What happened?"

"After talking and flirting for hours, we decided to go somewhere and spend more time together. He even passed up an opportunity to go to a club with my brother."

Monica nods and motions for me to continue my story.

"We left the party and made our way to the building's garage so we could go get coffee or something. Honestly, we didn't have a plan. After I'd gotten in his car, he reached over my seat and buckled me in. Who does that?" I squeal and look at her for acknowledgement. But all she does is stare at me with her mouth agape.

"Once in the car, things between us escalated quickly. Kissing turned into me straddling his lap and rubbing up against his erection while his hands anchored my hips. The pressure between us was delicious and addictive."

Monica lets out a breath and starts fanning herself. I laugh.

"That is so hot! When did you become a sexual deviant?" she teases, then laughs.

"Deviant, you say? Hardly! But it was the first time I have ever felt that confident and gone for what I wanted. And Lucas seemed really into it. Well, I guess *seemed* is the correct word, anyway," I reply.

"Seemed? What does that mean?" she asks, a confused look on her face.

"We were going at it pretty hard. Basically, I was dry humping him, in his car, in a parking garage. And he was hard as a pipe below me. I wanted to take things further, so I tried. And failed," I ashamedly confide, my head hanging low.

"Car sex? Is that what you were going for? Sam, that is so unlike you. But, hold up, what do you mean, failed? Did you slam down on his cock and hurt him before it even got fun?"

"No! I did not break his cock. But his reaction to me certainly stopped and shut down any future fun we could have had."

Her eyes widen. "What happened?" she asks, exasperatedly.

"After my second failed attempt, I felt completely humiliated. Assuming from his rejection, he hadn't wanted to be with me. Apparently, he was just looking for a good time and I wasn't it. Pissed, I got the message loud and clear."

Monica reaches across the table and grabs my hands. "Sweetie, I am so sorry." I just shake my head and mumble something about it being fine.

"No, it is not! Maybe if the situation had been different, things would have ended differently?" she questions with genuine concern in her voice.

I shrug my shoulders and answer, "Guess we'll never know. But what do you mean, if the situation would have been different?"

"Well, maybe he finally realized that fucking the heir of his new management team in his car, just hours after he signed his contract, could go horribly wrong."

I think about that and hang my head, feeling even worse. "Yeah, you're probably right. But what would've been the harm? He wanted me, I know it. Or can that be faked?"

Monica snorts. "Girl, you know better than anyone. That shit can be faked. Well, at least for women it can. But men can't fake a hard cock. It's not physically possible. If I were a betting woman, I would guess he finally realized the situation that you were in could be a career ender for him. And the thought of that sobered him quickly. I would guess that he reciprocated the connection and attraction that you felt."

"I don't know. I wasn't looking for a relationship. I wasn't trying to trap him into anything. I was just looking for a good time. Lesson learned, I guess. Instead, I just need to focus on me and what I want, and go after that," I tell my bestie. Although, I'm not sure who I'm trying to convince more, her or me.

Monica gives me a shit-eating grin, knowing exactly what I'm doing and says, "Sure." Her tone drips with sarcasm. I wouldn't even need to know her as well as I do to know she doesn't buy my redirection. She laughs and then rolls her eyes at me.

"Enough about me. What is going on with you? Any men you are embarrassing yourself with?" I laugh at myself, because at this point, what are my options?

"Seriously, Sam. No men in my life. I swore off them. You know that."

I roll my eyes because I don't believe her. She has a major lady boner for my brother. Still. "Even Christian?" I sweetly ask. They have insane chemistry, and it's been ongoing for forever. Monica has been pining over Christian, while he's been busy filling his time and bed with ditzy, self-absorbed, materialistic women. Someday—I hope sooner rather than later—he'll figure out those women are nothing like my best friend, a.k.a. his soul mate. Until then, he's settling for moments of pleasure and potential STDs.

At the mention of my brother's name, Monica gets quiet and looks away. Reaching over, I cover her hand with mine. "Monica. You know you deserve the best, right? He's out there. If my brother remains completely clueless, it only means there is something better out there for you. Okay?" Monica shrugs and her glassy eyes tell me everything I need to know. *He is losing her and it's his own damn fault. What an absolute moron.*

Seeing her in pain, I decide to switch the topic. "What are you doing two weeks from today?"

"Same time?" she asks, and I nod. "Nothing that I can think of. Why?"

"Outstanding. Pencil me in. I need the whole day."

Her eyes ask *"for what,"* which of course I don't

give her, and hesitantly, she agrees. "I have to cut this short because I need to get to the office to finish some paperwork before Monday."

As we say goodbye, we make plans to meet up in a couple of weeks. She doesn't know it, but I'm going to schedule some much-needed pampering. We both deserve it, and I am so beyond grateful my best friend lives in the same city as I do. I know I am going to need her, especially now.

Chapter 8

Lucas

Knowing I screwed up with Samantha and wanting to explain what happened between us a few weeks ago, I reach out to Christian. Hopefully, he can help a brother out.

Ring, Ring.

"Hey, Lucas. What's up, man?"

"Not much. Heading to Chicago for some games and I wanted to know if you were planning to come. Do you need tickets?"

"I'd love a ticket if you can manage it." Christian laughs. He knows I can manage that.

"Cool. Do you think Samantha would want to go?" *Can he tell I'm nervous as fuck?*

"Samantha? My sister? She doesn't do sports. I doubt she'd want to come." Again with the laughter. *What's with him?*

I breathe out slowly. *How am I going to get her to*

come? "I was hoping to take you both out to dinner after the game. You know, see some friendly faces?"

"That'd be nice. Better than a beer, for sure. I'll pick Samantha's favorite restaurant and she'll definitely say yes." Even though I can't see him, I know he's wearing a smirk. I can hear it in his voice.

"Oh, and Christian, maybe don't tell her it's with me. We can surprise her." Hoping my request sounds fun rather than creepy, I patiently wait for his reply.

"Sure, man. Hey, I've got to go. I have a meeting I need to get to. See you next week."

"Thanks, Christian. I'll have the tickets at will call for you and we can meet up in the tunnel after the game."

"Sounds good, brother. Bye."

Since the night we met, I've thought about Samantha non-stop, and I need to make things right. Now I just have to get through the games and to dinner. Every time I think about seeing her, I have two immediate responses: I want to puke because I'm beyond nervous, or I want to jump for joy and kiss her senseless. But, of course, that is after I beg for forgiveness for being an asshole.

The first night's game went well. I scored a goal and an assist. Tonight, the stakes are even higher, but I'm not talking about the game. Earlier today, my heart soared when I read the text from Christian informing me he'd convinced Samantha to attend the game and dinner tonight. I asked him to withhold that I, too, would be at dinner. Christian made reservations and promised it's Samantha's favorite. Hopefully, that alone will put her in a good mood. I'm incredibly nervous as I head to the arena. In a few hours, I'll have the answer to the question that's been plaguing me for weeks. When I explain what happened, will she listen? Will we be able to move past it? I've realized I'm still into her and, although that feeling is new, I'd like to explore it.

Chapter 9

Samantha

Christian has somehow convinced me to go to a Chicago Steel Hockey game tonight. I've never been a sports fan, despite being surrounded by it and professional athletes my entire life. When my father was in his thirties, he started Fox Sporting, and he has built it into a premier firm that represents athletes in all the major professional sporting leagues. Before college, I knew I'd have a place there if I was interested, and seeing that numbers always intrigued me, I found my niche on the accounting side of the business.

Last week, when Christian was attempting to convince me to join him, he promised me something he'd known I wouldn't pass on: dinner at Mateo's. Since finding it shortly after moving to Chicago, I'd eaten there almost monthly. It was the most amazing

Italian food, and the owners, Mateo and Josephina, were some of the nicest people I'd ever met.

Ding, dong. Ding, dong.

Opening my door, I'm greeted by my brother, who's smirking. "Ready to get this show on the road?"

Rolling my eyes at him, I reply, "Tell me again why we're going tonight."

"You mean other than I got free tickets?" Again, he smirks. *Why did I agree to this?* As if he's reading my mind, he says, "Remember I'm taking you out to Mateo's after this. Try not to have too much fun, sis. Anyway, let's go. We don't want to be late and miss something." Locking my front door, I follow him. *Maybe watching a bunch of attractive men geared up and flying around the ice will be entertaining. Hell, maybe there will even be a fight. That I can totally get onboard with.*

"Doesn't the game start at seven?" I ask, confused that we're already leaving. I mean, I don't want to be at the arena any longer than I have to.

Christian nods his head while we wait for the elevator. "Yes, it starts at seven, and yes, I realize it's almost six, but I need to check in with a player who is looking for new representation. He told me the best time to grab him is before they warm up tonight. Don't worry, I'll buy you a peppermint mocha for your sacrifice of additional time."

Smacking his arm, I mutter, "Smart ass." *Just for*

that, he's going to get me an extra-large mocha. That'll show him.

After we get to the arena, Christian gets me my drink before showing me where our seats are. Once I'm settled, he leaves me and heads toward the ice. Is he just going to walk out there? That can't be safe, especially with the shoes he's chosen to wear. At the last minute, he turns and heads toward a large opening in the stands, a concrete section, where he's ushered away by an arena employee. Waiting for his return, I glance around the arena, which is still relatively empty. Plenty of people look to be finding their seats, and kids holding signs have gathered where I know the teams enter from. A few sections away, I notice a family that must be visiting Chicago. They're wearing New York Chargers jerseys and enjoying a dinner consisting entirely of arena food. I pause when my thoughts finally register. *Chicago is playing the New York Chargers tonight?* It never occurred to me to ask Christian who the other team was. As the realization Lucas may be here settles, my blood runs cold, chilling me to the bone. *It's not like I'm going to see him up close.* Taking a sip of my drink, hoping it'll warm and settle me, the mint and chocolate duo dance on my tongue. "Mmmm, so good."

Christian barks a laugh to my left. While I was people-watching, he must've slipped into the chair next to me. "How's your coffee, Sam?"

With my hands wrapped around the white cup, I

take another sip before answering. "It's amazing, but I might need another if you expect me to survive the temperature in here. I'm about to be a Samapop."

Christian's confusion covers his face. "What are you saying?"

Even if I made the word up, I answer in an unquestioning tone. "You know, a Samapop. It's another word for a Samantha popsicle."

Christian shakes his head and mutters, "Ridiculous," under his breath. A smile spreads across my face. Even though my brother gets on my nerves, I'm thankful I have him.

"Hey, who'd you have to meet?" Nervous he's going to say Lucas, I hold my breath. I get they are friends, and I won't stand in the way of that, but I have no plans to either see Lucas or tell Christian what happened between us.

Motioning to the ice just as the teams take the ice, he points to number eight. "That's Johnny Stone. He's talking about switching agents, but I can't gauge whether he's actually agent shopping or not. I hoped that by talking to him on his own turf, I'd get the actual story, but no luck." Breathing out slowly, I go to take another drink of my mocha when he points to the other side of the ice. Following his finger, I see the one person I'm not the least bit interested in. *Liar.* "There's Lucas Bouchard over there. Remember, you met him a few weeks ago in New York at his signing. You two hit it off, right?" Swallowing hard, I wince, then quickly nod so Christian won't suspect anything.

Feeling like I need to answer him, I stutter out, "Y-yes, I remember meeting him. We had a friendly conversation, but it ended shortly after we left you. We didn't end up going anywhere together."

Christian replies with a surprised, "Oh!" *Had Lucas told him something different?* Obviously, he hadn't shared what really happened, because we wouldn't be here if he had.

Needing a distraction, I switch topics. "We're still going to Mateo's after the game, right?"

He nods. Once the game begins, we settle into our seats and watch as the teams battle it out on the ice. When it's over, Chicago beats New York, 2 to 1, and Lucas scored the lone goal for the Chargers. Even though I'm still hurt by what happened between us, I can admit that he is quite an impressive player.

After the game, Christian drags me into the players' tunnel to say hello to a few of the players Fox represents. While doing that, I distract myself on my phone with a new game I downloaded. Following that, we grab a cab over to Mateo's. As soon as we enter, we're greeted with hugs and cheek kisses by Mateo and Josephina. They whisk us off to their best table and tell us their top server will be with us shortly. My mouth practically waters at the thought of the meal that's just moments away.

Chapter 10

Lucas

After the game, I shower like usual. When I enter the players' tunnel, there's a nervous energy buzzing around me. *How will tonight go?* Reminding myself of the importance of this apology keeps me moving forward past my fears and worries.

As I wait for my Uber, I picture Samantha. Minutes ago, in the tunnel, she was standing only feet away from me, completely unaware of my presence. I'd noticed she wasn't dressed in anything fancy, but she was still stunning. The way her jeans hugged her made me jealous. I wanted to be wrapped around her. *Naked*. Apparently, my cock has an opinion. As usual, he wants to focus on the physical side of things. However, my brain just wants to be with her—to sit, talk, laugh, get to know her better.

I hop into the Uber when it pulls up and we head

to the restaurant. When I arrive, I take a moment outside, trying to get control over my unsteady heartbeat. I wipe my sweaty palms on the sweater I'd thrown on over my button-up shirt and tie. For once, I'm thankful for Coach insisting we dress up for games. Tonight, I'm grateful I went for something more relaxed than a stiff suit. Less intimidating, I hope?

When I finally make it inside, I'm only ten minutes late. A hostess leads me to the table, and as I approach, my tongue becomes thick and dry like the Sahara. My nerves are working overtime. I sweat more, and my brain stops functioning. Christian looks at me and smiles nervously. I probably look like I'm having a stroke. His uneasy look further worries me. I hadn't told him what happened the night Samantha and I met. I mean, how do you tell your friend, the big brother of the woman who you're interested in, that the last time you saw her, you fucked it up? No, not just fucked it up. You royally fucked it up. I didn't want to tell him that while we'd been getting busy in my car, I'd shut her down suddenly, with no explanation. Like an asshole, I'd left her completely clueless and possibly blaming herself for what transpired. If I would have told Christian any part of that, we wouldn't be cool. If he knew I treated his sister that way, I wouldn't be here. I know if he found out, it would piss him off. I don't know what he's going to do when he realizes I'm interested in her. Being here is a risk. But it's one I'm willing to take. I don't want to miss the opportunity to apologize and explain myself to Samantha.

Stepping up next to Samantha—she's facing away from me—I freeze, waiting to see if she'll notice me. Taking a breath and silently willing my anxiety to leave my body proves pointless. *Go on.*

"Hi, you two. Thanks for inviting me to dinner. It's great to see familiar faces." My words rush out. Looking from Christian's worried expression to the surprise on Samantha's face, panic sets in. *Danger. Danger.* Suddenly, I'm confident my dinner suggestion was a horrible idea. Samantha doesn't want to see me. The smart thing to do would be to leave immediately. Stepping back, I'm ready to run from the restaurant, when Christian quickly stands up and grabs my arm, encouraging me to stay.

"Thanks for joining us. You had a great game tonight. Too bad you still lost to the hometown boys," he jokes as if he is trying to extinguish the awkward mood that swarms around us. I'm beyond terrified, but I know I need to at least apologize. Samantha deserves that from me. Even if she never forgives me. Digging deep, I suck it up and press forward.

"Hey, Samantha! Is it okay if I join you?" I ask nervously as I rock back and forth on my heels—a habit I've had since I was a boy.

Always polite, she turns to me and simply nods her head. I pull out the chair next to Christian, trying to give her as much space as possible. I remind myself I need to be calm and not rush or force my apology. If only it were just the two of us, this would be easier. But beggars can't be choosers, so I'll take what I can get.

Christian orders meals for the table because he told me they come here often. He knows what's best. I've learned with all the traveling I've done that it's always best to defer to locals regarding what and where to eat.

"How's the season going?" Christian asks uncomfortably. He knows exactly how my season is going. We talk all the time.

Scratching my head, I reply, "It's fine. Thanks for asking. How's everything at Fox? Any new sponsorship connections for me?" I laugh awkwardly. Samantha remains silent.

"Nah, man. Just signed a new NBA player to my load." Christian smiles. Samantha picks at her nails.

"How are your parents?" I ask, hoping that will engage her. She looks up at Christian and smiles.

"They're great. Thanks for asking. In fact, Dad is planning to go to your next game in New York. Every time we talk, he tells me he has to 'monitor the new talent.'" We both laugh and I hear a titter from Samantha. *Maybe, just maybe, this will be my way in.*

Looking at Samantha's down-turned head, I ask, "How have you been doing, Samantha?"

Her big brown eyes look up at me, surprised I asked her anything. "I've been fine. And you?"

Making eye contact, I confess, "I've been alright, but I've definitely been looking forward to this dinner."

There. I didn't say too much, but hopefully, she'll read between the lines.

Our dinner arrives at the table, and the amount of food is massive. *There's no way three people can consume this much food.*

Pushing back from the table, Christian stands. "I just remembered a meeting I have to get to. Sorry, I can't stay. I'll take care of the bill. Lucas, call me next time you're in town. Sam, see you at the office." Then he strolls away without another word.

Samantha and I stare at each other, not fully understanding what's happening. It's beyond uncomfortable. Did Christian set this up? He didn't know I wanted to apologize. Maybe he's assuming something more, considering what we were like when we were last together. I don't know whether to be mad or happy. Samantha, however, could definitely be the mayor of mad camp. She forces a smile and whispers, "You don't need to stay for my sake. I can have them box this all up and you can head off to wherever you would rather be tonight."

I shake my head, disbelieving what she said. "Samantha, I know I majorly fucked up the last time I saw you. I want to be here with you. I asked your brother to arrange this, hoping that I could apologize for what happened that night."

She brings her light brown eyes up to mine, and they are so sad. Immediately, I feel like shit. I caused this. The night of the reception, I tried to be the respectful guy for once, and because I couldn't explain that to her at the time, I made her feel terrible. "You want to be here? Why?" she asks suspiciously.

"I do," I confess. I smile at her, hoping she'll take my words as the truth. "I would love nothing more than to share dinner with you. I want to apologize and explain my behavior the night of the signing. Would that be okay?" My eyes plead with her, begging for a second chance.

She pauses, as if she's considering it, then nods her head in agreement just as the server approaches the table to check on us. We haven't started our meal yet, but it smells amazing. The server notices the tension between us and backs away, not interrupting. I'm so glad she's permitting me to be here. She is the most captivating woman I have ever met. And there is no way I am screwing this up tonight.

We serve ourselves and then, as we eat, I notice how uncomfortably quiet it is. I lay my fork down, knowing I need to make things right. After all, this is my fault. All the blame is mine. I need to grab the bull by the horns and confront my fears. I breathe out slowly and throw myself into the fire, hoping I don't get burned too badly.

"Over the past few weeks, I have gone through this conversation hundreds of times in my head, and now that it's happening, I can't find my words," I confess.

"Lucas, you don't owe me anything. We can just share a meal and go our separate ways. No harm, no foul," she says. I don't know if she heard it, but I don't miss the waiver in her voice. It's almost as if she's trying to hold it together. My mom used to do the same thing when I was growing up. And just like it broke my heart then, it destroys me now.

"But what if I don't want that?" I say in a rush.

Before she can answer, I explain myself. "I want more, and I'm not sure what that means. I know I hurt you, and I'm sorry for that. I don't know how we got here." My words can cause her to react negatively. A scowl that makes me shudder covers her beautiful face. As I suspected, I've hurt her. Now, in my attempt to be honest and transparent with her, the realization sinks in. How I handled things, or didn't handle them, is what made me an asshole.

"You humiliated me!" she accuses with a bite in her voice. Her normally peach-colored skin turns flushed and tinged with scarlet.

She blows out a deep breath. "I'm sorry for how I behaved, too. I was already feeling raw and exposed, and you left me feeling rejected. With you, that night, I threw rational thinking out the window and I just was. What almost happened in your car... I've... that's new to me. Not sex. Sex isn't new. But car sex would've been."

"Samantha, I wasn't—"

She shakes her head. "Can I just finish, please? Before that night, I'd been humiliated beyond what I thought was possible. My now ex-fiancé cheated on me with his assistant... and I caught them. It was only weeks after we'd announced our engagement too. But the incident with you in the car was so much worse, even though we didn't have an audience and we aren't even a couple. It hit me harder because I felt an intense connection with you. One that I'd never felt with him."

I remain speechless after her confession.

At this moment, I honestly don't know what to do or say. I just sit there and fiddle with my napkin, afraid to make things worse between us. Samantha lays her hands on the table, defeated.

Not thinking, I reach over and cover them. Her hands look so small and vulnerable cradled beneath my much larger one. Her skin is pale and cool, warming beneath the heat of my palms. I sweep my thumb across the back of her hand, both in my desire to offer comfort and in utter selfishness, because I simply want to relish the smoothness of her skin. To test if she is as silky and decadent as I remember. I catch her eyes and stare into them as I admit, "I am so sorry, Samantha. I didn't intend to embarrass you. When things progressed in my car, I was completely in. But then I reminded myself that you are more and deserve something better. You are not the quick-car-fuck type. You deserve candles, roses, and a gentleman. And that evening, I was not that, so I told myself I needed to stop what was happening before I became something you regretted later. I don't know if you know, but I don't do relationships. But with you, I wanted something more than a quick hookup. And when I tried to slow it down, that's when everything turned for us." I wince, hoping my words don't cause more damage.

At my confession, her eyes widen and she takes a few moments to absorb all I've disclosed. Feeling vulnerable, I pull my hands back so I can keep them busy in my lap until she decides to either continue our dinner or end things between us. Truthfully, she's not giving any hints about what's going to happen.

And now, I'm the one embarrassed. I don't talk about feelings with anyone, and here I laid it all out to a woman I want more than anything. One who seems like she wishes we'd never even met. But I remind myself, if my confession and discomfort resolved the misunderstandings between us, it's worth it. I'm determined to sit here and take the consequences. Tears? Anger? Questions? Whatever she wants to throw at me, I'm here for it. Right now, I need to be the man she deserves and accept the repercussions of the pain I've caused. If I don't, I'm not worthy of a second chance with her. *Why is this all so confusing? Before her, I never once considered having a relationship, but now I'm willing to consider something different from what I've always had. Even though I can't define it.*

Samantha's eyes are gentle, kind, and full of questions. I wish I had a simple answer for her, but I don't. My reaction that night was confusing to us both, but I still want to explain what I figured out. "As things progressed with us, my words, feelings, and thoughts became jumbled. So, instead of fumbling through an explanation and making the situation more awkward, I just let you go. As far as that night is concerned, I wanted you, but the more I thought about what you deserved, I realized I couldn't be that. I don't date and you aren't a girl who is okay with casual, right?"

Even though I phrase my comment as a question, I'm hopeful she'll tell me she'd be fine with a casual hookup. Unfortunately, I suspect I already know her answer. After all, she was engaged, and nothing screams commitment more than that. Nothing I see before me tells me she would be up for something casual, and that's all I know or feel like I can offer.

Chapter 11

Samantha

He, too, is questioning whether I would be open to something casual. Would I? What does that entail? I need more details before I can decide.

"What would casual entail?" I ask and patiently await his response. I don't miss how his eyes light up with excitement at my question. It's like he's hoping I'm considering it.

He licks his lips and smiles, which instantly sets my heart to fluttering. "Casual is just that. No commitment. No formal relationship. Just having fun with each other."

I bite my lip as I consider his words. "Is that the only type of relationships you have?" I ask.

He nods his head. "I have never met any woman I wanted more than one night until I met you. And I don't know what that means." I can't help but smile at his confession. To him, I'm different, but in a good way. This is exciting and nerve-racking at the same time. The more I think about it, the more I tell myself, yes, I could do it. For a taste of him, I can try it. "Shall we get this wrapped up and go somewhere more private?" I boldly ask.

Lucas raises his hand, alerting our server that we'd like the check. Platters disappear quickly, and before I even have a moment to reconsider that I've just suggested we find somewhere to go have sex, everything is taken care of. Within minutes, the to-go bags land on our table. Lucas pulls a few twenties from his wallet—more than enough to cover a tip since Christian paid the bill—and drops them on the table. He requests an Uber, stands up, pulls me into him, grabs the bags, and leads me to the exit. We wait a few minutes outside until the Uber arrives. During the entire wait, Lucas has me cuddled into his side. He's nuzzling his nose into my hair, whispering against my ear how delicious I smell and placing chaste kisses on my temple. I feel my knees go weak and he supports me, helping me into the car. I give the Uber driver my address, knowing we'll have more privacy there than the hotel room his team put him up in.

Our drive through Chicago is hot because Lucas can't keep his hands off me. This car ride is taking too long for my lust-soaked brain to continue functioning. We need to be back at my penthouse before I mount him in the backseat of this Uber. Each touch and kiss set my body ablaze, and I fight the urge to rip my clothes from my body, giving our driver a wild show.

"Ahem." An obvious throat clearing from the driver's seat alerts us to the fact we've arrived at our destination. Lucas hands the driver some money to cover our fare and drags me from the car. At the last minute, I manage to grab our take-out bags.

Once we step into the empty elevator, I can feel the electricity in the air; something is about to happen. Excitement builds in my body. Just then, Lucas steps up to me, pressing me against the wall. After the doors have closed, he uses his body to secure me in place. With his knee wedged between my legs, I'm sure he can feel the heat radiating off me. Pausing for a moment, he stares at me before he leans in for a mind-blowing kiss. Too soon, a *ding* bounces off the metal walls, alerting us we've reached our destination. Gently, I lay my hand on his chest and nudge him. Lucas growls playfully and I giggle. "When we're behind closed doors, we won't be interrupted. Let's go, handsome," I say, leading us out of the elevator. Lucas's eyes are swimming with desire, and his firm touch on my waist guiding me down the hallway tells me he has plans for me. *I cannot wait.*

Upon entering my penthouse, Lucas walks in and pulls me out from behind the front door. He wraps his large hand around my hip and side-steps me away before he closes it. Then he twirls me so I'm facing him and my hands land on his solid chest. I giggle nervously. A sly smile appears across his face as he steers me toward the counter and duck walks me backward until I hit it. Excitement builds within me. I have never been with anyone so commanding. The thrill of that drives me wild. My lust and desire for Lucas are off the charts. It's apparent Lucas knows what he wants, and he plans to get it.

Usually, aggressive men put me on guard, but his aggressive nature doesn't alarm me at all. Instead, I feel safe. In all my life, I have never felt so desired. When my butt hits the edge of the countertop, Lucas places both hands firmly on my hips, locking me in place, and kisses me hard. Our tongues wrestle for control. I match him stroke for stroke, thrust for thrust. After he bites my lip, he pulls it with him as he dips down. He grabs my ass and lifts me up, setting me on the granite countertop. My kitchen has never seen this much excitement, and I am ecstatic to see where it's headed.

I widen my legs, accepting him between them. The realization that our centers line up perfectly is intoxicating. I feel drunk on him. He furthers this feeling when he presses his hips into me and I can feel how turned on he is. I wrap my legs around him and pull us even closer. We continue kissing throughout, and I feel him get even harder. I love knowing I've done that to him. My body responds and I grind my center against him. His reaction to that is something I've never experienced. He growls deeply and then tugs my hair tightly. My scalp tingles. It's both pain and pleasure simultaneously. My panties are soaked. I need this man, now.

I find the edge of his sweater and pull it up over his chest. Completely in sync, he releases my hair and tugs the sweater off his body. Mine disappears next. Then he loosens his tie and tosses it behind him. I move my shaky hands to the buttons on his shirt and undo them as quickly as I can. Never having undressed a man before, I fumble a little. When I get toward the bottom, I pull the shirt from where it's tucked in and spread it wide open. I pull my lips from his and sit back, absorbing it all. I'm met with the most breathtaking sight. Utter perfection is the only way to describe Lucas's chest.

My eyes graze over every inch. From his pecs to his abs and along the V that promises something heavenly below his buckle, it's all alluring. *Holy hell!* This man looks like he's carved from marble. His muscles are firm and well-defined. Unable to resist, I trace my fingertips over all his curves. As I do, I'm wishing it was my tongue doing it. *Wait! Where did that thought come from?* Must be all those romances I've been reading. The sex in them always sounds amazing, and I want that. Plus, if I were a betting woman, I have a feeling Lucas would deliver. Tonight, though, I want him to take me to new limits. I want to see what we are capable of without any boundaries. I want to feel an orgasm that's not self-induced.

After we rip each other's clothes off, the possibilities will be endless. Each time I look at Lucas, my libido does a celebratory jig. *Should you be doing this?* An inkling in the back of my mind cautions me. My mind and body seem to be in disagreement about what I should do. Yes, my wanting to lick all over Lucas is completely out of character for me. *This isn't you.* I chastise myself, momentarily feeling guilty. *Why not? What's there to be ashamed of? Licking, biting, fucking.* If doing that will bring me pleasure, then there is nothing wrong with it. We won't be hurting anyone. Lucas and I are two consenting adults who, at this moment, are acting on their insane attraction to each other.

I want this. I want *him.* Maybe Lucas came into my life for a reason. Maybe he'll be like my Jedi sex trainer. He can teach me the ways of the force, literally. Determined, I need to embrace this experience for all its worth. I promise myself that before the night is over, I will not be ashamed to try new things. Excitement bubbles up within me, leaking out as laughter.

"You're beautiful, Samantha," Lucas utters as he allows my hands to explore him freely. My fingertips trace down his treasure trail that disappears into the top of his slacks. When I reach his belt, I trace over the silver buckle, looking for his hesitation. There's none. Feeling brazen and unashamed in what I'm doing, the freedom I'm experiencing is exhilarating and empowering. *I am woman, hear me roar.*

Before I can continue undressing him, he reaches

behind me and unhooks my bra. Sliding the straps slowly down my arms, he pulls it free, revealing my average-sized breasts. As he cups each breast, he gives me a wide smile that reminds me of a kid in a candy store with money burning a hole in his pocket. Lucas bends forward and takes a nipple into his mouth. The heat of his mouth warms me to the core, and it feels incredible. He applies perfect suction on one nipple while he uses his hand to twist, pluck, and squeeze the other. Throwing my head back, my desire for him soars. As his lips and teeth scrape deliciously along my hardened peak, a wave of arousal pulsates all the way down to my clit. Every graze and nip of my breast is in sync with the throbbing rhythm between my legs. The signs of an impending orgasm work through my body, starting with the curl of my toes to the shake of my legs. Every suckle makes me needy and drags me closer and closer to the finish line. *Am I about to come from nipple play?* I think so, because I'm so wonderfully close. *Are Lucas's nipples as sensitive?* Reaching my hand up, I circle his pectoral muscle. Testing my hypothesis, I lightly twist one of his nipples. I'm rewarded with a low growl that erupts from deep within his throat. He pulls his head back, looks up, locks eyes with me, and gives me a wolfish grin. It's striking and oh-so-telling. Apparently, he likes what I've done. *Me too, Lucas. Me too.*

In my short time with him, I've realized he is full of surprise reactions. Mitch had never been this exciting, responsive, or thrilling in bed. If I'm being honest, he wasn't fun at all. In less than five minutes, Lucas has me more aroused than I had ever been with Mitch. *Why is that? Why the hell had I settled for something so mediocre?*

I'm pulled from my thoughts when Lucas bites my nipple sharply and then tugs at it hard. A desperate moan echoes through my penthouse, bouncing off the walls, and it came from me. *Holy shit!* I hear him laugh against my breast and I instantly become self-conscious.

Embarrassed, I push him back and throw my arms across my chest, covering myself. Lucas gently grabs my wrists and pulls them apart, revealing me fully. He releases me, then takes his large hands and places them on either side of my face, forcing me to make eye contact with him.

"Samantha, never be ashamed of your body. The sounds you make. The way you move. Or the way you feel. Every part is incredible, and I plan to enjoy all of it tonight. I plan to leave you completely satiated." His words are stern, and normally I'd react poorly to them. But tonight it does just the opposite, and I smile widely.

"Why did you laugh? Did I do something wrong?" I demand in a shaky tone.

He shakes his head no. "I loved your moan. Honestly, it just caught me by surprise. You have been so responsive and I'm savoring it. I can't wait to experience all the noises you have for me. I plan to revel in each of them." *All the noises.* Embarrassed, my cheeks grow hot.

Conflicted, I whisper, "I'm not very experienced. Everything we do tonight, other than the missionary position, will be new to me." Instead of being annoyed by my confession, Lucas smiles, making me feel accepted, especially when he lays his lips on mine and kisses me with unbridled passion.

"I'm looking forward to it," he mumbles against my lips.

He pulls away and then informs me, "You're going to need to communicate with me. If I'm doing anything you don't like or feel uncomfortable with, you need to let me know."

"I can do that," I promise him, then he goes back to exploring my breasts. Within moments, I'm writhing on my counter, moaning through the most powerful orgasm I have ever had. *That's a first, and I'm so ready for more.*

As I'm recovering, I realize I'm still partially dressed. I can't wait to see what happens when he gets me fully naked. Lucas lifts me, throws me over his shoulder, and asks where the bedroom is. Then he confidently strides down the hallway, smacking my ass. I giggle and he lets out a loud, hearty laugh that stirs up something within me. Unrestrained joy? It's a feeling I have never experienced before, but I like it.

Chapter 12

Lucas

Tonight, for the first time, I am desperate to leave a part of myself with someone forever. Just thinking about wanting that has me rattled. Talk about an absolute mindfuck. But I know I want Samantha more than I have ever wanted anyone.

When I enter her room, I see a king-sized bed with a white down comforter and I toss her onto it. "Ahhh," Samantha squeaks out as she lands easily and stares back at me with hungry eyes. I stalk forward, as if she's my prey and I'm ready to devour her. Because in all honesty, I am. When I get to the edge of the bed, I grab her ankles and pull her toward me. "Ohhh... he, he, he." Samantha giggles as I place my hands on her calves and slide them up to her thighs, making her squirm. Unsnapping the button on her jeans, I pull them off in one tug. Left behind is a tiny pair of lacy, black bikini underwear that matches perfectly to the bra I just removed and left abandoned in her kitchen. "You are so fucking sexy," I growl out while eyeing her center.

Samantha gasps as I trace up her legs with my nose. When I reach the V of her thighs, I kiss her over the lace, and I watch as shivers roll across her body. I nuzzle my nose at her core, and I feel her wriggling away. I place my hand on her stomach, holding her still. Dusting another few kisses across the lace, I look up her body until I find her eyes. They're filled with worry and apprehension. Maintaining eye contact, I kneel, then say, "Samantha, talk to me, please. Do you not like what I'm doing?"

"I do, but no one has ever done that to me. Touched me there. With their mouth. Do you really want to do that?" Her question is serious, and so I answer her by nodding and then placing a kiss on each hip bone. I hook my fingers in her sexy black panties and drag them slowly down her smooth legs, allowing her time to adjust to what is happening. With her panties off, I spread her legs open wide, taking in the magnificent sight before me. Making sure I make eye contact with her, I tell her, "You are beautiful, Samantha, and I definitely want to explore more, but if it makes you uncomfortable, I'll stop." Pushing back, I sit on my heels, waiting for her answer. I want her to feel totally respected, safe, and comfortable with me.

"Are you sure?" she squeaks out, a red blush

covering her gorgeous face. *She's curious. I can't wait to blow her mind.*

"I am. I've wanted you since I first met you," I confess. Then I move forward from the bend of her knee, back toward the juncture of her thighs. The trail I leave is full of kisses and nips as I make my way back to her center. When I reach it, I nuzzle my nose in her small, trimmed patch of hair and savor her unique scent. It's a combination of raspberry, mint, and musk, and it makes me feel intoxicated. "You smell incredible." This is a first for me. Usually, the perfumes and scents of the women I'm with aren't unique or memorable like Samantha's. Honestly, over the years, they all sort of smell, look, and fuck the same way. Which is damn boring and probably explains the rut I'd been in before Samantha.

From the start, I was confident that Samantha would be completely different, and I was looking forward to experiencing her. Embracing that, I languidly lick between her folds. "Ahh, Lucas... so, so good." Her deep, throaty moan encourages me on. After a few passes, I concentrate on her clit. I suck and nip at it, and she thrusts her hand into my hair, pressing me to her. Apparently, she likes it. I'm finding I like it too.

I'm committed to making everything pleasurable for her, especially this. Because she's so responsive, I tell myself I'm doing things right. I need to pay attention to what gets the best response out of her. My approach is to lick, nip, and explore her just like I would if I were kissing her mouth.

Slipping a finger into her rewards me with a moan. "Gaw," falls from her lips as she bucks against my hand. "You are so tight, baby," I tell her as I lower down to continue to devour her clit. Samantha rolls her hips, and I add another finger. Her body hugs my fingers in warm restraint. She bows her back and I add a third finger, helping to stretch her so that I'll fit inside her. I wasn't bragging when I said I was a big guy. At six foot two with a shoe size of thirteen, you could say I was packing plenty down below, and I didn't want our first time to scare or hurt her.

I'd met Mitch, and he was considerably shorter than me. He was smaller in everything, perhaps? I assume that because she's so tight; she hasn't been thoroughly fucked in a while—maybe ever—even though she'd been engaged. Samantha mentioned that she'd only had missionary-style sex. Thinking of all the positions I could use with her… I'm struggling not to blow. I'd definitely enjoy being the one to teach her about variety.

From everything I've experienced with her, I know that if I were ever to date anyone, Samantha would be it. After just one taste of her, you'd have to pry me off of her with a crowbar. I would fuck her on every surface, in every position we could manage, as often as possible. Being with her already feels like an addiction. She's a drug to me and one hit won't be enough.

Needing to deal with that thought later, I push it from my mind. Or maybe I'm wrong and after we have sex, I'll feel fulfilled, satisfied, and able to go back to my bachelor one-night stand ways. Even now, I suspect it won't be that easy.

Turning back into the goddess in front of me, I focus on her needs as I lick, suck, nip, and finger her to completion. When her muscles flex tightly around my fingers, I know she's moments away. Continuing my ministrations, I flick her clit back and forth and her body arches off the bed. "Lucas," she screams as her hips dance a wild samba across my tongue while I lap up all her juices. When her frantic moves begin to slow down, I slide my fingers from her and crawl up her delicious body. Knowing I'm covered in her come, I lick my lips. Samantha's eyes go wide and her cheeks blush. Slowly, I lean in for a kiss and she surprises me by reaching up, wrapping her hands around my neck, and pulling me into her. Breaking our kiss, I slide off the bed and remove my pants and boxer briefs. Again, Samantha's eyes go wide. I crawl back onto the bed and over Samantha, and in a matter of seconds, things change.

One minute, Samantha is a relaxed masterpiece, and the next she's a frightened doll. What had I done? I rack my brain, looking for what triggered the change, and nothing registers. Confused, I ask her, "What's wrong, babe?"

Desperate to know her answer, I breeze over the

fact I used a term of endearment. It wasn't something I did, ever. If I gave it any thought, I'd conclude I was fucked. This time around, I wasn't *failing* Samantha. I was *falling* for her.

Before I spiral down that rabbit hole, Samantha's whimper rescues me. She sounds scared, and I wonder if she is. Looking deep into her milk-chocolate eyes, I see it clear as day: pure, undiluted fear.

"Please talk to me, babe. Tell me what's got you scared."

I wasn't normally so attuned and talkative with the women I slept with. Honestly, I had never spent enough time with them or cared about their feelings. I never called them names like babe. Hell, by the end of our hookup, I was lucky if I remembered their names at all. That makes me sound like a dick, which is probably accurate. But from the moment I met her, I knew Samantha was different. This time, I really cared. In fact, I cared more than I wanted to admit.

I'd never had to put in so much effort with a woman. They were everywhere, never warranting a second look. Before Samantha, all I was ever looking for was a onetime thing.

But she isn't like those women. Already I know she is worthy of so much more of me. This one time, I want to listen, understand what she's feeling, thinking, and desiring. I want to please her in every way possible. As she orgasms, I want to whisper sweet nothings into her ear. I want to call her babe. I want her to be mine.

My thoughts scare the shit out of me, but despite the anxiety they stir up within me, I force myself to stay in the moment, waiting for her answer.

Finally, she speaks up, settling my anguish. In a quiet voice, she confides, "I'm scared, Lucas. You... you're enormous, and I'm afraid you'll hurt me."

I smile and kiss her cheeks before whispering against them, "That's what I was getting you ready for. I'll go slow. If you need me to stop, or if it hurts too much, you tell me and I'll stop, okay?" Waiting for her go-ahead is agonizing. What if she changes her mind? I would never force her to do something she didn't want or wasn't ready for, but the blue balls I'd be sporting on my way back to the hotel would be excruciating.

She nods. And that one movement puts me out of my misery. Samantha pulls me close. "Kiss me, Lucas." Her command is like a balm to my aching heart. I waste no time lowering myself to her and kissing her deeply. I feel like a starved man who's found his manna from heaven, and I intend to greedily savor every bit. And I do. Slowly. I cherish the gift she is giving me.

After kissing for a while, I feel her start to relax. Her hands travel down my sides and brush against my throbbing cock. Under her ministrations, I harden beyond what I'd ever experienced. I could feel myself dripping pre-come. I'm beyond ready for her, but again, I want to make sure she's still ready.

I move my hand down to her center and plunge two fingers inside. They slide in with ease. Despite her fear, she's soaked and more than ready for me. I thrust my drenched fingers in and out a few more times, warming her up to the movements I hope my cock will emulate in moments. She opens her legs wider and thrusts her hips into me. Her inner muscles tighten, gripping my fingers boldly. And it's one of the most incredible feelings I've ever experienced. I feel euphoric. The only thing that would feel better is if my cock were filling her.

I remove my fingers, roll off her, grab a condom from my slacks, slide it on, and climb back over her. I look into her deep, dreamy chocolate eyes, kiss her nose tenderly, and ask, "Are you ready?"

The smile she gives me lights me up entirely. I nudge her legs farther apart and line myself up with her. Then I slowly guide myself into nirvana. She's still tight, but she doesn't flinch as I push inside. "Samantha, you feel incredible." I groan and she surprises me by wrapping her legs around my waist, driving her heels into my ass, and forcing me inside faster than I had intended. Moments later, I bottom out inside her and the hug her channel wraps around my cock makes my body sing the Hallelujah chorus. I'm in absolute heaven. Taking it all in, I enjoy the moment. I'm with Samantha. Inside Samantha. Worshiping Samantha. Nothing could be better than this moment right now.

We move slowly at first until we get in sync. It feels amazing, and before long, I feel the telltale signs of an orgasm building within Samantha. I slip my hand in between our writhing bodies and find her swollen clit. I alternate between pinching and massaging it until her orgasm explodes around me. I continue thrusting my hips until she relaxes below me. Throwing her hands above her head, she's exhausted. But I'm not. I'm just getting started.

Pulling out of her, I flip her over on her stomach and haul her hips up in the air toward me. She settles on her knees with her perfect heart-shaped ass high in the air. I take a moment to appreciate the magnificent view before me. The slope of her back is incredibly sexy, and I run my fingers up it. *Slow down, man. This is new to her. Be gentle.*

In our previous position, I couldn't get deep enough. But with her positioned like this, I can. Thrusting back into her, she tightens around me again.

"This is amazing! Samantha, you were made for me!"

Not long after I start moving, a throaty moan comes from her, and my heart almost explodes. It's the best sound I've ever heard, and I want to hear it again and again. *I made her do that.* Then she does something that blows her moan out of the water. She begs.

"Harder, Lucas. Please."

I give myself a mental fist pump. *Hell yes!* I could totally do that. My hips piston faster, thrusting harder. *Anything for you, Samantha.* Even with the lack of blood in it, my brain keeps spiraling. Before me is the only woman I have ever wanted to please. And keep doing it for the rest of my life. *Holy shit! Where did that come from and what does it mean?* Not allowing myself to think too much, I continue to drive into her. Chasing the high relentlessly, I feel my orgasm build. After a few more thrusts, I explode within her, triggering another orgasm for her.

Pulling out, I collapse next to her. I haul her on top of me and hold her tight to my chest until our breathing regulates. I nuzzle my nose into her hair and whisper, "That was unbelievable."

It's official. Thomas Rhett had it right. Being here with Samantha, I could die a happy man. Sex with Samantha is unlike anything I have ever known. But now, I know that once will never be enough. She has ruined me for anyone else. No way am I ever going to feel like this again. Instead of just chasing an orgasm, now I want to drive her wild, over and over again, never stopping.

Chapter 13

Samantha

Experiencing sex doggie style was even more than I'd imagined. Having Lucas anchor my hips while he pounded into me felt unbelievable. With me, he was so controlled, commanding, and undeniably sexy. After we had both orgasmed—my fourth of the evening—he collapsed on the bed next to me. My body felt like a cooked noodle. He pulled me into his chest, snuggled me a bit, and spoke my exact thoughts. "That was unbelievable."

After some time, he climbs out of the bed to dispose of the condom. Then he climbs back in next to me and pulls me to his chest. I listen to his heart beat erratically and realize mine is doing the same. I raise my hand to his chest and trace my finger along the various ridges and bumps of his muscles. Lucas must manscape because only a small scattering of hair dusts his pectorals, and it's slightly damp. *I'd made him sweat!* I find I can't help myself from running my fingers through the coarse hair. Moving to his nipples next, I circle them with the manicured nails of my pointer fingers. Instantly, they respond, hardening. As they pebble, Lucas squirms. Is he ticklish? I keep at my ministrations, testing my theory, and after a few more circles, his hips respond by thrusting upward. Before I can further explore, he reaches up and stills my hand against his firm pec. Before today, I had never played with a man's nipples, but his are adorable. I had to touch them, wanting to see if they were as sensitive as mine were. Thanks to Lucas, I am now aware of a lot of new erogenous zones all over my body. He laughs and says, "Babe, doing that drives me wild. But I need a few moments to recover before I can do anything about it. You aren't playing fair."

I laugh too. Is he serious? He couldn't be. I have never had back-to-back sex before. I lift my head up and lock my eyes with his before squeaking out, "Wait, are you serious?"

He just nods. My mouth flies open in surprise. *Holy shit!* And I smile like a beauty pageant contestant, wide and bright.

His eyes sparkle with promises of things to come, and my heart skyrockets. I squeal my excitement. Or at least I think I do, because he again laughs. Embarrassed by my childish excitement, I drop my head onto his rock-hard chest, hiding. He pats my head, comforting me while mumbling under his breath, "Glad I'm not the only one who's excited."

Hearing him confess his eagerness for more gives me a confidence that is completely unfamiliar. I rise to my knees and straddle him. His expression tells me my actions surprise him. However, in an instant, an enormous smile spreads across his devilishly handsome face. I lick my lips, and he wraps his large hands firmly around my hips. With me firmly anchored in place, he taps my hip bones with his thumbs. I circle my hips slowly and, with each rotation, I feel him growing harder beneath me. His undeniable response encourages my own, and I lower my lips to his. Our kisses always seem amazing, but this one appears to hold a magical charge that combusts when our lips touch. Instantly, my body goes hot and needy. I grab around Lucas's neck and pull him farther into our kiss. His fingers spread wide around my hips and he tugs me tighter to him. He then slides my hips back and forth, rocking me against him. His body further responds after only a few slides, and mine does the same. I'd never been this responsive. It was as if Lucas freed a needy sexual deviant, because right now, I needed him, *again*.

I lift my hips, slip my hand between my legs, and circle my clit, encouraging the orgasm already taking hold of me. I roll my hips, using the pressure of my hand on my clit, and moan. Lucas lifts his head, breaking our kiss, to see what I'm doing. When he sees my hand, he growls, and it's incredibly hot. He lifts me off him, and before I can protest, he explains, "I need you now. But shit, Samantha, I need a condom. What you're doing is fucking hot, and I need to be inside you. I want you to ride me."

Totally lost in the moment, I breathlessly pant, "We don't need a condom. I'm on birth control and am clean. Are you?"

"I always use protection and I tested clean months ago at the beginning of the season. I haven't been with anyone since before then. Full confession. I haven't wanted to be with anyone since the night we met," Lucas whispers.

As soon as he utters that, I rise and line us up. Before I lower onto him, I memorize the look of intensity blazing in his eyes. They're full of emotion; lust, desire, and trust. When our centers finally kiss, I feel a charge course through my entire body. In an instant, I feel complete. Lucas's tight grip centers me, and I shimmy my hips. As this is another new position for me, I find I feel nervous, curious, and enthusiastic. "Can you help me?" I ask.

Lucas's devastatingly handsome grin is his reply, and it makes my nerves melt away. He shows me exactly what he wants of my body and, after I repeat it a few times, he loosens his grip on my hips. I love the feel of his hands, possessively anchoring me to him as I rise and then sink back down. At first, my movements are slow and disjointed, but it doesn't take long for me to find my rhythm. I'm loving this new position. I place my hands on his muscled chest and grind down onto him. Lost in this exquisite feeling, I take a bit to notice his tightened grip on me. My movements become restricted and I discover I can't lift my hips, so instead, I circle them, rubbing my clit against his pubic bone. The friction feels absolutely incredible. He keeps my ability to move limited until pleasure envelopes my body completely. Another orgasm crashes into me and I moan. "Lucas, that feels so good."

"Mmmm, Samantha." Lucas then releases the tight hold he has on me. "I want you to ride me, babe."

It doesn't take long for an orgasm to ravage my body. With it still pulsing through me, I resume lifting my hips up and down, and this time around Lucas lifts his hips, thrusting up into me. Every time our bodies connect, he grunts deep from his throat. The sounds he's making are so raw and primal and my pulse climbs. I need more. Of him. Of that sound.

Chapter 14

Samantha

Lucas is extraordinary. Not only is he a superior athlete, but he's also charitable, kind, and caring. He's beyond attractive, with a fantastic body. And by my thorough research, I've also discovered he is a certifiable sex god. I don't know if that's a real thing, but he has my unwavering support and stamp of approval. Never before have I felt so relaxed and sated in my life. Actually, I'm not even sure I can climb off him. I wonder if he'll let me sleep on him. Instead of sleeping, though, he strokes my hair and suggests a shower and a snack before bed. Lifting the only part of me I can, I look into the face I'm rapidly becoming attached to. My eyes fall upon a flirty smile and I feel my heart pitter-patter. Nodding, I slowly roll off him. It's official. I'm stuck, lying spread eagle across my comforter, and not caring how unladylike I look. *What has happened to me?* Lucas rolls onto his side and pushes my hair out of my eyes. He tugs my chin toward him and then lowers his lips to mine. He places the most tender and loving kiss on my lips. Then he gets up off my now well-used bed and pulls my completely satisfied and deliriously happy body up. "Ahhh." I groan as I register aches in places I haven't had in a long time, or maybe ever. It's a delicious ache, so I won't be complaining about it.

When we walk into my bathroom, he steps toward the large shower. A twist of his wrist turns the water on and he lets it get warm before he pulls me in. He backs me into the waterfall pouring from my shower head. I savor the feel of the hot water cascading over my body. Once I'm sufficiently wet, he moves me out of the direct spray, turns me away from him and washes my hair. "Mmmm," falls from my lips as he massages my scalp. *I'm in heaven.* Next, he washes my body, and I love the feeling of his hands dancing across my skin. He pays especially close attention to my breasts, hips, ass, and center. After he rinses me off completely, he quickly washes himself.

When done, Lucas wraps us both in my large, fluffy towels. Once dry, I slip into my black silk robe that hits mid-thigh and then I head out to my kitchen for something to eat. Lucas follows with the towel tied low at his waist. *Oh, my goodness.*

Pulling open the fridge, Lucas peers inside.

"We brought home leftovers, right? I think we

burned up some serious calories the past few hours." His playful, flirty tone revs my body up.

"Hours?" I squeak, completely surprised. I hadn't realized so much time had passed since we returned to my penthouse, but when I read one thirty on my oven clock, it registers. Lucas smiles at me. I quickly try to account for the last few hours. But all I can come up with is how pleasurable the time was. And that I want a repeat.

"O-oh, okay!" I stutter. "We can heat the leftover lasagna," I quickly suggest while he grabs it from the fridge. I collect plates, forks, napkins, and cups. With the lasagna heating, I fill our cups with ice water. It will be refreshing and potentially cool my hormone-crazed body down.

With our heated food, we head to my couch and settle in to eat. When I'm finished, I place my hand on my belly. Lucas notices, stands up, grabs my plate, and heads back to the kitchen, where he washes the plates and loads them in the dishwasher. *Seriously, could this man be any more perfect?* He returns to the couch, steps between my legs, then pulls me up to him. When we're face-to-face, he kisses my nose and tells me, "We're going to bed. I have a mid-morning flight."

Back in my bedroom, he strips off the towel still wrapped around his trim waist. He unties and removes my robe, letting it flutter to the ground. Together, we crawl into bed, naked and unembarrassed. I settle on my side and he moves in behind me, spooning me.

Having him that close, I can't help but wiggle my hips. "Samantha," he growls. Seconds later, his large hand is firmly on my hip, stilling me. "Babe, we need to get a few hours of sleep, and that won't be happening if you keep that up." His warning comes out in a gruff, growly bite. I giggle. Lucas kisses my neck and whispers against my ear, "Goodnight, babe. Thank you for the best night of my life." I sigh at his words. It's been the best night of my life too. Thinking about that, I cuddle into him. The body heat he's generating is insane, and in no time, I drift off to sleep, completely exhausted and sated.

I'm having the best dream, replaying the events of last night, when I feel Lucas placing chaste kisses on my neck. It's tough not to get lost in the many ways he knows to touch me. Blinking my sleepy eyes open, I feel him pulling me tightly into his waist and... *oh my*! He's hard. But not just hard. He's like steel, and he's settled his cock between my ass cheeks. Looks like I'm getting an amazing start to my day. I mean, I'm not wrong in thinking there isn't anything sexier than your man letting you know just how much he wants you, right? *Hold on... did I just call Lucas my man?* Thoughts zip through my head at warp speed. *Why did I call him my man? What does it even mean?* It's too soon to put a label on him—on us—right? I honestly don't even know what he wants from me. Maybe it's just the one night? That's his M.O., isn't it? I need to slow down the crazy train I apparently boarded.

Between the four sensational orgasms he gave me last night, the insanely graphic dream I've just awoken from, and a very large and in-charge man behind me, I'm feeling a bit out of sorts.

Taking a moment to register where his hands, his lips, his body are in relation to mine, I shiver at the thought. This man... he wants me again, and he's not being shy about letting me know. *Sexy*. Reaching my hand up, I run my fingers through his hair. When I grab it and tug it, my movements pull him closer and he growls playfully against my ear just before he traces his tongue down it. At the same time, he skims his hands down my sides. When he reaches my hips, he grabs them possessively and thrusts against me. *Holy hell!* Every move he makes sends me higher and higher.

I turn my head and snag his gaze. Immediately, I notice his eyes are heavy with desire. We lean into each other, and the kiss we share is electric. Our tongues wrestle, each battling to maintain control. Lucas slides his hand over my hip and toward my center. Since I'm already naked, he skims through the small patch of hair as his fingers continue their exploration. Once he finds my clit, he slowly circles it. "So good, Lucas," I say on a moan and arch back into him.

He nuzzles at my neck and says, "Do you know how incredibly sexy you are?" I shake my head no, because he is the only man who's ever told me he finds me sexy. "You are, babe. You drive me absolutely wild," he confesses against my neck. His day-old scruff rubs against the sensitive skin, sending goose bumps all over my body. At this moment, he's the sexiest he's ever been. Reaching behind me, I wrap my fingers around his cock and squeeze it. It twitches in my hand. "Samantha," comes out in a throaty groan.

He tested my readiness by dipping his finger inside of me. His wide grin against my neck tells me everything I already know: I am more than ready for him. His hand runs back up to my hip and down to my thigh. He lifts my leg, pulling it over his. He uses the head of his cock to tease my entrance, and the anticipation sends shivers across my body. Pushing myself back toward him, I angle my hips, asking for him to take me, and he does. The feeling of him finally pushing inside me is both dizzying and euphoric. I feel so full. Then he thrusts behind me and my body melts into him.

Lucas anchors his arm around my waist, pulling me closer against him, controlling his thrusts. He knows his body so completely, and the way he moves makes my body sing. It doesn't take long to feel the beginnings of an orgasm, and I unashamedly moan. "Right there, Lucas. I'm so close. Please don't stop." He chuckles but continues thrusting. He releases the hold he has on my leg and finds my clit. His movements are incredible. Lucas circles, flicks, and pinches my clit, forcing the orgasm building within me to explode. I turn my head and pull his head toward me, kissing him ferociously. When he bites my lip and pinches my clit, he sets off another tremble that rocks through my body.

Chapter 15

Lucas

It's hard to settle down after the high I find myself on following the best sex of my life with the most incredible woman I've ever met. Samantha is an anomaly, for sure. Not only is she breathtaking, but she is driven, smart, kind, and funny. In all the years I've been having sex, I have never, and I mean *never*, had morning sex. Currently, I can't imagine why the fuck not. *That was unbelievable.* Lying here in Samantha's bed, I am completely gobsmacked. What we just did is hands down the best sex I have ever had. And that's even taking into consideration the marathon of earth-shattering sex we had last night. *What have I been missing? Was it the time of day? The position? The woman?*

The heat our bodies are manufacturing together, the sounds of me rutting into her, the moans we both make, the feel of her skin against mine. It's all overwhelming and devastating at the same time. This can't last, right? Has Samantha ruined me for other women? Does she want more of me? If so, what would that mean? Can I give her what she needs? Realizing I need some answers before I head back to New York, I ask.

"Samantha, I think you are amazing. But I have to ask, where do you see this going?" *I'm terrified of her response.*

She looks nervous, and my heart pounds out with an unsteady beat. *Shit! Did I screw this up by asking for her to define us?* Honestly, when we met at my signing, I never imagined we'd be here now. When I begged Christian to bring Samantha to my game and dinner, I was just looking for an opportunity to apologize. Now, I feel like I'm at a major crossroads. Do I confess my feelings, even if they're scattered, disorganized, and unknown? Do I once again suggest staying casual? Do I act like this was a onetime thing and walk away? Her answer will determine mine. I'm willing to try casual if she wants to. I just don't want to seem desperate, looking for something more if she isn't. Plus, I'm not even sure I know how to do more.

"I think you're amazing too, Lucas, and this was completely unexpected. I honestly don't know what to think. I can't argue that we're combustible together, but I have to be realistic. You live in New York and I live here. How would it even work? What would it look like? Is that what you want? What would it entail?" She gazes at me with hope in her eyes, seeking answers for all her questions. But I don't have them. I'm just as confused as she is.

"Yes, you're right. Living in different states creates some logistical issues, but it's not impossible. I travel here for work, you travel there for work, and we have the finances that would accommodate other trips to visit each other, right?" I form my response as a question so I can see if that is an option she'd entertain. Once she decides whether she's in, I'll answer the rest of her questions. Otherwise, there's no point.

When Samantha makes a move to roll out of the bed, I stop her by placing my hand on her hip and pulling her back toward me.

"Please, let me finish. I have never wanted more with someone. I don't know what that means, but I know I'm not ready to say goodbye to you. I want to stay in your life, whether it's through phone calls, visits, or something more. I'm committed to trying." I look into her eyes, and I see my fears reflected. She's scared too.

Both unsure, she finally asks, "So, how do we do this?"

The conversation we're having is terrifying. I've never been in a relationship, but with her, I'm intrigued. I just don't know how it will go.

"What about if we do casual?" I suggest. I've heard about it before, but regarding the specifics, I'm clueless.

"Casual? Huh. How does that work exactly?" she asks pointedly. Her tone makes me believe that she's withholding reservations she has. I know I need to be careful with how I respond, so I don't give her additional reasons we might not work.

"Well, I guess it means I travel to you and you travel to me. Based on our schedules, we carve out time to spend together," I vaguely suggest, hoping she'll read between the lines. Draw her own conclusions.

"Okay, so what's upcoming on your schedule?" she asks hesitantly. I mentally run through all my commitments and realize that only one weekend is free for me to travel to her in the next three months. But she can visit me in New York, if she wants to.

"I'm really busy the next few months with the end of the season and some sponsorship commitments. I could come visit you in a month. Could you come visit me in a few weeks when I have a series in New York? I'd have my games and practices, but the rest of the time, I'd be all yours," I hesitantly offer, hoping she'll agree.

She's tentative. But after comparing the dates I suggested, we agree to give it a shot. Looking at the clock, I realize how late it was. "I need to head back to my hotel to get packed up before I have to report to my team." She nods and we dress. When she walks me to the door after my Uber has arrived, saying goodbye is harder than I thought it'd be. I'm not ready to go.

On the way back to the hotel, the last kiss she gave me still burns on my lips. *I already miss her. How is that possible?* In a few weeks, she's traveling to me.

She'd mentioned planning a few business meetings at the end of that week since she'd be in the city.

Back at the hotel, I ride the elevator up to my floor, wondering what she'll say to her parents about visiting New York. As far as I know, she stayed with her parents the last time she visited. I'll ask her when we talk tonight. Because I'm not sure how her parents or brother would take it if they knew she was planning on staying with me.

After I get to my room, I pack my bag quickly and head back down to the lobby to catch the team bus for the airport. Unable to keep my eyes open, I sleep through the two-hour flight. Last night was exhausting but so worth the sleep deprivation. Another bus picks us up from the airport and delivers us to the arena, where I grab my black Audi R8 and head home.

Arriving back home is eye-opening. It's so empty, and I don't like it. After being surrounded by Samantha for not even twenty-four hours, I realize it's lonely without her. Grabbing my phone, I'm ready to call her, but I pause before I dial... I don't want to seem desperate. Instead of calling, I drag my suitcase into my bedroom to unpack. When I was in Juniors, I learned to unpack and take care of my dirty clothes before doing anything else. I've actually become neurotic about it. I can't physically rest until the suitcase is empty, laundry has been started, and I have placed a grocery order. So that's just what I do.

Before I know it, my stomach growls, reminding

me I skipped lunch and that dinner is rapidly approaching. I chuck the last of my laundry in the dryer, stow my suitcase, and order a meat lover's pizza from Joey's. My teammate and our captain, Owen, raves about it. He says it's the best, and he's right.

As I wait for my delivery, I plop down on my leather couch and dial Samantha. While waiting for her to answer, my heart rate picks up, my hands sweat, and my thoughts spin. *Have I ever been nervous about calling a woman? No. So why now?* Because she isn't just a woman; she's Samantha. And that means something to me.

We didn't make us "official." Honestly, I'm not even sure what to label us. We're more than a one-night stand, more than a booty call, but we aren't dating. *What are we?* Being new to this, I don't know all the rules. All I know is that I really like Samantha, and I'm interested in seeing where this goes.

Chapter 16

Samantha

Lucas and I had to say goodbye this morning, and I have to admit, it was harder than I expected. We've decided to try being casual. I'm still unclear what that means, but I feel like that was the only way to keep him in my life. After Lucas left this morning, I went back to bed for a nap. When I woke up hours later, I realized how empty and lonely my penthouse seemed without him here. He promised he'd call tonight, so I've busied myself with household chores, grocery shopping, and some work tasks to keep me busy until then.

Just as I'm about to figure out dinner, my phone rings and his picture flashes across the screen. My heart flutters and excitement runs rampant through my body. I try to calm myself before I answer. "Hello." *Damn it! Why do I sound breathy?*

"Hey, babe," Lucas responds in his deep, sexy voice.

"How was your flight?"

"Fine. Someone kept me up most of the night, so as soon as we took off, I passed out and slept the entire way," he teases.

"Hmmm... someone kept you up all night? I hope you weren't doing anything too terrible. Good thing you're now home and can get a good night's rest," I counter.

"I'm not sure good is quite the word I would use. Yes, I'll probably get some sleep. But last night I had someone amazing to snuggle with, so tonight, I'll be missing that."

Smiling wide, my heart beams. He loved snuggling as much as I did. I've never had anyone to snuggle with and it felt beyond incredible to be wrapped in his muscular arms, pulled tightly into his unbelievable body. "I'm going to miss you tonight, too. After you left... my bed felt empty, lonely, and huge." My admission is tinged with sadness. *How can I feel so connected to someone I barely know?*

While talking, I order a deep-dish veggie pizza from my new favorite spot, Luigi's. Growing up in New York, I have always had a love for pizza. But now, being in Chicago, I had to give the deep-dish pie a chance. And I absolutely love it.

When my pizza is delivered, we switch to Face-Time so we can have our dinner together.

"Do you have pizza too?" I ask, while holding up a slice.

Lucas nods. "Of course, I do. Living in New York, it was that, hot dogs or pretzels, right?" He chuckles. But then his expression suddenly changes to a more serious one. "Samantha... is that deep-dish pizza?" The low register of his voice startles me until I realize what he asked and bark out a laugh.

Wiping tears from my eyes because that... that was funny. "Yes, Lucas. It is a deep dish. I live in Chicago. It would be a crime to have anything else."

Over our pizza dinner, we talk about everything and nothing. The entire conversation is so easy and effortless. Around nine p.m., my brain halts. Between the constant yawning and the inability to recall basic words, I'm exhausted. I need to call it a night, but I don't want to.

"Babe, I think you're tired and probably need to go to bed," Lucas quips.

Then I yawn again while shaking my head. *I don't think I've ever been so tired before.*

"You aren't tired?" Lucas asks, but I hear the humor in his voice. He isn't ready to end our call either.

Like a toddler who's had her favorite toy taken away, I pout. An adorable smile spreads across Lucas's face, so tell him, "I am tired, but I'm not ready to say goodbye yet. I know it'll be tough to connect this week, and I've had such a fantastic time talking to you."

"I've had a great time talking to you, too. We can text and figure out what works best for us. We'll connect, I promise."

His words ease me. "Okay, you're probably right. I'll text you tomorrow after my meeting."

"That sounds great. I have a light day tomorrow, so unless I'm in practice or working out, I should be able to respond easily." *I'm counting on it.*

Releasing yet another yawn, I can't help but giggle. "I guess I should go to bed. Thanks for calling, Lucas. It was so great to talk to you tonight."

"Sweet dreams, Samantha. I'll talk to you tomorrow." Again, his saying goodbye hits me hard. *I really like him. I hope he doesn't hurt me.*

Chapter 17

Samantha

Talking to Lucas tonight was almost the perfect way to end the weekend. The only thing better would be if he lived here and we were going to bed together. Thinking about that is too much, too fast, though. I need to stop before I get too far ahead of this... whatever it is. Otherwise, I'll be paying the price.

The next morning, I start strong, thankfully, because I'm putting out fire after fire. Before I know it, it's six in the evening and I grab my cell phone to see if I've missed any texts or calls from Lucas. Throughout the day, I had been away from my desk more than I'd been there and it's possible I missed him if he tried to get ahold of me. Looking at the screen, I see I missed a call from Christian and one from Monica, but nothing from Lucas. I try to tell myself that he's probably busy, as they just returned from a weekend away and he had mentioned that he knew he'd be busy with some sponsorship commitments. But I can't help feeling a bit slighted. He must be busy, I tell myself as I straighten up my office for the evening. I call Christian back, but instead of answering, he texts back that he can't talk right now, but he'll find me tomorrow at the office.

I head to my penthouse. While I'm making a salad for dinner, I call Monica back and we catch up on what happened over the weekend.

"So, what did you do this weekend?" she asks.

"I went to the Steel game with Christian."

"That sounds... fun?" *I love Monica. She gets me.*

"Yeah. Last thing I wanted to be doing, but Christian said he was scouting a new client and he promised me dinner at Mateo's afterward."

Monica clucks her tongue at me. "Ha. You only agreed because of Mateo's." Her accusation has no bite. Instead, it's filled with mirth.

"You got me. I was sold as soon as I heard their name. But it was a strange night," I confess.

"Strange night? What does that mean?"

Rip off the bandage. Tell someone. "You remember Lucas?"

"Car Lucas? Yes, I remember him. Why are we talking about him?" Her tone hints at her distaste for him.

"Funny story... I kind of had dinner with him and... and..." My stomach plummets as I stutter through my conversation with my bestie.

"Spit it out, Sam. I'm already in shock. What more can you say? It's not like you slept with him, right?"

Silence fills the line. *How do I respond to that?*

A gasp filters over the line. "You slept with him? After the whole car situation?"

"Yes," I squeak out.

"Sam, what happened?"

"He showed up for dinner. Apparently, my brother invited him." *I'm still mad at Christian. I can't decide if I should kick him or hug him.* As far as I know, he's still unaware of what happened between Lucas and me the night of his signing. And I plan to keep it that way. No brother needs to know the intimate details of his sister's sex life. "If things aren't uncomfortable enough, after Lucas joined us, Christian made some work excuse and left."

"What?" Monica screeches.

Holding my hands up, even though she can't see me, I say, "It needed to happen. Lucas and I talked about what happened and he apologized for what did and explained that he didn't just want fast and dirty with me but something more."

"Eeeek," Monica squeals. "What happened after dinner?"

"Hmmm." I make a non-committal noise in my throat. "Only the best sex of my life."

After dropping that truth bomb, I hear Monica gasp. "Holy shit. No words. I literally have no words. You slept with Lucious Lucas?"

Still trying to wrap my head around it, I confess, "Lucas and I are going to try a long-distance casual arrangement."

"A what? I've never heard of it. Is it like long-distance fuck buddies?"

"Maybe we can come up with a less crude term." I laugh.

"We can totally do that, but let's get back to you telling me about the best sex of your life."

Even though she can't see me, I can feel my cheeks turning red and hot. "I'm only going to give you minimal details. Lucas has an incredible body, and he knows how to use every part... remarkably... well."

Monica sighs into the phone. "Okay, I know you won't discuss specifics, but what will you tell me?"

"Hmmm... It was amazing. It's like he knew my body and what exactly to do to it to leave me a squiggly noodle, and when all was said and done, after he delivered no fewer than four orgasms, he snuggled me to sleep. It was perfect."

"That sounds perfect," she whispers. "And now you're casual. Will that work?"

Hesitantly, I answer, "I hope so. I really like him. Guess we'll see." Glancing at the clock, I notice it's after nine.

"Monica, I'm exhausted and I need to do some things around here before bed. Mind if we talk in a few days?"

"No problem. Talk soon. Love you."

"Love you too. Night."

I quickly finish up my chores before heading to bed. As I place my phone on the charger, I realize I still haven't heard from Lucas. Bummed, I fire off a quick text to him before crawling into bed.

ME

Missed talking to you today. Hope your day was okay. Maybe we'll connect tomorrow? Good night.

Chapter 18

Lucas

When I wake up to my alarm on Tuesday morning, I'm already feeling like I'm running behind. My assistant overbooked my Monday but didn't tell me until that morning. I barely had time to breathe, and today I'm playing catch up. Today, I have practice, weight room, and a photo shoot with one of my sponsors. Hurrying through getting ready, I grab a protein shake before rushing out of my penthouse, barely seeing the doorman as I fly out of the building.

In my car on the way to the arena for morning practice, I ask Siri to read any missed messages. She informs me I have one. When she reads who the sender is—Samantha—my heart drops. Sitting at a stoplight, I realize I didn't talk to or text her at all yesterday. I had been so busy. Thinking back, I'm not even sure when I would have squeezed it in.

When I got back to my penthouse at ten last night, I was exhausted. Falling into bed shortly after undressing and brushing my teeth, when my head hit my pillow, I passed out. I had every intention of calling her. *Shit. I hope she isn't mad.*

Siri reads the message to me, and as I listen, I notice she sounds both sad and disappointed. I don't enjoy letting her down. I need to call or at least text her today. Running through my daily schedule, I'm desperate to figure out when I can do that.

Relationships are tough, even when they're just casual. Never having done this before, I'm unfamiliar with being concerned about hurting someone I care for. The only person I've ever wanted to make a priority was my mom. That was until Samantha came into my life. For her, I want to put in the effort. Even though that scares the shit out of me, I know she's worth it and deserves it. To me, she isn't just a hookup, but something more. I can't define what "more" means, but I know it's something that I haven't done or wanted before.

When I arrive at the arena and am about to head into the locker room, my phone rings. It's a call from my assistant, Stacey.

"Morning, Stacey." I huff while climbing out of my car.

"Morning, Lucas. Just calling to remind you about the photo shoot you have this afternoon. Also wanted to let you know I scheduled a business dinner tonight with Christian and some reps from Gatorade. They'd mentioned something about a potential campaign and they'd like to meet you." Her words put an instant smile on my face and extra pep in my step.

Fist pumping the air, I clarify, "The dinner is tonight? Where and when?"

Stacey hums to herself for a moment before answering, "Ahh, yes. Christian is flying in this afternoon and will meet you at the restaurant he selected. It's new and I've never been there. I'll stop by your penthouse and grab a suit that I'll send over to the shoot. You'll need to get ready there because the shoot will probably run late."

This is amazing. "Can you please text me the addresses of both the shoot and dinner? I'm heading into the locker room now."

"Sure thing. I hope the dinner goes great."

"Thanks, Stacey. Me too."

Pushing into the locker room, I'm greeted by some of my teammates with their favorite taunt. "Hooker!" I smile and shake my head, dropping my bag at my locker. I fist bump my best friend and co-captain of the team, Jackson (Jack) Blue. He mutters in my ear, "You better wipe that perma-grin off your mug, or Coach is going to give us extra drills. You know he can't stand to see us too happy!"

"Is he still pissed? I thought he got it out of his system with yesterday's practice from hell and the torturous weight room workout," I question, my smile still clinging to my face. Between Samantha and the potential new relationship with Gatorade, I feel like I'm the king of the world.

"He is. He's become a testy devil since his wife served him divorce papers last month. It's almost like he blames us for the fall of his marriage. Hell, relationships are hard. Especially because of our schedule, but it's something you have to really work at, making sure you aren't neglecting your partner. That's on him, not us."

Knowing Jack is cautioning me about Coach's mood, I'd be wise to listen. What he said about relationships seems pretty sound, too. But since I don't do relationships, it really doesn't apply. Or maybe it does apply? What did he say? Something about not neglecting your partner because of the time requirements of our job. That thought registers hard. Wasn't that what happened on a smaller scale with Samantha yesterday? I wouldn't consider Samantha and me in a relationship, per se, but I certainly knew I'd have to put in some effort regarding my time with her. I already had a taste of her disappointment regarding that when I'd gotten her message this morning. And it had shaken me to the core.

Tweet! Tweet! The sharp squeals of the coach's whistle get my attention. My back snaps up, and I rush to tie my skates. That didn't sound good. Coach is in a mood. *Fuck.* I only hope we survive it without throwing up on the ice. I can't give too much thought to my predicament with Samantha when I hear Coach storm through the locker room with his whistle pinched tightly between his lips. His breath labored and his round, pudgy face red like a Hot Tamale candy. If he isn't careful, he'll stroke out. *This isn't good.*

From his appearance, I know I'll need to be on the ice in seconds or there will be hell to pay during drills. Even though I'm slightly terrified, I still feel the remnants of the smile I'd had only moments ago. It'd be smart if I could wipe it from my face, but it won't budge. I cover my face, knowing my happiness will piss off Coach and earn extra drills for the rest of the team. And that would suck ass. Not only would my teammates retaliate if I were the culprit behind more drills, but they'd find another way to make me suffer. With them, it'd be worse than a freshman pledging a fraternity house. In fact, I had some ideas of what they might do: put tape on my blades, cut my laces, or the notorious jockstrap-filled-with-Icy Hot prank. I need to lose my smile because anything I come up with would be dreadful. On top of that, Coach's ass-chewing with an audience would be frightening and humiliating. Quickly, I school my expression and turn back toward where Coach is already hollering out his plan for our ice time.

Following another grueling practice, Coach expected us to spend at least an hour in the weight room. Once I've showered and changed, I see a text from Stacey.

STACEY

> The photo shoot is at the arena at one. They are getting shots of you in new gear on the ice. I will place your suit in the locker room for dinner tonight. You are to meet everyone at Formaggio's at eight.

The shoot starts in twenty minutes. My stomach growls. I'm starving and I need to hustle. Thankfully, I can grab lunch in our cafeteria. After I load a plate with grilled chicken and roasted vegetables, I devour it while the photographers set up.

While eating, I scroll through my phone. I'm about to send Samantha a text apologizing for last night and informing her of my business dinner tonight, when I'm called over to check the gear I'm expected to wear for the shoot. I want her to know, even though I haven't talked to her, I've thought of her often. I end up pocketing my phone without finishing or sending the text. My remaining lunch goes into the trash and I get changed for the shoot.

The photoshoot takes longer than expected, just as Stacey predicted, and I rush to shower and dress before having to scramble across the city to Formaggio's. I've heard from some teammates that it has amazing food, but I'm suspicious. From the name, I assume it's an expensive cheese bar. Hey, I'm Canadian, so unless we are talking poutine, I eat very little cheese. *This is going to be interesting.*

Arriving outside the restaurant, I hand my keys to the valet before heading inside. Working out my nerves, I fidget with my tie while I wait for the hostess. When she returns, she gives me her best bedroom eyes. She's definitely attractive and exactly my usual type. Well, at least she was before I met Samantha and we became something more. Now, the only woman I want is Samantha. I give a curt nod to the hostess to let her know I'm not interested, but am ready to meet with my party. She gets the message and, after a moment, guides me to a back room that's filled with men in suits.

Christian strides over to me and shakes my hand. He leans in and whispers, "Follow my lead." I nod and follow him over to a group I presume are the executives of Gatorade; the men I need to impress. As he introduces each man, I give them a firm handshake and tell them I'm glad to meet them. After introductions, we sit around the table and order drinks. Not much of a drinker, I order a beer. Beer goes with cheese, right? If I remember correctly, that's a thing, especially in Wisconsin.

After Christian orders a variety of things for us to sample, we get down to business. The executives waste no time peppering me with questions about me, my career, my passions, and my future plans. Throughout the evening, I stuff myself full of wonderful food. I hadn't realized that cheese could be used so diversely and tasted so good. I really enjoy the toasted almond and fig baked brie, mini cheesesteak sandwiches, mac and cheese, and something I think is called a charcuterie board.

The dinner goes beyond great, and we've made great strides toward developing an endorsement agreement. The head executive, Jim, tells Christian and me he needs to get back to his office to run some numbers. He says he'll forward a contract over later in the week for review. My body is buzzing with excitement.

After all the Gatorade executives leave, Christian and I toast with two fingers of Wild Turkey bourbon. "To a new endorsement deal." Christian says.

"Thanks, man." Lifting the glass to my lips, hearing the clank of the ice cubes, I savor the first taste. It's full of spice that morphs into a sweet finish. It's delicious and the perfect way to celebrate our deal for the Gatorade endorsement.

I finally realize how late it is when I look at my watch after I finish my drink. "Headed back to Chicago tonight? Or staying in the city for some fun?" I ask with a smirk.

Christian laughs and shakes his head. "No, I have to head back for meetings tomorrow. Next trip is for fun, right?"

Smiling, I answer, "I'm not sure I can keep up with your fun. Travel safe." We fist bump and he heads to a cab while I wait for the valet. When my Audi drives up, I climb in and make the short drive to my penthouse.

I'm still riding high on adrenaline, but as soon as I cross into my penthouse, it wanes. Suddenly, I'm dog tired. I practically crawl to my bedroom, removing my clothes as I go, leaving an embarrassing trail behind me. When I reach the bathroom, I'm completely undressed except for my boxer briefs. I hurriedly brush my teeth, plug in my phone, and fall into bed. These last few days have been exhausting. Between my practices, sessions in the weight room, a photo shoot, the business dinner, and the bourbon, I am a noodle and sleep comes easily.

Chapter 19

Samantha

Today promises to be a little easier than yesterday, and I'm thankful for that. Minutes after I arrive at work, as I'm addressing emails, Christian strolls into my office with a wide smirk on his face. *What's that about?* He's done something. I know it because he's strutting around like a peacock, showing off his plumage.

I sit back in my leather swivel chair, cross my arms over my chest, and give him my most questioning look.

He notices, points to my posture, and says, "What is that about?"

I smile and answer, "You tell me. You're smiling like the cat that ate the canary. What are you up to?" He lifts his shoulder as if he doesn't know what I'm referring to. I give him my most intense stare and mentally will him to tell me what he's up to. After a few moments under my gaze, his demeanor crumbles and he raises his hands in defeat. Christian has never kept secrets from me, and right now, he's about to reveal a good one. It's obvious by the way his now relaxed state has morphed into him bouncing on his heels. He's trying to contain his excitement and at any moment, it's going to explode out of him.

"Sam, this is hush-hush. We haven't made a deal yet, but it looks promising, and it's huge," he brags.

"Does it have anything to do with why you couldn't answer my call last night?" I inquire while tapping my manicured fingers on my biceps.

He nods his head. "Exactly. I was having dinner with the executives at Gatorade and I sold them on an idea. Lucas as the rep of their sports drink. In fact, I'm flying back to New York on our jet and taking them and Lucas out to dinner tonight."

"That's an incredible opportunity. I hope it goes well. Please tell Lucas congratulations for me if it all works out." I try to sound supportive, but I'm internally groaning. Great, another night where I'll miss talking with Lucas. I wonder if I'll hear from him at all today. Christian might have shared the good news with him, but who knows? I don't even know if he organizes his own schedule. He mentioned an assistant, and that seems like something she'd be responsible for.

"I bet Lucas was excited about the potential opportunity. Gatorade is huge," I admit.

"Actually, I'm not even sure he knows yet. I just

called his assistant, Stacey, on my way in, so he's probably finding out right now, before practice begins."

"That is truly an exciting possibility, Christian, but I'm swamped. You don't need me to run any numbers before you fly out, do you?" I say, giving my brother a polite brushoff. Christian looks at me with confusion pulled tight across his face.

He shakes his head and answers me abruptly. In a clipped tone, he spits, "No, I don't need anything. I just wanted to share the good news. I'll get out of your hair." Quickly, he retreats from my office like he's being forced out by an invisible hand.

Grabbing my phone, I send a quick text to Lucas.

ME

Hey. I just heard about the Gatorade dinner. Wanted to say good luck. Talk later.

The rest of the day gets away from me, but it's filled with endless meetings. When I arrive home late, I have no energy. Cheese, crackers, and fruit are the perfect dinner. My bed is calling my name, and without a second thought, I succumb to my overly exhausted state.

The next day when I get to my office, Christian is already there with his feet kicked up on my desk, wearing a million-dollar smile. *Here we go again. Game face on.*

"What?" I ask, my words laced with heavy sarcasm.

"I may have helped our newest hockey client set the foundations for an epic deal with Gatorade," he brags.

My mouth falls open and I dramatically clutch my fictitious pearls. "Wow. That's impressive, and here I thought you were going to tell me you bedded an heiress to some empire."

"Don't sound so surprised," Christian defends, rolling his eyes at me. "Geez, Sam. Way to ruin my excitement." He groans as he dramatically kicks his feet off my desk.

My head dips in apology. "You're right. It's really great. I'm sure Lucas is thrilled, too."

Christian stands and saunters past me. "Who peed in your cornflakes this morning? Why are you in such an awful mood?" Without even waiting for an answer, he strolls out of my office. And I'm left wondering why hearing about this from my brother rather than Lucas bothers me so much.

As the day stretches on, thoughts of Lucas continue to invade my brain, taking up more headspace than I should allow. Is this how it's always going to be between us? Me, always waiting? Waiting to see if I'll hear from him? Waiting for any scrap he'll toss to me?

I shake my head defiantly. *No, I refuse to be that girl.*

After work, I head to a yoga class near my penthouse to help myself unwind. I'm hoping an hour of hot yoga will help me destress. After class, I find I can breathe a little easier and I realize I'm starving. Stopping by the corner market, I grab a pre-made dinner. Just because I'm feeling better doesn't mean I want to go through the hassle of fixing some elaborate meal. For one. *Shit. That's depressing.*

When I enter my home, I can't help but notice how desolate it seems. When Lucas was here over the weekend, we filled it with so many joyful noises. But now it's eerily silent. Needing to change that, I turn on my sound system and pick a country station. Music fills my penthouse, erasing the silence, and after a few songs, the void seems nonexistent and I feel more comfortable.

After finishing my dinner, I decide a relaxing bath is just what I need. I hope to loosen the rest of the knots that have been holding my shoulders hostage for the past few days. And when I emerge from the citrus-scented bubbles, I'm completely relaxed, refreshed, and ready for bed.

As I'm lying there waiting to fall asleep, I realize Lucas still hasn't reached out. Normally, this wouldn't bother me, but we'd specifically talked about it. My fragile heart stutters and I curl into a ball. Hugging my pillow that still smells like his aftershave is painful. But I can't seem to unwrap my grip from it. I fall into a night of fitful sleep.

Chapter 20

Lucas

When I hit the arena this morning, I was still reeling from my dinner. On the agenda for the day is a team meeting, practice, and a weight room session. Our team heads to Philly at the end of this week for a two-game series and Coach is amped even higher than yesterday. Unfortunately, it doesn't look like we'll have a chance at the Stanley Cup this year, but we're still determined to show up and play well.

As I'm strapping the last of my gear on, it occurs to me I didn't hear from Samantha yesterday. *Shit.* I wonder if I missed her call while I was at dinner. Last night, I was so exhausted, I barely got my phone on my charger before I passed out.

Now, sitting on the bench in front of my locker, I'm confused. Backtracking, I replay my day. Before the photo shoot, I remember sending her a text. At least, I think I did. *Did I?* Not feeling one hundred percent confident, I quickly check through my texts and realize that the message I'd carefully crafted is still waiting to be sent. "Shit! Shit! Shit!" I mutter under my breath. *I'm an asshole.*

"Lucas."

"Lucas."

"Lucas," Jack calls out, a tinge of panic in his voice.

"Yeah," I croak back. My head swimming.

"Time for practice. If we aren't out there in a minute, we're all going to get extra drills."

Ugh! "You're right, I'm coming," I answer, while grabbing my jersey and pulling it over my head. Exiting the locker room, I tell myself everything will be fine. But apparently, I don't believe it because maintaining focus during practice proves difficult.

"Lucas, get your head in the game." Acknowledging Jack barking at me, I give him a chin lift. Later, Miles checks me in the shoulder and growls, "Focus." *Damn, I'm distracted. I need to focus and get my head in the game. And off Samantha.*

Despite the guys' best efforts, Coach still notices I'm distracted. Thankfully, he doesn't punish the whole team, only glaring at me. Knowing I'll deal with that at some point, I finish practice.

After stripping out of my gear, I pull on some athletic shorts and shoes to get a workout in. "Let's do this," Miles hollers at Jack and me on our way out of the locker room.

When I'm even with Coach's door, he snarls out, "Bouchard. Get your ass in here." Jack and Miles snicker, knowing Coach is pissed with me. *Fuck me. Here we go.*

"See you later," I tell my best friends as I enter Coach's domain. With my fingers, I rub at the tension that's settled in my neck. I mentally catalog what I need to say to get this flogging over as quickly as possible.

"About time," he grumbles as I make my way to an uncomfortable plastic chair he has for guests. "Lucas, where the hell was your head during that practice?"

"Sorry, sir. I have some personal things on my mind today, and I allowed myself to lose focus. It won't happen again."

"You're damn right it won't. You are one of my best players. But if you've got your head in the clouds, you are useless to me. Understand?"

"Yes, sir. I understand completely."

"Okay. You're dismissed. Get your ass out of my office and go get your workout in."

"Yes, sir."

Quickly, I make a beeline for the weight room. It's relatively quiet except for some grunting, weight plates settling, and the low chuckle of my best friends. *Assholes.*

"Guys. Cardio done?"

Jack and Miles both nod. *I'll do that tonight.* Today is a dedicated leg day, and the sooner we get to it, the sooner it'll be over. The trainers scheduled it for today because they want us fully recovered before we head out of town for a series of games. We fill our next hour with deadlifts, lunges, squats, and hip thrusts. By the time we're done, my legs feel like rubber.

"Damn, my legs feel like Gumby." Miles groans as we head into the cafeteria for lunch.

"How do you know about Gumby? You're, like what, nineteen?" I jest as I grab my lunch of grilled salmon, baked potato, broccoli, and salad.

"Twenty-one. And while I was growing up, I spent a lot of time with my grandparents and they had some Gumby toys that they'd let me play with. No matter how many times I bent and twisted him, he never broke," Miles confesses with a smirk on his face. *Little shit. I bet he tried to break it.*

During lunch, Miles tries to convince me to join him at a club the following weekend. Looking at my calendar, I realize it's the weekend that Samantha mentioned coming to see me.

"I have something that weekend. I can't be your wingman." Miles pouts. "Can't you ask Deacon? He's always up for clubbing," I suggest in an overly friendly tone. Secretly, I'm hoping they don't ask about the plans I mentioned. I'm not ready to tell them about Samantha. This thing with us is new, and I'm not looking to invite harassment from them about a woman. Apparently, though, I'm not that lucky.

"What do you have that weekend?" Jack asks with raised eyebrows. He's like a dog with a bone. His ability to smell out half-truths is fucking weird. But before I come up with an answer, he focuses back on his food, only half listening.

I shift nervously in my seat. *How do I spin this?* They're my best friends, but they know I don't do relationships. So... how do I explain Samantha? I decide to go with casual, hoping they won't ask for details.

"I have a friend coming to visit since we don't have any games that weekend."

Miles smirks at me. "A friend, you say? Is this a male or female friend?"

Jack whips his head up, suddenly disinterested in his salmon and intrigued with the conversation. He stares at me, waiting impatiently for my answer.

Panic sets in. My palms sweat. Clearing my throat, I answer in a squeaky tone that's reminiscent of puberty. "Female."

"What?" Jack shouts loudly as he shoots up from his chair. It clatters next to him and the entire cafeteria focuses on our table. Realizing he's drawn the attention of everyone, he quickly apologizes for the disturbance. He picks up his chair and settles back into it. Then he stares at me again and whispers, "What?"

Next to me, Miles laughs like a hyena, and all I can do is roll my eyes. Even though he hasn't been with the team long, he still knows what's coming. Jack the Inquisitor is about to make an appearance. A very unwelcome appearance at that. Grumbling, I dip my head, pretending my lunch is utterly fascinating. *Come on salmon, help me out.* Chancing a glance up, I'm hopeful. *Maybe they'll forget I said anything and move on to something else?* I refuse to make eye contact, because if that happens with Jack, I'm totally screwed. He is capable of extracting every bit of information from me. I remind myself that Samantha is something I want to keep private. Especially if I'm right in assuming that I've already majorly fucked up with her over the past few days. She might be so hurt that visiting is no longer in the cards. An even worse thought is that we're through before we've even started.

Jack asks, "What female friend is visiting? You don't do female friends. Hell, you barely do friends, period. If Miles, Christian, and I hadn't taken pity on your sorry mug, you'd be all alone." I laugh because what he said is true. As a general rule, I don't do friends or relationships. Those I have befriended, I keep close. Truth is, when I think of Samantha, I don't just want a friendship with her. I want more.

Then the thought occurs to me that if I'm serious about wanting more with her, I should probably give them a heads-up about it. Eventually, they'll have to meet, and I don't want her to think I'm hiding her or us. So, I bite the bullet and answer them.

Leaning forward, I murmur, hoping they'll understand I want to keep this quiet and private, "Yes, I invited a female friend to visit me next weekend." *Stop talking, Lucas. That's enough.* Limiting what I share right now is the only plan I have. Unfortunately, my best friends are amateur sleuths and bombard me with questions.

"What's her name? Where is she from? What does she do?" Jack pries.

"Jack, those are important questions. But I need to know... How is the sex?" Miles demands as he pulls himself closer to the table. He's gyrating next to me like an excited little puppy who's desperate for a toy.

Little does Miles know I don't talk about sex with anyone. Actually, I guess that's not entirely true. Talking to Samantha about her lack of experience was definitely a first for me. But it was a necessity. I needed to know that she was totally comfortable with me and with everything we were doing together.

I breathe out slowly and finally answer some of their questions. "Her name is Samantha, and she works on the financial side of Fox Sporting. I invited her here so I could get to know her better. She's a native New Yorker, but she lives and works in Chicago." Just thinking about her brings a smile to my face and a lightness to my chest. *I probably look dopey.* Just then, I remember that I still need to call her. *Shit.* Grabbing my phone from my bag, I hurriedly gather my dishes and hop up out of my chair. *I've got to go.*

"Wait! Where do you think you're going? You just dumped a lot of information on us. We need pictures, details," Jack tells me as he grabs my forearm, trying to keep me from leaving.

"Guys, I have to go. I need to call her. For the last few days, I have been a distant asshole. I've been too busy. This needs to be fixed before I destroy everything." I hope they'll sense the urgency and desperation in my plea.

Jack removes his hand and cautions, "Pissed off, hurt women are the worst. You need to stay on top of that shit! Trust me, I've learned that lesson the hard way. Grovel big."

After putting my dishes away, I run out of the cafeteria like my ass is on fire and hightail it to my car. Before long, I'm back in my penthouse, pacing and mentally running through what I need to say to Samantha before I actually call her. I know I'm to blame for any hurt feelings she has. I need to make it right. Grabbing my phone, I hit her contact. Now, I only hope she answers so I can apologize and grovel. Repeatedly. Until I earn her forgiveness.

Chapter 21

Samantha

I'm just about to head into another meeting when my cell phone rings. Unsure who is calling me, I grab it. Everyone knows I'm at work and to call my office line. Everyone but Lucas. My heart flutters at the thought that maybe he's finally calling. Turning it over, his handsome face fills my screen. Just as I'm about to answer, my assistant, Suzette, pops into my office, reminding me that everyone has gathered in the conference room and is waiting for me. Even though it hurts, I decline the call, set the phone on my desk, and grab the paperwork I'll need. As I head out of my office, I focus on making this the quickest meeting I have ever had. I'm desperate to get back to my phone and see if Lucas left a message. We need to talk.

What was supposed to be a quick financial review of some of our representation in athlete endorsements, turns into a two-hour-long bitch session about how salary caps are making it difficult to secure some of our clients with the best contracts. I remind them we have no control over that and we just have to work harder to secure endorsement deals for those clients who are interested in more money.

Trudging back to my office following the shit show that just combusted in the conference room, I'm exhausted.

As I pass Suzette, she reminds me I have a charity event later at the Museum of Contemporary Art for the children's hospital. Thankfully, I remembered that before I'd left my penthouse this morning and brought my dress, shoes, and jewelry with me. I scoot into my personal restroom and touch up my hair and makeup.

I dress in a red Oscar de la Renta floral cutout sleeveless A-line dress and matching Ruby asymmetric 90mm sandals. I plan to leave my briefcase in the car so I don't have to worry about holding on to too many items. Loaded in my wristlet are all the things I'll need for the night: phone, ID, cash, business cards, and lip gloss. When I walk back into my office, I run into Christian, who catcalls me. I laugh. "Hey. Want to fill me in on the meeting you and Lucas had with the Gatorade people?"

"How about I tell you about it while I walk you out?" he suggests.

Grabbing my briefcase from my desk, I answer, "Sounds great!" Putting my arm through his, we both say goodnight to Suzette before heading to the elevator.

"The dinner went fantastic. They want to make a deal with Lucas. We totally impressed them, just as I knew we would. I took them to Formaggio's. They hadn't been there yet, so I think that helped too." Christian's smile radiates. He's pleased with himself.

I have always been proud of my brother and how hard he works, but this bit of information rubs me the wrong way. Honestly, I struggle to celebrate this with him. Why wouldn't Lucas want to share this with me? I frown, thinking I must not be that important to him. I kind of get it, we're still new. "I bet Lucas is happy," I say, with a bit of snark in my voice.

Christian turns toward me, eyeing me suspiciously. "He's excited, for sure. I'm confident he will be the next NHL player to represent Gatorade. We celebrated after the executives left, and he was definitely happy, but something seemed off with him." *What is Christian holding back?*

"Seemed off?" I question. *Maybe he's regretted making our arrangement? Maybe he already wants to be free of it? Of me? Maybe that's why he hasn't called me since we talked on Sunday night. Maybe that's what his call was about this afternoon. He was probably calling to break it off.*

Not wanting to deal with any of the emotions stirring up within me, I push my feelings and thoughts about Lucas out of my head. Needing to maintain control, I squeeze my brother's arm. "I hate to cut this short, but I really need to get to the charity event. I am really proud of you." Tears well up in my eyes and I attempt to blink them away as I give my brother a kiss on the cheek. He can't see me upset.

He hugs me hard and tells me to have fun tonight before he ushers me into my car. As we drive away, I watch Christian. He's calm and has a bit of bounce to his step. Where's he headed? Rolling my eyes, he's probably going to meet some nameless woman for a hookup or to hit a club where other random women will crawl all over him. His behavior disgusts me. Then, like a gut punch, I remember Lucas is just like him. My air rushes from my lungs. Fearful, I rationalize that he must have recognized all he'd be missing out on. If he hasn't yet, he will and he'll end things. Honestly, I never had a chance with him. Why settle for average when extraordinary is always throwing themselves at you?

The charity event for the children's hospital is just as I expected. And I'm thankful I arrive late, causing me to miss the boring speeches at the beginning. Throughout the fundraiser, I network with some of Chicago's most influential CEOs and CFOs. Even though this isn't typical business for the sports representation world, it never hurts to have influential and powerful people in my arsenal of affiliates.

When I finally make it home, I'm exhausted. I strip off my dress and heels just after my front door closes. My feet ache and I amble into my room. I clean my face, brush my teeth, and charge my phone before I crawl into the sheets and pass out.

Thursday morning begins too early. Still rubbing the sleep out of my eyes and yawning like I haven't slept for days, I wander into my shower. Thankfully, the water warms quickly, and after I peel off my bra and panties, I climb in and let the water cover me.

Slowly, after the hot shower, I wake up and get ready. Snagging my phone from its charger, I notice the unretrieved message. *Who called?* Flipping to the voice mail, I remember Lucas called as I was heading into a meeting and I couldn't take the call. Thankfully, he left a message. My nerves are on edge as I push play. *What will he say?* Butterflies take flight in my stomach as his deep, sexy voice fills the air.

> *"Hey, Samantha, it's Lucas. I can't apologize enough about the fact it's Wednesday and you're just now hearing from me. I have been incredibly busy, but it's no excuse. I know I fucked up, and I hope you can forgive me. Please call me back so I know you got this. I am truly sorry and I can't wait to talk to you. Bye, babe."*

My knees go weak when I hear the emotion in his voice. Not only does he sound sorry, but there is a tinge of sadness and anger too. He's genuinely upset. The only way that we can resolve this is by talking. Sitting on the edge of my bed, I push his contact.

Ring, ring, ring...

When he doesn't answer, my heart drops. It's just another missed opportunity for us. Will it always be like this? If so, should we stop this... whatever it is, before anyone gets hurt? Taking a quick inventory tells me my heart's already invested. Losing Lucas now would be painful. I'm already somewhat attached. My phone flashes and I look down and see a text... from Lucas.

LUCAS

I just saw you tried to call. I can't answer because we're in a team meeting on the plane, about to head to Philly for a pair of games. Can I call you tonight? I really, really, really want to talk to you. Miss you, babe.

Lucas's text halts my racing mind, and I can't help but smile. I quickly answer back, not knowing how long he has before they taxi.

ME

I got your message. I too have been incredibly busy. I'm free tonight, so I'm all yours. I look forward to talking to you. I miss you too!

Chapter 22

Lucas

Fighting the urge to shout "wahoo!" and fist pump because I'm supposed to be listening to the team meeting, I am ecstatic. We are finally talking! Well, kind of. Looking over our conversation, it's my turn to answer her, and my fingers fly across the keys.

ME

All mine? Is that a promise? You know, I'm a greedy man and I want all of you.

What am I saying? My words shock me even as I press send. However, I don't feel panic or anxiety about the suggestive nature of my answer. Instead, a warm, comfortable sensation settles in the middle of my chest. *That's new.* Samantha responds just as the pilot informs us we are next in line for takeoff.

SAMANTHA

I'm going to hold you to it. I have to get to work. Have a safe flight. xoxo.

Holy shit. She just signed her last text with xoxo, hugs, and kisses. *Breathe.* Again, I'm feeling no panic. For the first time in my life, I am enjoying the affection a woman is showing me. To make matters even more confusing, I want to reciprocate her feelings. With a giant smile spread across my face, I turn my phone to airplane mode before I'm tempted to respond with something cheesy and romantic. I need to play it cool, not show her how much I already care. Heated stares and the obnoxious chuckling of Jack and Miles across the aisle let me know I'm the source of their humor. Their antics earn them each the bird before I pull on my headphones, blocking everything else out.

Despite the short flight, I watch part of an episode of the latest season of *Manifest* on Netflix. I get lost in the show, and before I know it, we're touching down in Philly. After we deplane, we board the team bus for a quick trip to the Wells Fargo Center to run a practice before being delivered to our hotel.

At the hotel, I grab lunch and a nap before heading to their weight room for a workout session with Miles and Jack. With them, we manage an abbreviated session. After that, we're free until the next morning, when we have to report to the arena for a short practice and team meeting. I plan to fill my evening with room service and some FaceTime with my woman.

Talking to Samantha tonight is just what I need to center myself. According to Jack and Miles, over the past few days, I have been a moody bitch. Today, since texting her, I'm in a much better space. They, of course, ask if I've gotten laid. *That'd be a hard no.* When the only woman you want is states away, you suffer alone. The distance between us will not be convenient for working off excess energy, but I know we'll figure it out. *Maybe phone sex?* I've never done it, but with her, I'd give it a go.

Chapter 23

Samantha

All day long, I've been expecting Lucas's call. Relief hits when I step into my penthouse and I find myself giddy with excitement. After ordering my favorite meal—a Brussels sprouts & kale salad from Archer Farm Stand—I busy myself with meaningless tasks, trying to distract my restless mind.

When my dinner is delivered a half hour later, I have enough time to set it up before Lucas's call.

Moments later and mid-bite, I receive a FaceTime from Lucas. My heart beats frantically in my chest. I swallow, check my teeth for clingers, and take a few calming breaths before I accept the call. Instantly his gorgeous face fills my screen, and I can't help but smile widely. Thankfully, his lips are adorned with the same. Feeling giddy, I laugh. Tipping his head to the side, he silently questions it. However, his eyes dilate when I reach up, touch my mouth, and confess, "I'm sure I'm smiling like an idiot."

"Well, that makes two of us." The deep timbre in his laugh does weird things to my insides. "Samantha, you're beautiful."

I have missed him so much, which I can't seem to understand. We barely know each other, but I know my feelings. "I've missed you, Lucas," I admit.

His smile grows even bigger and my heart flutters.

"Babe, I've missed you, too. I'm so sorry that we haven't been able to connect until now. But right now, I'm all yours," he reassures me.

"Okay. What have you been up to?"

"Let's see... after we last talked, I had a billion practices, team meetings, and visits to the weight room. Survived a photoshoot and ate so much cheese I'm now probably half cow."

I giggle. "Did you just say you're half cow?"

He nods, his perfect face confident in his words.

"Okay, let me hear your best moo."

Lucas clears his throat, puckers his lips, and, with a straight face, releases a clear "mooooo" from his mouth.

Unabashed laughter fills the call. Gripping my sides, I croak out, "That was hilarious. You know my bestie Monica was raised on a dairy farm. Should we patch her in and get her opinion on it?"

His laughter halts immediately. He gets a serious look on his face. "You wouldn't dare," he growls out with a snicker.

Still giggling, I answer, "Yes, I totally would. That's a great moo you've got, and the entire world needs to know about it."

"I'm good. We can keep my hidden talent between us."

"Really? Your PR team could have a *hay*day. See what I did there? They'd keep you mooving forward. Come on Lucas, don't be a cow-ward."

Lucas just laughs at me. And a warm feeling spreads across my body.

"So then, why did you eat a bunch of cheese?" I ask, genuinely confused.

"Christian came to town. We had a meeting with some Gatorade executives about potential sponsorship and we met at Formaggio's, a trendy cheese bar."

"That sounds promising. I know Christian mentioned it briefly at the office. He seems confident it'll work out, and he's usually right," I tell him.

Lucas breathes out deeply. "Enough about me. What have you been up to?"

I smile warmly. "Business meetings, crunching numbers, and yoga."

Lucas moves his device closer to him as if he's studying it intently. "Yoga? Are you wearing yoga pants right now?" A seductive smirk follows his question.

I nod. He says nothing but makes a spinning motion with his pointer finger. His waggling eyebrows are everything I need to understand his silent request.

Setting my iPad so it's propped up on my coffee table, I walk a few steps away and slowly spin for him, guessing he wants to see what my pants look like on my ass. I take my time turning around. When I'm faced the opposite way, I bend over as if I'm grabbing something off the floor.

"Holy shit. You have an incredible ass." Lucas's breathing is labored and I spin around, suddenly feeling flush just as he licks his lips.

Shrugging, I say, "It's all the yoga I do."

"Well, it does your body good." My cheeks heat as his words penetrate my heart. "Babe, I wish you were here." Lucas's confession makes my heart soar.

Letting out a shaky breath, I answer him. "Me too. Soon."

Before we say goodbye, I notice he suddenly grows nervous. Instead of making eye contact like he's done all night, his focus has shifted down to his hands that he's wringing together. *What's he nervous about?*

"Is everything okay?"

"Yeah. I guess," he finally relents.

"You guess?" I ask, more defensively than I mean.

He shifts his position and I notice the tension he's holding in his shoulders.

Lucas lets out a shaky breath, looks at me, and tries not to grimace. "Do you still want to come to New York next weekend?" he asks nervously.

I look deeply into his eyes, which are pleading with me. Smiling, I try to temper the edginess I feel rolling off him. Before I answer him, I check with myself. Asking myself the same question. The answer is glaringly obvious to me. "Yes! I'm still planning to come and visit you," I happily exclaim. I'm practically shouting with excitement at him.

Instantly, his face morphs, showing the relief he's feeling. His eyes twinkle and a sexy smile spreads across his handsome face. I can't get over how incredibly irresistible he is. "Good. I'm glad to hear that." Gone is the tension and discomfort of moments ago.

We talk for a few more minutes about what we plan to do while I'm there, and it seems we're in sync. Aside from a few business meetings I have scheduled and his hockey commitments, we plan to spend most of our time just getting to know each other better. Probably in his penthouse and probably naked.

Lucky me. Having just one night with him was not enough to feed the insatiable sex beast he's unlocked. I remind myself to stop by Victoria's Secret before I leave. Visits to my hair stylist and esthetician are already scheduled.

He yawns and then grumbles, "I probably should go to bed. I need to be rested for the game tomorrow."

I nod, understanding, even though I'm not ready to say goodbye. We've gotten so comfortable with each other and I wish he were closer. I'm glad to be going to New York to see him soon. "You're right. You need your rest so you can beat Philly tomorrow."

"Planning to watch?" he asks.

"I'm not usually one to watch sports, but I looked up the games and downloaded the ESPN+ app on my laptop. Monica and Christian are coming over with pizza," I tell him.

"Monica? Does Christian have a girlfriend I don't know about?"

I shake my head before answering. "No. He's too busy chasing ass to notice that the perfect woman for him is right in front of his face. Monica is my best friend from college, and he refuses to admit their insane chemistry. Instead, he'd rather have meaningless hookups without commitment or feelings. Because of that, he'll probably lose his shot with her." I probably shouldn't have said anything about it to him, but it spilled out. I am beyond annoyed with my brother's manwhoring ways, especially when it affects my best friend. So, I guess he can suck it if Lucas ever teases him.

Lucas winces. "I've not been an angel with women and what my past intentions have been with them, but I'm sure Christian will figure it out. When he's supposed to. Trust me on that." He smiles, and my heart flutters. *Is he talking about me?* Sigh.

I hear what Lucas is saying, but I'm afraid he'll hurt Monica in the interim. I wish I could convince her to move on, but they are made for each other. "I know you're right, but I wish I could save her the pain of watching it all go down. Literally in front of her." I'm truly heartbroken for my best friend. She deserves the absolute best. And my brother is capable of so much more.

"Honestly, all he's doing now is meaningless. Once he figures that out and finds 'the one,' there will be no comparison. He'll forever be ruined for every other woman." He follows that statement with a wink that releases a thousand butterflies within me. *Why did that feel like he was talking about himself?*

Begrudgingly, we end our conversation and say goodnight. We're planning to talk again once he's back in New York after this series with Philly. Later, while I'm lying in bed, I can't help but smile when I recall the way he calls me babe. *Swoon.* Terms of endearment have always seemed silly, but when he says it, I feel the emotion behind it penetrating deep within. Like it's touching every part of me and making me feel alive.

Chapter 24

Lucas

Sweeping the series, I manage three goals and two assists; an average haul for me. Chores and a nap are on my agenda before I call Samantha. Back at my penthouse, after my laundry is started and before falling asleep, I place my dinner order at Kimball's Deli so it'll arrive right before our call. Tonight, I am going with a Reuben sandwich, and because we won the series, I'm celebrating with a black and white cookie.

While waiting for my dinner, I switch my laundry and hop in the shower. I want to look decent for my FaceTime with Samantha. During the shower, my mind drifts to our upcoming weekend and, of course, that makes me think about all the sex I hope we'll be having. Even just the thought of Samantha's hands on me has my dick throbbing. Closing my eyes, I allow myself to become immersed in that dirty fantasy, my hand grabbing hold of my shaft, squeezing hard.

After only a few strokes, I'm hard as stone and about to topple over the edge. Imaging her naked body covered in hot water and suds makes my balls draw up and tighten. This coming weekend, I want to wash and caress every inch of her magnificent body before pushing her up against the tiled wall of my shower. A zing runs up my spine, alerting me to what's ahead, and I squeeze myself at the base of my shaft, wanting to prolong the feeling. However, when I imagine lifting her legs up to wrap them around my waist before I push into her, I explode. Pumping my hand over and over, I drain my orgasm from me. Once empty, I collapse against the shower wall, breathing heavily, wishing she were here with me. Fantasizing about making her come harder than ever is nothing like experiencing the real thing, and I'm desperate to experience it again. One night was not even close to enough.

Thinking about Samantha as I pull on my gray sweatpants—I want her panting tonight. *Yes, ladies, we are aware of what they do to you*—my doorbell rings. Collecting my dinner, water, and laptop, I head to my couch to get situated before our call.

As I'm trying to connect, Samantha's contact picture fills my screen. On the one night we were together, I snagged a shot of her, looking dreamy and incredibly sexy. Even though I'd just had some fun in the shower, memories of her that night flood my brain, making me painfully hard. Just as I'm trying to shift my boner to make it less obvious in my pants, the call connects. Her giggles fill the air and I know I'm busted. All I can do is shrug and laugh.

"Is someone happy to see me?" she teases mercilessly.

Not being one who gets embarrassed too easily, I decide to roll with it. "Yep! Two somebodies miss you very much." A red blush covers her cheeks, causing my heart to pound. *Man, I've got it bad for her.*

Without missing a beat, she replies, "Is that so?" She licks her lips, and my boner that was fading comes raging back, leaving a rather noticeable tent in my sweats. Unembarrassed, I confidently challenge her. "If you were here, what would you do about it?"

She looks up through her lashes and lowers her voice to a whisper, as if she's afraid or embarrassed to admit her desires, and tells me, "I'd strip those sexy as fuck gray sweatpants and briefs down your muscular legs. I'd trace my tongue all along your abs before traveling back down your treasure trail to what waits below."

Not even letting her finish, I yell out, "Fuck. That is hot! As you can see"—I motion to my crotch—"I am totally onboard with that plan, but we have a slight problem."

The seductive smile on her pink lips falters, and questions appear in her eyes. "What?" she asks.

"Babe, you're in Chicago and I'm in New York.

Unless you have Wonder Woman's invisible jet or The Flash's speed, I don't see it happening right now." I frown and pout like a toddler.

"You're right," she says sadly. "Can I offer a rain check?"

I nod eagerly like a bobble head who's hit a speed bump. Her smile grows, which makes my body respond in unfamiliar ways. A heat builds within my chest, my heart races, and my stomach ripples. *Am I having a heart attack?* The thought of Samantha's hot, wet mouth wrapped around my dick is mind-blowing. *Yeah, I know. My body and brain are short-circuiting.*

Our conversation hasn't exactly been phone sex, but the visual images she's given me will certainly entertain me long after our call ends. I'd be stupid not to hope she'll follow through. But as I think about the upcoming weekend, I find myself wanting to please her, even more than I want my own pleasure. Talk about doing a one-eighty. Complete mindfuck, right?

Switching topics to something less exciting, she asks what I'm eating for dinner, and I pull my dinner over my lap, covering my tenting situation.

"Is that a Reuben from Kimball's Deli?" she inquires. I should have known she'd recognize it, seeing that she's a native New Yorker.

"It is. Jack introduced me to Kimball's when I first joined the team, and I love their Reubens. I even spoiled myself with a black-and-white cookie. It's my reward for the goals and assists I got in Philly." Holding up the delicious treat, I watch as her eyes grow comically wide.

"Those are my favorite," she mumbles.

"These?" I tease, pretending to take a bite.

"Jerk," she counters as she rolls her eyes dramatically before she laughs.

Chapter 25

Samantha

Talking to Lucas has definitely become one of my favorite things ever. It doesn't matter what we say, even when I tried dirty talk. It wasn't humiliating like I thought it might be. Lucas actually really seemed to enjoy it. He shared his thoughts with me and I felt comfortable sharing mine with him. He especially seemed to enjoy hearing what I wanted to do to him. In my defense, it wasn't fair. He showed up to our FaceTime in low-slung gray sweats that left nothing to the imagination but plenty to fantasize about.

From our one night together, I had only a snapshot of what he could do. And I wanted more. All his moans and growls. I was turning into a sex-crazed maniac, but it's only because I've never felt this way before. Lucas brings something deeper out of me, and I like it.

Needing a break from my hormone-driven fog, we

switch topics to dinner and then to his games this past weekend.

"How'd the games in Philly go?"

"They went fine. Did you watch?" he counters.

"I did. Christian and Monica both watched too." Lucas laughs.

"Why is that funny?" I ask curiously.

"How'd it go? Didn't you tell me they have insane chemistry? Anything happen? I'd be happy to hassle your brother."

"They're so annoying. They spent the entire game flirting and exchanging casual banter. I swear my brother is an imbecile," I complain.

"Maybe he isn't ready? Maybe he doesn't see her that way? Maybe they see each other as friends or quasi-siblings?" I shake my head at all his suggestions.

"Okay. Have you ever gone out to bars or clubs with them both? If so, has he ever seen her get attention from another guy? Maybe, if she seemed disinterested, that would finally force him to acknowledge the feelings you believe he has," Lucas suggests.

I sit there and think about what he's said. "We have gone to a club together once, but he brought some chick with him. So, his focus was elsewhere. The entire time, the barbie look-a-like hung all over him. We didn't stay long because it was too painful for Monica to watch."

"That seems to be his type." Lucas's grumble surprises me. I hadn't noticed my brother has a type and that they are the opposite of my best friend. *Interesting*. Is he purposefully avoiding girls like Monica?

"And the one time Christian knew Monica was on a date with someone, he acted really bizarre. He was really moody and short-tempered. When I called him on it, he tried to play it off like he was filling the protective big brother role for her. But I don't buy it. She has three older brothers and they've never gone that alpha when she's flirting with some guy. Plus, he's my big brother, and he's never reacted that way for me. Christian's always let me make my own mistakes. He's pretty hands off." *Hence my relationship with Mitch the Dick.*

Lucas just shrugs his shoulders. And so, I continue on.

"Really, none of it makes much sense to me. It's just so confusing. I don't know why he won't admit anything." Then it hits me, the perfect plan. Snapping my fingers, I say, "I got it. The best way to test my theory would be that when you come to town, we all go out. Then you can tell me if you see it too." I shrug my shoulders. "Maybe I'm just hopeful and seeing something that isn't there."

Lucas seems to consider my suggestion, and after a bit, he answers with, "We could do that. It might be fun, but I'm not sure how much I'll see. Full confession, if you're there, I'll be incredibly distracted. Especially if you're dressed in something sexy; my brain will be entirely useless. Unable to process any new information." He laughs like he's kidding. *Only, I don't think he is.*

When I think about how good it would be to have his focused attention on me, shivers break out all over my body. And suddenly, I feel antsy and horny and I shift in my seat.

He cocks his head, focuses his eyes on me, and slowly asks a question. "But wouldn't this 'outing' put us on display? You want people to see us together? You want your brother to be in the 'know' about us?"

His questions rattle me. "Oh. Okay." It's tough to hide the surprise in my voice. In seconds, I go from being completely turned on to feeling like someone has thrown a bucket of ice-cold water on me. *Is he hesitant about going out together? Ashamed of what we're doing? Being with me? Am I just an itch to scratch and he doesn't want to be seen with me?* As far as I know, Lucas has never been linked to any woman socially, and I guess if we went out, that might happen. Is he afraid of that? He probably doesn't want the added hassle or extra exposure, seeing that he's probably already assigned us an expiration date. If so, why am I getting so invested? This is why I don't do casual. I don't know the rules and don't know what to expect.

I clear my throat, not really sure what to say. My mind's flooded with thoughts and insecurities, and if I address them, I don't want to come across as needy or clingy. But this whole thing we've got going on has me confused. *What exactly are we?* For someone like me, having no label is maddening. Lucas, however, seems just fine. Maybe that's the answer. I am taking this more seriously and I need to slow it down or end things before I get hurt.

"Samantha." Lucas' gruff voice saying my name brings me out of the mental chaos I've been drowning in. "Where'd you go?" he inquires.

I just look at him, confused, unable to find words. He mirrors my expression and asks, "Why do you look like you're trying to solve a complex problem?" I don't answer. There are no words for what I'm feeling. He laughs nervously, like I'm making him uncomfortable.

Unsure of my feelings, I remind myself I need to get them sorted before I invite more chaos into my head. Once I figure all the pieces out, it'll be fine. Feeling confused like this in a relationship is new for me. The uncertainty of it is just like a gigantic puzzle that needs unscrambling. At work, I'm great at solving problems, and I'm certain that once I can wrap my head around it, the answer will reveal itself.

My confusion all started because Lucas asked me if I care if my brother knows about us. *No. I don't care.* But if Lucas is asking, does he? Maybe he's afraid of dating me because my family's company represents him. Maybe his idea is that we don't get involved past casual fucking, and being seen together would make things complicated. Maybe he just doesn't want my brother to know. At this point, I'm not sure how to approach Lucas with all my confusion and insecure feelings. Instead of wavering, I choose to pull back so I can determine where I stand. He's yet to tell me how he feels, so I want to figure out how to navigate this relationship smartly. Otherwise, I may get destroyed.

The only thing I know without a doubt is that I'm falling for him.

"Lucas, I need to go," I murmur.

Looking confused, he nods and wishes me goodnight before I end the call. Realization storms in. I am beyond screwed. *How am I going to do this—just be casual—when I want so much more?*

Chapter 26

Lucas

The call tonight with Samantha started off amazing. She'd filled my mind with seductive offerings, making me want her even more. And then it had gone to shit.

When she'd looked at me with her big brown eyes full of surprise and sadness, it gutted me. The way she muttered "night" let me know she'd already pulled away. Not knowing what to do, I responded with "night, babe." Had she heard it? Babe was what I called her. And that night, it hung heavy in the air. Normally, nicknames and terms of endearment weren't my thing, but with Samantha, it just felt right. I wanted something special for just her. *But why? That* I couldn't answer.

After a sleepless night, the only thing I concluded was that I needed to proceed with caution. Last night was confusing. Hoping everything is okay between us, I send her a good morning text.

ME

Morning, babe. How'd you sleep?

Being six thirty, I'm already running late. Dressing quickly in a New York Chargers hoodie and sweats, I rush to make my smoothie before I head out the door. While jogging into my building's elevator, Samantha's response comes in.

SAMANTHA

Fine

Fuck! Her one-word response lets me know she's anything but. My mom always told me that if a woman told you she was "fine," she wasn't.

While drinking my smoothie in the elevator, I search Yelp for a florist in Chicago. Calling the first one I see with plenty of 5-star ratings, I order a cheerful-looking bouquet to be delivered to Samantha's office that morning. They're including a card with the message:

Babe- Just thinking of you makes my day brighter! I can't wait for you to visit me next weekend. I'm sorry for what I said last night that hurt you. It wasn't my intention. Can we talk about it? Please forgive me. ~Lucas

"Today is going to suck," I mutter to myself as Coach calls yet another drill. So far, we've run supermans, 1x1 dekes, and countless versions of sprints and relays. Even when he's not blowing the damn whistle, I still hear the sharp trill of it ringing in my ears. *What is going on? Is his personal goal to make us all vomit?* "Is he especially aggravated today, or is it me?" I whisper to Miles when we face off during one drill. Instead of answering, Miles just shrugs, but his grimace matches my own.

Maybe Jack would know. I wait until a water break and skate over to our captain. "Is Coach, okay?" I ask quietly.

Jack shakes his head before muttering, "No, but we'll talk about it tonight." I nod, ready to finish this punishing practice so I can get to the rest of my day.

Today seems to last forever, the hours dragging by. *Come on.* All I want is to find out if Samantha received her flowers and if she liked them. But following the world's longest practice where Coach ran drill after drill, working over the ice like he has a personal vendetta against it, we have a team meeting and sessions in the weight room. Then tonight, I'm having dinner with Jack. Since he's married, maybe he has some advice for me. Perhaps he can see the error of my ways with Samantha.

My workout following practice is difficult. But as I look around the weight room, I'm not alone. It's supposed to be an easy session, but we all seem to be grunting and groaning. Prior to a shower, I head to the meeting with the team's social media coordinator, Robert. He fills us in on a mind-numbing list of upcoming events and activities management expects us all to attend.

One event sticks out. A gala hosted at the American Museum of Natural History that's during the weekend of Samantha's visit. Talk about short notice. Would she go with me? Who will I say she is? My date, girlfriend, fuck buddy? Nothing fits or feels right.

Thoughts about the upcoming gala and my required presence consume me as I step into the shower. I'd love to bring Samantha as my date, but the thought of that makes me anxious. But why? Whispers of the tense ending to our conversation last night flit through my mind, triggering me.

I have questions, the most important being, how do we define us? Neither one of us has done that. Are we ready to go public as something? When I'd hinted at that last night, Samantha hadn't answered. *Did she want that?* Stepping out together would definitely thrust whatever we had going on directly into the spotlight. *Could she handle that? Could I? What would it mean?* Attending black tie events in the past, we'd always had to walk the red carpet to be photographed and interviewed. That was probably the worst part of my job. I was a private person. Other than my mom, I'd never stepped out in public with any woman before. Was I ready for my first time to be with Samantha? Saying yes felt pivotal, but it was the only answer I had.

But with that decided, I know that Samantha and I need to have an important conversation where we define what we are. We need to be on the same page, so that if anyone asks, our answers match. My stomach rolls and heaves at the thought of telling her what I feel for her. Feelings are tough for me. I don't share them with anyone, mostly because I struggle with identifying them. My emotions have always seemed elusive and unclear, but I need to try to understand them so I can tell Samantha what I feel and want. She deserves that from me.

Chapter 27

Samantha

This day was the absolute worst. After the FaceTime with Lucas, I'd tossed and turned all night. When my alarm had gone off at five, my sheets were twisted tight, kind of like my heart. Despite ruminating all night long, the only conclusion I'd come to was that I need to prepare myself for when this—Lucas and I—ends. It was apparent to me that the depth of our feelings for each other are vastly different. And because of that, I fear the end is inevitable. In fact, if I were smart, I wouldn't prolong it any longer and call it quits before one of us gets really invested. But I don't want to. I don't want to let him go.

"Good morning, Ms. Fox," someone says to me in a cheery tone as I stomp off the elevator with my head down. *Do not make eye contact. That will only encourage them.*

"Hmph," I grunt. I can hear a group of ladies to my left gasp, but I tell myself not to care and I push ahead.

When I'm almost to my door, a male clears his throat. Looking up, I scowl at my brother. He instantly throws his hands up and calmly says, "Whoa. Samantha, are you okay?" This time I manage to make some awful, unladylike, snorting sound as I plow past him and into my office.

"Excuse me," he replies with a hint of snark.

When I finally reach my desk, I toss my bag on it and sink into my leather chair. *This chair feels so good.*

Turning around toward my brother, I growl, "Did you want something?"

He grimaces. "You, my sister, are in a terrible mood." Christian's right. I'm cranky, grumpy, and short-tempered and that's probably picking the more flattering descriptions. People wouldn't say I'm normally a bitch, but today, I've got that label wrapped up tight. Walking through my door as I'm getting ready to start my day, he nudges it shut. "How about we leave this closed today? I can let everyone know you're preoccupied with an important project and shouldn't be bothered unless absolutely necessary. Yeah?"

He tries a smile, and it just makes me want to cry.

"Okay, that's probably best," I agree.

After I've scared everyone off, I spend the afternoon stewing in my office. I try to drown myself in paperwork. Hours after my self-imposed silence, I hear a knock at my door. *Someone dared?* Another knock comes. Again, I grunt something that is supposed to sound like "come in." Without looking up, I hear faint footsteps enter my office, and I know it's a woman. Before me stands Janice, a newly hired front desk assistant, carrying a huge, colorful bouquet.

"Where can I set these?" she asks while her eyes comb over my office, looking for some surface that will accommodate the extremely large vase. The bouquet is beautiful; with a rainbow of colors scattered throughout the arrangement. Instantly I wonder who sent me such an exquisite present.

"You can place them over there on the table, Janice," I state while pointing to the table I use for small impromptu meetings. She plucks the enclosed card from the center of the bouquet and walks it over to me. After she places it on my desk, she backs away slowly, as if I'm a dangerous animal.

After reading the card, tears begin to fall from my eyes. They're heavy, just like my heart. Swiping them away, I call Lucas.

Ring, ring, ring.

As I wait for him to answer, I notice it feels like my heart has been plucked from my chest and sent through a grinder. When the call finally connects, Lucas sounds nervous. *Why?*

Chapter 28

Lucas

The second Samantha received the flowers, I knew. Thank you, technology and delivery verification. However, what I didn't know was whether she liked them and if she'd call. I was hoping for both.

While riding the elevator to my penthouse to change for dinner with Jack, my phone rings. It's Samantha, and instantly I'm filled with a variety of emotions. Not only am I anxious and nervous, but I'm also happy and excited. I try to calm my racing heart before I answer her, but it's no use.

"Samantha," I rasp, then quickly clear my throat. "It's good to hear from you. After our call last night, I wasn't sure where we stood." Hearing the directness in my voice, I didn't want to come across as aggressive, but I'm definitely looking for some clarity that only she can give.

"Yeah. I'm sorry, but something you said really made me pause, and I needed to do some thinking about how it made me feel." Even though she hadn't admitted anything specifically, it still cuts, making me feel even more uncertain.

"Okay, can you share it with me now? I'm not experienced with relationships at all. And I know I hurt your feelings last night, but I don't know how."

Wanting to see her, I question whether this conversation would be easier over FaceTime. Reading between the lines isn't my forte, but at least I'd be able to see if she's upset. She wears her emotions on her sleeve.

Stepping up to my door, I ask, "I just got home. Can I switch this to FaceTime?"

"Sure," she responds hesitantly. Answering my call quickly, I couldn't miss her red and puffy eyes. *Has she been crying?* My heart pinches and I wince. I'd done this to her. Feeling horrible, I desperately want to fix things between us.

"Babe, talk to me," I beg.

Forcing a half-hearted smile, she winces. "These types of talks aren't part of our 'just casual' status. They're emotional, messy, and complicated." Her look is questioning me as to whether I want her to keep going.

Unsure what to do, I stare at her and nod my understanding. *What do I say?* She's right to question me. I don't do emotions and feelings with women. But with her, I want to. Unfortunately, I haven't got a clue what to say. I've gone mute. And I'm not sure what that means. Instead, I purse my lips and look at her, willing her to understand. Moments tick by, she wrings her hands in her lap, and I watch as she transforms from sad to withdrawn. *Lucas, speak up before you lose her.* Opening my mouth, nothing comes out. *Fuck.* I can feel her slipping away.

Finally, she breaks our uncomfortable silence. "Last night was a reality check for me. Although I'm trying to get my emotions back in line, they aren't behaving." A weak laugh falls from her soft lips and hits me right in the chest, making me feel things I don't understand. *Tell me what you're feeling.* I notice she's really trying hard to avoid having a conversation with me about her feelings. *Why? Oh, that's right. I told her that I don't do emotions.* Does she want to share them with me? *I want to listen.* Has she assumed I don't care? *But I do. Again, Lucas, that's what you told her.* When she mentioned our casual status, it felt like someone stabbed a hot poker through my heart. Searing pain that's blistering and agonizing rips through my chest, causing severe damage. But I don't quite understand why. We barely know each other. *Why am I already feeling this way? Why are my feelings for her so intense?* Hopefully, Jack will have an idea, because I am so fucking confused.

Not wanting to make her any more uncomfortable, perhaps a more casual approach is needed. Moving our conversation into more neutral territory, or into the friend zone is smart. Is potentially safer, right? Honestly, I don't know. I've never had a female friend before. Isn't that kind of what we are? Actually, we're more like frenebits—friends with benefits. Regardless of that, if anything is going to get better between us, I have to make things right.

Connecting with her sad brown eyes, I apologize. "Samantha, I'm sorry I hurt you." She only nods, keeping her silence and leaving me clueless.

Hopeful, I ask, "Are you still planning to come to New York next weekend?" Even I can hear the desperation in my words. *What about the gala? Patience, bro. We'll cross that bridge when we know she's still coming to New York.*

"I still have those meetings scheduled, so yes, I'll be coming." Her answer is quick but emotionless. *What's going on? What am I missing?* My heart thunders in my chest. Giving her a minute to see if she'll elaborate on her plan is absolute torture. But time ticks by, leaving us again in uncomfortable silence. Panicked, worried thoughts race through my mind. *What isn't she saying?* Darkness sets in. But the silence continues. *Are we done?* Staring at her, I wish she could read my mind and give me the answers I desperately need. My stomach twists and rolls, and I feel like I'm going to puke. Unable to handle the deafening silence any longer, I ask the only question I can. "So, what does that mean?"

Chapter 29

Samantha

"Isn't it obvious?" I snap. Obviously, I'm ending things, but maybe that's not clear to him. After all, Lucas doesn't have experience with relationships. He's never been through a breakup before. Can we really even call what's happening a breakup? We weren't dating, so maybe it's called something else, like "drop your hookup" or "boot the extra baggage." I don't know. Casual isn't my thing, so I'm not familiar with how this works or the correct terminology. Looking at him, I see him just sitting still, looking confused. And for some reason, that annoys me. Then I see him shake his head back and forth repeatedly. *What is he doing?* But instead of asking, I proceed forward, not wanting to prolong this anymore. Ending this, whatever it was, now, will hurt less later.

Swallowing past the boulder lodged in my throat, everything feels wrong. Especially the words written on the tear-stained paper in front of me. Words that sound empty, even though I agonized over them all day. As I begin speaking, I don't allow myself to look him in the eyes. It's the coward's way, I know. But otherwise, just the sight of him would kill me.

"Lucas, you're a great guy, but this—being casual—isn't working. We had some fun, but I've realized I'm not comfortable with it. Maybe I'm not programmed for it. I don't know. Yes, I'll be in New York next weekend for business meetings, but I don't think it's a good idea to see each other. No hard feelings, okay?"

I glance up to gauge his reaction to what I've just dropped, and I can't read him at all. In fact, he doesn't look like he's moving at all. Wondering if the FaceTime call is frozen, I tap the screen. Did he hear anything I just said? I hope so, because I can't possibly do it again. I think I'd rather die than go through that.

Before too long, I see him sink back into his couch. He looks like he's lost in thought. His eyes blink rapidly and he curls his hands into tight fists. He remains quiet and it makes me fidgety. I can't gauge if he's mad, sad, confused, or relieved.

"Lucas," I whisper.

He shakes his head furiously and angrily growls, "I've got to go, Samantha. Have a nice life," then he ends the call.

Needing air, I quickly shut off my computer, grab my coat and purse, and escape out of my office, avoiding everyone. One foot in front of the other, on autopilot, headed for my blessed freedom when my escape route is blocked by none other than Christian, of course. Stepping in my path, he scrutinizes me. Unblinking, I stand there silent. "Where are you headed, Sam?"

"I'm not feeling well. I'm taking a personal day." Trying to step past him, he mirrors my every move, finally relenting when I refuse to give him more.

Heading down to the lobby, I see my driver Jeffrey and he rushes to my side. "Ms. Fox, you look to be in a rush. Do you have an appointment you need to get to?"

Shaking my head no, I say, "I'm not feeling well. Could you please take me home?"

"Of course. Do we need to stop anywhere to get anything? Do you need to go to the doctor's or hospital?" His offer is kind, but a trip to the doctor's, hospital, or drug store won't fix how I'm feeling.

"Thanks for offering. I just need to get home." Pulling the door open, I climb into the back of the car and melt into the leather seats for the short ride home.

When Jeffery pulls up, he opens my door for me and again asks if I need anything. Thanking him again, I slowly walk into my building. The ride up in the elevator is a blur. Once I've crossed into my penthouse, my carefully constructed walls collapse, taking my heart down with it. My body follows shortly after and I sink into a sobbing puddle only steps from my door. Time loses relevance as I wallow in my pain. Christian finds me wrecked and tear-stained when he walks into my penthouse some time later.

"Samantha... what is going on?" he whispers to me.

As if I cried thousands of tears, my eyes ache. My throat feels as dry as a desert, but getting a drink seems monumental. My whole body is in pain. I'm not sure how long I lay there alone until my brother found me.

It's kind of prophetic, right? Since alone was probably the way I would remain forever. Never would I be happy again. Scared, I'd turned my back on the shot of finding happiness. Lying there on the floor in my penthouse, I imagine what life could have been like with Lucas. If only he'd wanted the same things. But he didn't and now it's over. I'll likely be single and unhappy for the rest of my life. And the only person I can blame is me.

When I try to open my eyes, to respond to Christian, it proves difficult. Reaching up to rub them, hoping that will help, I notice they're puffy and sore. "Owww," I moan.

When I finally manage to pry them open, I struggle to focus my vision on anything. My eyes are horribly dry and raw. Finally, I direct my attention to Christian. He has his hands on my leg and he's speaking in a low tone that I can hardly make out. *What is he saying?* Focusing hard, despite the migraine pounding behind my eyes, his words finally register.

"Sam. Are you okay? Why are you on the floor?

Are you hurt? Do I need to call for help?" Noticeably worried, my brother bombards me with questions.

"I'm fine. Really," I croak out. "Why are you here?"

Exasperatedly, Christian pulls his hands through his hair. "You looked pale at the office and something seemed off, so I came to check on you."

Pushing up to sitting, I force out a deep breath and it all comes rushing back. My call with Lucas, ending things between us, feeling destroyed, and the anger in Lucas's voice as he told me to have a good life. When I start to cry again, my brother moves next to me, pulling me to his side while he whispers, "It's going to be okay." A while later, my mom and dad appear. *Am I dreaming? Why are they here?* My mom drops to her knees, and with a shaky voice she says, "My precious girl, what's wrong? Let me make it better. What can I do?"

"It hurts so bad," I mumble against Christian's chest. Already wrapped in his muscular arms, he pulls me in tighter. My mom caresses my hair while she speaks calm words to me. I hear my dad on the phone ordering from Soupstone. My stomach growls, and I try to remember the last time I ate or drank anything. I can't recall.

When Dad answers the door some while later, the smell of chicken noodle soup and freshly baked bread fills the air. Still nursing a migraine, I massage my temples, seeking relief.

"Do you have a migraine? Would it help if we left?" Mom asks.

Nodding yes, she rises to standing and goes over to my father. After a quick discussion, they are back in front of me. "Samantha, we are going to leave you to rest. Please let us know if you need anything," Dad says.

Releasing the hold I have on my brother, I shakily stand up, grabbing them and giving them both a hug. Christian is next.

"Sam, you want me to stay? I can hang out and watch TV quietly." My brother only watches sports, and he does it loudly while also adding his own commentary. If I hope to get rid of my migraine anytime soon, it would be better if he left.

"Thanks, but I'll be fine. I just need to get some sleep and I'll be better in no time." His questioning look tells me he wants to say more, but he doesn't. Giving me a hug, he departs too, leaving me alone again.

The silence of my penthouse is deafening. Needing to escape it, I head to my room so I can crawl into bed. Slipping into my en suite bathroom to undress and pee, I look in the mirror. The vacant-eyed woman staring back at me causes me to shudder. I look horrendous. My eyes are sunken, swollen, and red-rimmed, and my cheeks are tear-stained. My mascara is streaked, making me look like a weepy raccoon. And my hair looks like a bird is actively trying to construct a nest in it. I grab a hair tie from my vanity and gather my locks into a messy bun. I'll deal with it when I have more energy and the incessant pounding in my head is no longer making me nauseated and off-balance.

Splashing cold water on my face is refreshing. At least I can scrub off some of the evidence of my sobbing. After doing so, I glance back at myself. What I see looking back at me knocks me further down. Instead of the happy, confident woman I usually am, I see a shattered shell remaining. As heartbroken as I feel, I again remind myself that I'm the only one to blame. I'd chosen to get involved with the wrong guy, became attached, then ended things with him because I was afraid of the possibility of future pain. Now, though, I'm miserable and second-guessing my decision. If I'd handled things differently, would my future have been more painful than what I'm going through now? My crystal ball's broken, so I have no way of knowing.

After downing a bottle of water and taking some migraine medicine, I slip out of the bathroom and into my bedroom. Crawling into my sheets, my weary body succumbs easily to sleep. *Tomorrow will be better.*

Chapter 30

Lucas

During our call, Samantha comes across not only as direct, but heartless. I would have never thought she had a mean bone in her body. But when she rips my still beating heart from my chest and stomps on it, she effectively disproves that. I'm completely floored by what she says. I couldn't have prepared myself for that.

She gives me some bullshit about how I'm a great guy but what we're doing isn't working. She even says it was fun. *What in the actual fuck? Really?* I'm angry, hurt, confused, and sad. Basically, for the guy who never acknowledges his emotions, I am a mess of them right now. *Ironic, isn't it?*

Not believing it could get any worse, she surprises me when she drops her next bomb. In a voice that's completely devoid of feeling, she informs me she's still coming to New York, but she doesn't think we should get together. *WTF? No problem, sweetheart. After you just shredded my heart, you are the last person I want to see.*

Everything she says comes out in a flat affect. *Who does that? Psychopaths, that's who.* Adding insult to injury, she tops it all by flippantly saying, "No hard feelings." *Really? No. Hard. Feelings?* Everything Samantha's said enrages me. Apparently, she's already decided we're over. Nothing I do or say can change her mind.

Still feeling hopeful, I think maybe I didn't understand. Looking at her, I wonder if I misheard. But when I take a moment and replay her words, I know I heard her correctly. She ended things between us.

Throughout her spiel, she shows me she's nothing like I'd thought. Instead of kind and caring, she's cold, calculated, and precise. *She doesn't want you.* Kind of like a surgeon with their scalpel. She's expertly cutting me out of her life. Her words making a direct slice to my heart, destroying it.

Sitting back on my couch, letting it all sink in, I feel unrestrained anger course through my body. I need to end this call and get as far away from her as possible. I'll give her what she wants and get her out of my life for good. I don't need to spend any more time with someone who doesn't want me.

Wringing my hands together, I try to keep myself from forming them into fists. But I'm unsuccessful, and soon I'm clenching them tightly and openly raging. I want to hit something hard. Pummel it, leaving only a pile of destruction in my path.

Her whispering my name pulls me from the anger-induced state I'm in. *This conversation is fucking over.* Samantha conned me, completely tricked me. She isn't anything like I assumed. Instead, she is a conniving bitch, and I am done with her. She means nothing to me anymore. I won't show her she hurt me. I'll take all my feelings onto the ice and channel them into my workouts. Because of this, I will make myself a better hockey player. Instead of living with it, I will funnel the pain and anger into something productive. Samantha's doing me a favor. I won't miss her at all; I won't allow it. She was just casual and nothing special. This is why I don't get involved with women. It's too much damn trouble. She isn't worth any more of my time. I need to get off this FaceTime call. Right. Fucking. Now. "I've got to go, Samantha. Have a nice life." Stabbing the screen, I end the call.

"Fuck!" My lungs burn as I rage into the open space after I hang up on Samantha. This. This is exactly why I've never done relationships. I'm in misery, and although it's a new feeling for me, I already know I'll make sure I never feel it again. One and done, thank you very much. That will not be a mistake I'm repeating.

I'm shaking from all the extra adrenaline pumping through my system. Clenching my iPad in my hand, a notice pops up and her gorgeous face appears, enraging me all over again. Just last week when I got this, I set the one and only picture of her as my screen saver. Needing to be as far away from her as possible, I throw it across the room. The new device smashes into my television, shattering them both. Sitting here, staring at the destruction I've created, all I can think is I'm broken into a million tiny pieces, too.

Restless and angry, I pace my home like a confined jungle cat. Refusing to acknowledge how incredibly sad I am. These feelings are eating me up. I need to distract myself. Unfortunately, practice isn't until tomorrow, but I need something now. I'd call Jack, but we just got home from an out-of-town series, and I don't want to get him in trouble with the missus. We were supposed to grab a quick dinner tonight, but with the way I'm feeling, no conversation would be quick.

ME

Hey, man, something came up and I can't make dinner tonight.

JACK

Okay. No worries. See you tomorrow at practice.

After tonight's shit show, I plan to swear off women entirely. Still agitated, I call Miles to see if he wants to hit up a bar with me. I mean, in the past, a few drinks were always the trick to clearing my mind of any lingering issue. After a few rings, he answers. "Hey, Hooker, what's up?"

"What are you up to?" I ask, trying to register what I hear behind him.

"Just hanging out at the new sports bar, Layup. Why?"

As a rookie goalie in the NHL, he takes full advantage of going out and indulging in the "benefits" it offers. In fact, of all the times we've been out together, I don't think I've ever seen him pay for a drink or go home alone. Miles has a jovial personality that everyone seems drawn to. Right now, he is exactly what I need to distract me. He'll provide great entertainment. "I'm heading your way. I need a drink," I confess.

"You need a drink? Really?" he asks, genuinely confused.

"I do. See you soon." I end the conversation before I say anything else. Dressing in jeans and a polo, I quickly fix my hair and brush my teeth before I'm out the door. Thirty minutes later, after my uneventful Uber ride, I walk into the bar and there sits Miles. The man looks like he's holding court. Both men and women within a few feet of him are hanging on his every word.

When I catch his eye, he pauses with the story he'd been animatedly telling, and waves me over. A few ladies, who seem to track his every move, follow the flick of his hand, and soon their gazes fall on me. Their overdone eyes grow comically large and seductive smiles spread across their pouty, fake, red lips. *Shit. I'm their new target.* Not wanting their attention, I look away.

Walking up to the crowd surrounding Miles, I give a little wave and say, "Hey." Miles makes a confused smirk and he mouths, *"You, okay?"* Even though he's a rookie and I haven't known him for long, he's become one of my best friends. Already he knows me well enough to know that what he's witnessing is entirely out of character for me. I'm known by my teammates as hardly drinking and never being social, especially at a bar. Just another example of the new me. I have Samantha to thank for that. To Miles, I nod a yes and then order a Heineken. The beer is ice cold and goes down too smoothly.

Returning to my penthouse a few hours and beers later sucks. It's impossible to miss the destruction I left in my wake after Samantha's call. Shards of glass pepper my hardwood floors, but I can't find it within me to care. Exhausted and unwilling to deal with it, I walk straight to my bedroom to crash. Before climbing into my bed, I remove my clothes, dropping them at my feet. Tossing my phone on the charger pad, I don't even look to make sure I set the alarm. As I pull my pillow closer, I curl into my sheets and am thankful Samantha never visited because I couldn't handle it if everything smelled like her. Despite my exhaustion, sleep is impossible and I toss and turn.

When I finally succumb to sleep at four a.m., it's restful until my alarm goes off two hours later for practice. My overly exhausted state turns to anger when I realize I'd been dreaming about Samantha and I'm rocking a hard-on from hell. As I lie there, I close my eyes, willing it to go down. A cold shower won't even help at this point. Still groggy, I drift back to sleep and head right back into the dream I'd been having.

I'm lying naked in bed and Samantha is crawling toward me. As she reaches my ankles, she slowly trails open-mouthed kisses up my legs, moving slowly toward my hips. Each touch she places on me is electric, like touching a live wire. My body craves what she's doing and my dick grows impressively hard. Standing tall and proud, reaching for her. I wrap my fist around it, needing it to be patient. Slowly, I stroke from base to tip as she comes closer and closer. A seductive smile graces her delicious lips. When she reaches my waist, she licks her lips and then drops her head and places a kiss on the tip of my dick. My dick flinches in my hand and I reward it with a tight squeeze. He's more than ready for any attention she'll give. Samantha moves past my waist and continues kissing up my abs and chest, giving each nipple a quick nibble.

When she reaches my collarbones, she stops. As she languidly licks across one and then puckers her lips to blow over where she just traveled, my body comes alive. Shivers spread across my body and my dick throbs in my hand. Needing to touch her, the fingers in my free hand flex before grazing her breast and plucking a nipple. The throaty moan that falls from her lips is like the best symphony; rich and deep. While momentarily preoccupied, I release my dick and work my hand down to her waist. Squeezing her makes her flex her hips, which only makes me want to push things forward. Our bodies are both humming with need. I trace my fingers down to her center just as she leans up to nibble and suck on my earlobe. A deep moan erupts from my chest.

When she places a chaste kiss on my lips, I decide I've had enough foreplay. Dragging my fingers through her folds, I know she's beyond wet and ready for me. And I need her now. Samantha's driving me crazy. She is an absolute temptress. I can't hold back any longer. I take my hand from her breast and wrap it around her neck, pulling her to me tighter, requiring a longer, deeper kiss. She moans and bites my lower lip. I growl. Grabbing her hips, I trace her hip bones with my thumbs and then lower her onto me. At initial contact, we both moan. I want her wrapped completely around me. That is what I need. Being with her is the best thing I have ever experienced, and it's something I crave and always will. I want this woman completely.

Just as I'm about to slide her all the way down onto my shaft, my backup alarm goes off and rips me from my dream. My dick throbs and I wrap my hand around it tighter. Looking for relief, I stroke my aching shaft, gaining speed as I go. I picture the Samantha of my dream. Her creamy skin. Her soft hair and perfectly round breasts. The curve of her hips makes my mouth water. When I've completed the picture, my orgasm slams into me, and I come harder than I ever have before.

As I'm coming down from the orgasm high, my brain comes back online, reminding me of the previous night's heartache and aftermath. *What have I done?* Dread sits heavy in my heart as I lie in my bed, in sheets soaked with my desire for her. My shoulders shake and my chest rumbles as a loud, boisterous laugh builds up within me. The sound bounces off the empty walls of my bedroom. Apparently, my dick still wants her, even with how badly she hurt me. *Hey, idiot, your heart does too.* But my brain definitely does not. *Who are you lying to?* That's it, I am cursed. Am I doomed to a life of jerking off to images of the only woman I've ever wanted, who doesn't want me? If so, what did I do to deserve that? It must be karma for something I've done, but I don't know what. Slapping my hand on my bed, I shout, "Dammit!" *I am officially screwed if I can't move past her.*

As I get out of bed, I angrily rip off the dirty sheets and throw them on the ground. I'll wash the evidence of my Samantha-induced orgasm out later. First, I have to get to hockey practice. At least there I can hit some guys, and work out some of my pent-up aggression.

Getting to the arena is a blur. When I walk into the locker room, I can't believe I'm actually hoping Coach is in a foul mood. I need to pump, push, and drive myself harder than I have in a long time. That's the only way I'm going to get through this. Coach delivers and practice is punishing, but even it doesn't seem to get me out of my funk. Even a brutal session in the weight room does nothing to lighten my mood. Earbuds have kept me from having to interact with anyone because I can guarantee it wouldn't be pretty.

After my shower, I dress slowly. The idea of going back to my empty penthouse is depressing. Originally, I had planned to go shopping for new sheets and a few other things to spruce up my place for Samantha's visit. Now, considering everything that's happened, it seems pointless. Grumbling to myself, I aggressively pull on my boots.

"Hey, Hooker, what did those boots ever do to you?" Jack asks playfully.

"Nothing," I growl. I'm not ready to have this conversation with him. He doesn't know anything that's happened between Samantha and me because I haven't told him. Right now, I'd rather walk across hot coals than talk about anything having to do with her. Sounds less painful, at least. But Jack doesn't drop it.

"Dude, throughout practice, you looked pissed. In the weight room, you looked about ready to explode, and now you look like you're about to commit murder. What's going on?" he asks as he sits beside me.

He's too close. Am I suffocating.? I need out of here.

"It's nothing, man," I force out through gritted teeth.

Puffing out his chest, he challenges me. "Bullshit. Try again, asshole."

My anger is at the boiling point, and I stand up and

posture toward him. Daring him. Feeling like a trapped animal, my body shakes involuntarily with anger and pain. The desire to fight quakes through me. My knuckles are curled in tight, begging to hit something.

Jack stands up. He purposefully steps back, giving me space. Maintaining eye contact, he says, "Lucas, I know something is up and I'm here for you. When you're ready, yeah?"

I snort, grab my bag, and storm past him. As I leave the locker room, I look around and am thankful it's mostly empty. I don't need my teammates to see me losing my shit. It's bad enough to have Jack witness my downfall. Hopefully, Miles wasn't in the locker room, too. After the bar visit last night, I don't need him sniffing around. If those two suspect anything, they'll get together like a couple of old ladies and tag-team me until I spill. And I'm not ready for that. Not now. Not ever.

Eventually, after I've wandered around aimlessly, I return to my home and crawl back into bed. The soiled sheets, still lying abandoned on the floor, are a painful reminder. *Damn, Samantha.* Grabbing my down comforter, I pull it on top of me. Hopefully, sleep will erase the constant ache in my chest and the chaotic feelings waring in my head. All day long, my emotions were erratic. I spent equal time feeling anger, depression, confusion, guilt, shock, and hopelessness. This has all been too much, and I feel like I have whiplash. Closing my eyes, I force myself to take a break.

Tomorrow is another day and another chance to exorcise her from my life.

Between practices and visits to the weight room over the next few days, I'm desperate to remove Samantha from my thoughts and feelings. But, despite my best efforts, it's impossible. In a few days, she'll be in the city and I need to prepare myself. That way, if I cross paths with her, I'll seem unaffected by what happened between us. She'll never know how much she hurt me. I refuse to give her that power over me. She doesn't need to know she's destroyed me.

Chapter 31

Samantha

I skipped work for a few days and drowned myself in Ben & Jerry's ice cream. Did you know they can deliver it to you at any time of the day? That's been a lifesaver. Calls would surely have been made to the authorities if I wandered out in the clothes I pulled on days ago after arriving home. My outfit of choice is a faded black, holey t-shirt and stained pink sweats. As if that's not enough, the bird-nest hairdo I've spent hours perfecting perfectly complements the smell I'm sure I have. But at this point, I don't care. I'm beyond shame. Why, you ask? Because it was absolutely mortifying to have my brother find me curled in a pathetic, weepy ball on the floor. Having my parents witness my self-destruction was amazing, too. Even days later, I'm still somewhat confused about why they were here and not in New York. While I'd been lying in my brother's arms, I remember hearing my dad mention being in town for a fundraiser. I guess if I had to plan a mental breakdown, I picked the right time. Their visit worked nicely for me. Because even if I want to be alone, there's comfort in having your parents close when you feel like your world is imploding.

Over the last few days, I've heard my phone alert me to messages, and when I finally checked them this morning, most of them were from my brother and parents. Even though I know they are worried, I can't bring myself to respond. The only person I want to talk to is Lucas, and that won't ever happen. I made sure of that when I made the biggest mistake of my life. Despite things being new, I already feared how strongly I feel toward Lucas. I was scared and convinced that if given the chance, he would hurt me. Figuring if the distance didn't ruin us, Lucas's not wanting anything serious would. Knowing that he'd easily move on once he was finished with me would destroy me, leaving me worse than I am now. So, I ended things. Hoping to save myself from even greater heartache. But I'm not sure I did.

In all the messages I received during my heartbreak hunker down, or HHD, my brother and parents warn me I'll see them when we fly back to New York Friday morning. I have some business meetings I scheduled when I intended to visit Lucas, and now it's too late to reschedule most of them. My current plan is to stay at a hotel close to Fox Sporting's headquarters. By doing this, I won't have to commute from my parents' estate. I know they probably won't like it, but I'm an adult, and considering all that's happened, I really don't care. I'm calling the shots. Today, though, HHD continues on. Tomorrow is Friday and another story.

When Friday arrives, I get myself as together as I can. I shower, dress, and pack a reasonable bag. Boarding the company's jet, I fly to New York looking like a fully functioning adult. Even if that's the entire opposite of what I'm feeling. The quick flight allows me to keep everything surface level with my brother and parents. As soon as we land, I grab a car and head to my first meeting. Thankfully, I'm just there to verify numbers for some upcoming contracts and I can easily lose myself in the distraction.

After the meetings, which I'd had my assistant schedule back-to-back, I go to my hotel to check-in. Dropping my bag in my room, I decide to head down to the bar to drown my worries in a drink or three. *Don't know who wouldn't think that was a brilliant idea.*

While there, hidden away in a corner, I see Lucas walk in. Panic overwhelms my body. Swallowing becomes difficult. He looks devastatingly handsome. Christian strolls in moments later to join him. Apparently, they're meeting for a drink. After fist bumps, they move over to the bar, and I hope neither one will notice me. As they wait for their drinks, I unashamedly stare at Lucas, and an unbearable ache grows in my chest. I wonder if I should leave, but my curiosity gets the better of me. Is Lucas as upset as I am? Has our split rocked his world like it has mine? I take in his appearance, and the answer is glaringly obvious. No. He looks perfect. He talks and jokes with my brother like he doesn't have a care in the world. Like what happened between us hasn't affected him one bit. Meanwhile, I'm struggling with absolutely everything, even the basics. Living has become a chore. Sleep is non-existent. I've only showered and gotten out of slobby pajamas because I had to. I've eaten so much ice cream in the last few days, I'm sure I've probably gained weight. And, truth be told, I'm an emotionally shattered hot mess.

Dabbing at the tears I feel in the corners of my eyes, I notice a couple of attractive women approach them. Instantly, I'm seething with jealousy. At first, it seems Lucas pushes off the advances of the woman who's targeted him, and I'm slightly relieved. But then his head whips around and his eyes narrow on me. *Shit. I've been spotted.* When recognition hits, his not-quite smile morphs into a grimace. He's glaring at me, baring his teeth, and it's downright scary. The oblivious woman, still attempting to flirt with him, doesn't notice his change, and she touches his chest suggestively. My body responds immediately. I glare and am about to rise out of my chair, when something stops me. Looking back at the mysterious woman, it appears like she's trying to get his attention focused back on her. Lucas misses nothing. Noticing my response to her touching him, he quickly masks his anger. Aware that I'm watching, Lucas shifts his focus back to the woman and smiles at her. *Asshole.* She giggles, most likely assuming he's given her his full attention. *He hasn't.* He's giving her a smile she hopes will lead to something. *It won't.* It certainly is attractive, but it's completely forced and filled with disdain. In the short time I've known him, I've noticed he gives the same smile to reporters and those he finds annoying. It's not at all genuine or real. But it does the trick once again and convinces the woman he's happy to be with her. *He's not.* In response, she smiles and then licks her lips suggestively as she caresses his biceps. *I think I'm going to be sick.*

Lucas looks over to gauge my reaction to his obvious flirting with the overeager woman. His eyes say *"you didn't want this, so eat your heart out."* Meanwhile, the woman's aggressively trying to wedge herself between Lucas's muscular legs. My blood pressure rises and I feel nauseous. I grab the edge of the table to stabilize myself. I'm sure my discomfort is evident all over my face. A sly smirk appears on his lips and he winks at me. *I can't believe him.* My heart aches. In fact, he appears to be enjoying my displeasure.

Just as I'm about to storm out of there, hoping to shield the tears that are threatening to fall, my brother leads the entire group away. Lucas follows, holding his head high, with that woman tucked into his arm. And, once again, I'm utterly destroyed.

When the coast is clear and I'm sure they're gone, I dash back up to my room to drown my despair in the minibar. I've never been much of a drinker, but tonight, getting trashed sounds like a hell of an idea. Despite my wrecked emotional state, I'm perceptive enough to place the do not disturb sign on the door, so housekeeping will leave me alone. My reservation is for the entire weekend. There is no need to bother me.

The next couple of days are a blur. Room service has kept me well-supplied in ice cream. I tried drinking that first night, but all it earned me was a killer headache, vomit galore, and a horrid crick in my neck. Note to self: sleeping on the cold tiled bathroom floor, wrapped around the toilet, is not conducive to one's alignment.

On Saturday afternoon, after I sort of recover from my first ever bender, I plan to leave the city. I want to find a commercial flight back to Chicago because I can't be in New York anymore.

While Lucas and I were quasi-dating, I'd set up a Google alert on him, hoping to keep informed on everything that was said about him. However, as I prepare to search for flights out of the city, that backfires on me. Alerts bombard my phone, informing me of the new woman in Lucas's life. Surprise, it's the same woman I'd seen him with at the bar. *Fabulous.* He stepped out with her. Realization of that slaps me across the face. Guess I know how he truly felt about me. I was just a secret fuck. Nothing more.

Before I can tell myself no to any more internet searches, I locate all the notifications. And all the photos and articles that accompany them. Each one rocking me to the core. It feels like a single blow delivered by a steel-toed boot directly to my heart as I discover them all. From the pictures, he looks to be living his best life, and it makes me sick. My stomach heaves and all the ice cream I'd consumed threatens to make another appearance.

Lucas, the antisocial guy that he is, is splashed across all media outlets. Pictures taking prime real estate in gossip venues show him close and cozy with the blonde from last night. But not just her. Over the course of the night, he'd apparently been photographed multiple times with different women at various clubs. Further torturing myself over the next few hours, I scroll through picture after picture. It's become a perverse obsession. I can't look away no matter how badly it hurts. And it's fucking agony.

Never scheduling a flight, I instead call in more of my trusty reinforcements to help me deal with the heartache that just seems to get worse with each day that passes. Ben & Jerry, the only men I vow to ever love again, arrive at my door and ease my broken heart. Or maybe they ease me into a sugar coma. However, instead of feeling empty, I'm cram packed with chocolate fudge brownie, which is making me feel poorly in another way.

When I don't respond to any of my brother's texts

after I missed our return flight Monday morning, Christian arrives by midafternoon with the hotel security to perform a safety check. With the manager in tow, he storms into my room, barking orders. I don't listen because I don't care. I'm an absolute mess who's surrounded by containers of half-eaten, melted ice cream. The once-stark white sheets are now crumpled and stained brown from missed bites. Housekeeping will probably curse me; I'm not sure the bedding is worth saving. This right here is not how I usually behave. But considering everything that's happened. I'm finding it difficult to be embarrassed by my lackadaisical behavior.

Looking over at Christian, I notice he looks stressed out as he stands in the middle of the room with his hands on his hips. His tie is pulled loose around his neck, and his hair is ruffled, like he's been running his hands through it over and over. My big brother, who's normally calm and collected, is looking flustered and overwhelmed. Then he calls our mom and rats me out. Again. She comes running, as she's only a few blocks away at Fox's headquarters. My family doesn't know what to do with me. Even with the broken engagement and cheating by Mitch, I never behaved like this. *That should tell you something*. They know nothing about Lucas and never will.

In no time, my mom is standing next to my bed. She wastes no time coddling me but rather drags me to the bathroom, hollering to Christian that he needs to call down to the hotel's personal shopper to have them get me some clothes. Sitting me on top of the toilet, she makes sure I'm steady before stepping away. Once she's confident I'll stay put, she turns the shower on.

Knock, knock.

"Mom, what clothes does Sam need?" Christian speaks loudly through the door.

I roll my eyes as my mom grumbles under her breath, "Seriously?"

Pulling the door open, Christian stands there with his cell phone pressed to his ear.

"Let me have it," she demands, taking the phone and instructing someone to bring me cashmere yoga pants, a tank top, and a sweatshirt. Christian looks over her head and shoots me a telling wink. *What a little shit.* He doesn't want to do what Mom asked him, so he's giving her the wounded chicken act. The employee she's speaking with must ask additional questions, because before I know it, Mom has also requested underwear, a bra, socks, and shoes.

"Thank you. I appreciate it," my mom says before she hangs up and hands the phone back to my brother.

"Thanks, Mom. You made that look simple," Christian croons at her. *I wish she could see through his bullshit.*

Retreating back into the bathroom, Mom checks the water temperature before she turns to me and orders me to strip. Because it's my mom, I do what she asks. When I'm naked, she pushes me into the shower, telling me to enjoy. Once I'm out of the way, she gathers up my clothes and puts them in the hotel's plastic dry cleaner bag and seals it tight. Not sure if she's going to trash them or wash them, I shrug my shoulders, not caring either way. When she tosses them out to Christian, I hear a loud "hmmmph" and I imagine she's hit him with it. A smile breaks out across my face. It's the first one I've worn in weeks.

While waiting for my new clothes to be delivered, Christian orders me breakfast. The clothes and food arrive while I'm finishing showering. Christian delivers the clothes to my mom and sets the coffee, fruit, omelet, and toast on the table in the room. After dressing, I try to eat my breakfast, but my stomach just rolls in protest. It's probably unhappy about the amount of ice cream I've gorged on the past few days. While I push the food around my plate, I notice my brother hidden in the room's corner, whispering to someone on the phone. Leaning in to listen, I overhear him say three words that stop me from any further eavesdropping.

"Monica, it's bad," he whispers. *Why is he talking to my best friend?* Annoyed, I stab at the omelet. *That feels strangely good.* Christian's hushed conversation continues while my mom flits around the room like a hummingbird, visiting here and there while finishing my packing.

After a few calming breaths, I again try to eavesdrop and hear him clearly mention my breakdown the previous weekend. "Really?" I mutter under my breath. My mom sits down next to me, and when I look over at her, her eyes and jawline are tight, telling me she's concerned about me.

"Darling, after you're done with breakfast, I'm going to take you out to the estate to give you some more time to process whatever you're going through. Your brother is flying back to Chicago today to attend to the office's daily work until you're ready to head back. Please know that anything you need, your dad and I will take care of." Her voice is full of kindness and love, but I don't feel like I deserve it. After all, I caused my heartbreak. I need to figure out how to deal with the emotional fallout I'm suffering.

She grabs my hand, bringing me back to the here and now. Encouraging me to look into her eyes, what I see is that they reflect my desolation. Her sadness for me makes me feel even worse. She doesn't know everything I'm dealing with is all my fault. That is the reason I still haven't told anyone what happened. Not even Monica.

My brother ends his call and strolls over to check on me. When he's beside me, he looks down and laughs. "What?" I question. *Who can be joyful or happy right now?* Lucas can be, I remind myself. He looked happy Friday night, especially in all those pictures taken at the club. Then I remember Lucas was with my brother. I want to be mad at him, but I can't be. All I can seem to focus on is the thought of all those women surrounding Lucas. And that's what sets me off, because once again, tears fall. Christian squats down so he's eye level with me, swiping at the tears. "Sam, I wish you'd tell me what's going on."

"You laughed," I angrily accuse him.

He nods. "I laughed because it looks like you've done a fantastic job massacring your omelet. What's got you so upset that murdering your breakfast seemed like the best option?"

I look down at my plate and see he's right. My omelet, smothered in ketchup, looks like bloody chunks of flesh, both grotesque and gruesome. "I'm not ready to talk about it," I mumble.

He smiles and nods his head, letting me know he understands.

My mom squeezes my hand in unwavering support and asks, "Are you ready to head to the house? Your room is ready and Jacque is on standby to cook whatever your heart desires." All I can do is nod.

Chapter 32

Lucas

Well, I tried my best to prepare myself for seeing Samantha, giving myself pep talks and all. But when it finally happens, nothing helps. Seeing her is agonizing. Every part of my body hurts, and I want nothing more than to wrap my arms around her. But my pride steps in, refusing to show weakness, and tells my destroyed heart to shut the fuck up.

After Christian arrived in town, I agreed to meet him for a drink at the hotel closest to Fox Sporting. On my way to the hotel, I remind myself I can't mention what happened between me and Samantha. I know that she's in the city. Christian told me so. Because I'm desperate to avoid her, I hope she isn't staying at the hotel we're meeting at.

While sitting in the bar having a beer with Christian, an unnerving feeling washes over me. My shoulders bunch and goose bumps scatter over my body. *Is someone watching me?* I push it aside as a few over-done women approach us. The way they're eyeing us, I assume they're responsible for the way I was reacting. My shoulders remain tight and my body is in a heightened state even after they arrive.

Still feeling uneasy, I turn around, allowing my eyes to wander over the entire bar. When my eyes fall on the most beautiful woman I've ever seen, I immediately feel like someone's struck me in the head with a two-by-four. Blinking rapidly, trying to clear my vision, I realize it's Samantha. *Is she a mirage?* Shaking my head to clear it proves pointless. What I see before me is devastation. The always radiant woman with a gorgeous smile spread across her face, wears a frown. Her expressive eyes harbor dark circles and she is sickly pale with tear-stained cheeks. *Samantha is here and only feet away*. Fighting the urge to run to her, pull her in my arms, and comfort her, I stay frozen in my chair. There's no denying it; I still want her desperately. But the feeling isn't reciprocated. Like being drenched with ice-cold water, that feeling triggers my pain and anger.

Distracted, I don't notice when Christian and the ladies make a plan to head to Inferno, a trendy new nightclub. Once there, we're escorted to the VIP section because Christian knows the owner and I'm, well, me. Before I know it, we're surrounded by a huge group of people. If I was ready to move on, I could take my pick. But no part of me is interested. The night drags on, and instead of going home to my empty penthouse, I sit back in the VIP section and people-watch.

The next day, practice comes too early and I curse Christian when my alarm goes off. Even though its Saturday, Coach was on a tangent yesterday and ordered some extra ice time. I hit snooze twice before I drag my semi-hungover, exhausted ass out of bed.

I stumble through getting ready, then rush to practice, still feeling charged up from seeing Samantha. When I get to the arena, I dress quickly and hustle onto the ice. I'm looking forward to working out some pent-up aggression that I can't seem to shake. Halfway through practice, Miles skates up to me.

"Hitting the weight room after practice?"

"Course I am," I answer with a quick snarl.

He hits me in the chest with his gloved hand, stopping me before I skate off. "You seem on edge. Everything okay?"

I shift my weight on my skates and answer in a gruff tone, "I'm fine." Pushing off to skate away, he again skates in front of me with a concerned look.

"Lucas."

"Don't!" I growl.

He holds up his hands in surrender and skates away while shaking his head in disappointment. I don't miss the "jackass" comment he makes under his breath. He's right, but I don't care.

Returning to the blue line for more drills, my

adrenaline is pumping as Coach blows his whistle, signaling the start. I focus on pushing myself harder and faster than ever. Physical exhaustion is exactly what I need in order to pass out. I don't need to get stuck on the mental garbage that's already taking up way too much space in my head.

Later, when I enter the weight room, I avoid both Jack and Miles and hop onto the treadmill to get my thirty minutes of cardio in. Putting in my AirPods, I silence everything and turn on some Skillet. While I listen to "Monster," I ignore everyone and everything around me. For the first time in weeks, I have a moment of peace.

Sweat drips off me and my lungs burn. I push myself on my run. This time my goal is to complete five miles in under a half an hour. When I wobble off the treadmill with rubbery legs, I know I need to take a moment before starting my leg workout. Being smart is how I keep myself from sustaining unnecessary injury. Leg days are always the worst, but I know that strengthening my legs will only help me do better at my job.

After my mini break, I set myself up to start with Bulgarian split squats. I grab my dumbbells and start my five sets of three. Waiting fifteen seconds between each set seems like forever. I'm impatient. My body vibrates with nervous energy. I want to get through my workout and get out of here. It's getting uncomfortable being under the scrutiny of Jack and Miles. Considering my attitude recently, they've given me a wide berth, especially because I keep ignoring them.

My death box jumps are next. These take focus and precision, which today seems impossible. Samantha invades every brain cell. Finally, mentally and physically exhausted, I make it through my last set, even though it takes longer than normal.

Jack taps my arm as I refill my bottle at the water fountain. I glare at him and he glares back. I blow out a deep breath and remove an earbud.

"What?" I angrily ask.

He puts his hands up and mutters, "Are you done pouting, or is this what we have to look forward to for the foreseeable future? Are you planning to be a dick to everyone? What is going on with you? I thought your girlfriend was going to be here this weekend. If so, why are you so pissed off?" He rapid fires his questions at me.

Not wanting to deal with his inquisition, I slam my earbud back in my ear, turn around, grab my stuff, and stomp out of the room, refusing to answer him. He chases me down and catches me off guard. He pins me up against the wall with his forearm under my neck.

"Let me go! Get the fuck off me!" I shout. Miles joins him and they both stare me down, challenging me. I thrash my body, trying to get loose, but I can't. I'm fucking exhausted. I'm not a small guy, but Jack has a few inches on me and about twenty-five pounds of solid muscle. Plus, I'm not only physically drained from practice and my workout, but I'm emotionally spent from the past week.

"No!" he roars at me. He never loses his cool. His demeanor and tone snap me to attention.

I finally calm myself down, and when I stop flailing, he releases his grip on me. When he's sure I won't bolt, he steps back from me and joins Miles. Again, they both stare at me, their faces covered with complex emotions.

"What is going on, Lucas?" Miles asks.

I hang my head and slump down the wall. They both drop to a squat next to me and wait until I finally look up. I don't answer. I don't know what to say.

"Isn't Samantha here? Why do you look like you want to kill someone? What happened?" Jack asks.

"She broke up with me!" I spit out.

I hope I don't need to say anything more, because I'm not ready to relive it all. Not with them or with anyone. Both their faces fall, and I know they won't push me any further. Jack extends his hand to me and says, "Let's go. We'll grab something to eat and meet you at your place."

Jack and Miles arrive with the pizzas and cream soda, and we make a huge dent in it. The pizza is delicious, and I shove five pieces down, hoping it will fill the empty space I've had since Samantha walked away. It doesn't work. But this is the first actual meal I've eaten since that dreaded night. Before now, I couldn't stomach food. I've been mainlining coffee just to keep me awake enough to function. I've eaten a few protein bars that I've got stored in my locker or gym bag, but I know I've already lost weight. As I grab another piece of pizza, I notice that Miles and Jack aren't eating. Dropping the slice on my plate, I'm suddenly nervous. "What?" I croak.

Jack and Miles share a look, silently deciding who's talking first, while I sit there being held hostage. *At least my captors brought food.* When they finally decide, Miles shifts in his seat. I watch as he nervously fiddles with the grease-stained napkin he has grasped in his large hands. "She broke up with you? Want to tell us about it?" For a big dude, his almost whispered question catches me off guard.

Sitting still for a moment, I look around my penthouse. When my eyes fall on the pile of rubble below where my flat screen used to hang, I wince, embarrassed. My friends notice and follow my eyes to the pile of broken electronics. They exchange worried looks but say nothing. I'm not normally the angry guy, let alone the uncontrolled angry guy, so I'm sure what they see scares them. I need to tell them what happened. Then they'll understand. Maybe they can tell me how to get over her, because seeing her the other night was torture. And constantly thinking about her is wearing down every part of me.

I lift my pizza to my lips and thoughtfully chew a bite while I try to compose what to say. When I swallow, I look at my two best friends and tell them about what happened with Samantha. From the beginning.

Starting with how we met and the misunderstanding in the car. I tell them about convincing Christian to get Samantha to a game and out to dinner with me afterward. I'm tight-lipped about our night together but confess it was the best I've ever had. When Miles tries to pry for more details, Jack punches his arm and tells him to shut up, which makes me laugh.

"Wait. I'm confused. Didn't you say she was coming here?" Jack asks, confusion spread across his face.

"Yes, she was supposed to come this weekend. Well, I guess she did. She's in the city now. She just ended things with me before she got here."

Miles tips his head and asks, "How'd she end it?"

After I tell them about the phone call and the bullshit reasons that she gave me for why she thought we should break up, they're just as appalled as I am. Knowing they have my back, I lay it all on the line, sharing all my thoughts, feelings, and issues concerning Samantha. When I'm done, they look shell-shocked. I'm not known to be a relationship guy, and what I've just unloaded sounds exactly like relationship drama. Their confusion is completely warranted. Before Jack settled down with his wife Janie, I would have responded to him the same way they're now looking at me. Because Miles is a young rookie, I know he's far from wanting to settle. I had always felt that way too, until Samantha. Now, I just feel destroyed, and I want to know what to do to stop the constant pain.

Spilling my guts to my friends is strangely freeing. Jack smiles at me like he understands. And Miles just smirks like he's either uncomfortable or gassy. I look back at Jack and hesitantly ask, "Why are you smiling like that?"

He lets out a deep laugh and answers, "Because, Lucas, you have it bad, and that shit is funny!"

Confused, I ask, "Have what bad?"

"Dude, Lucas. You love her, and she broke your heart." He smirks at me, as if he's solved all my problems. Just like that.

I shake my head and stutter, "E-excuse me? Love her? Did you listen at all?"

He nods and looks over at Miles, who also seems to be keyed into the craziness Jack's spouting. Miles nods enthusiastically and says to Jack, "Yep, I see it too."

"Love? No, you don't fall in love with someone you barely know after only a few weeks. Sure, she's hot as fuck, and I was totally into her, but I wasn't even close to loving her. I don't do relationships, remember?" I hadn't explained to anyone that I was afraid I would be just like my sperm donor father: an abusive asshole. Just look at what I had done to my iPad and television. All over a woman. What was I capable of if it was something more serious than a casual hookup? *But was it a casual hookup?* Jack's statement has me questioning things.

My best friends silently stare at me and let me mull it over. Do I love her? No, it's too soon to be in love. I was really into her, but that isn't enough. I know I have minimal experience with relationships, but I can't possibly already love her. Admitting I care for her deeply is a big step, but even they can agree, we barely know each other. Sure, I feel completely comfortable with her. With only her, I could finally be myself. I didn't feel like I had to maintain my constant walls. But that doesn't mean I love her. Instead of feeling better about coming clean to my best friends, now I feel even more confused. Pushing back in my chair, I wonder how to navigate this clusterfuck I'm in.

Trying to keep themselves busy while I contemplate everything, Miles cleans up dirty dishes and wraps up the extra pizza. Jack bravely tackles the fallout of my emotional explosion. I'm totally lost in thought when my phone rings. Jack grabs it and answers. He looks over at me nervously, begins whispering, and walks away. Normally, I'd be pissed at his intrusion of my privacy, but today I don't care. I can't imagine who called, but I know it's not the one woman I want to hear from. Even though she destroyed me, I still want her. And just the thought of that scares me. She told me she doesn't want me, so why do I still want her?

When Jack doesn't return after a few minutes, I wonder who it is. "Jack, who's on my phone?" I holler down the hall at him. He appears from my office and whispers, "Your mom." He grimaces as he hands me the phone. *Shit!* What did he say? What will I say? I know she'll immediately know something is up. It's the reason I haven't called her in over a week. It's probably why she's called. My mom has a sixth sense and can tell when something is up with me.

"Mom," I force out, trying to make my voice sound as normal as possible.

"Lucas, why haven't you called me?" she asks in a concerned tone. Her voice hits me straight in the gut. Guilt floods through me and mixes painfully with the grief and anger already overwhelming me. I sag against the wall and sink to the floor.

"Sorry, Mom. I just have a lot going on and I didn't want to trouble you with it," I confess honestly.

"Lucas, it's no trouble for me. I want to be there for you. What's going on? Jack was trying to catch me up, but then you hollered at him," she chastises me.

I cover the receiver and growl at Jack, who's still standing near me. "What did you tell her?"

His eyes grow wide and he answers, "I was telling her about Samantha and what happened. But you cut me off before I could tell her you're in love with Samantha." He raises his voice at the end, hoping my mom will hear him.

"Dude," I caution him.

"Whatever. Someone has to get it through your head, and your mom is the best bet." He walks away, grabs Miles, and they leave without another word.

I bring the phone back to my ear and walk back into my living room, saying, "I guess you heard Jack just now?"

"I did. Is he right? Do you love her?" Having this conversation with my mom is difficult. My dad was a bastard who abused her in every way. Their relationship was horrible. And I'm not sure she is the best person to get advice from. I don't think she's ever been in a healthy long-term relationship. Honestly, I was trying to avoid mentioning Samantha to her until I fully understood how I feel. Until everything doesn't feel so raw and painful.

"I don't know, Mom. I know I had deep and intense feelings for her. Even though we weren't together for very long, I wanted more. Things I had never considered wanting with anyone else, I suddenly craved with her. Unfortunately, she didn't feel the same way and ended things. Now I just have to figure out how to pick up all the pieces. So, when you ask if I love her, I don't know. Everything I'm feeling now is colored with hints of pain and anger, and I'm sure it will influence my true feelings. If you were to ask me before, I would say I was falling for her. That's probably why this hurts so bad." My mom is the strongest woman I have ever known and I hate to admit this weakness to her.

"I have a question for you," she whispers.

"What is it?" I ask, genuinely curious about what she wants to know.

"You said she doesn't feel the same way? How do you know? Did she tell you that?" The sadness in her voice is palpable.

Her questions stir the pain and anger within me, and I fight the urge to snap at her. I let out a breath as I count down from ten before I say, "Why would she end it if she felt the same way? It doesn't make any sense. She can't have felt the same way as I do, or she wouldn't have broken up with me."

She sighs, as if she's also annoyed with me. "Before I answer you, I need to ask a few more questions that will hopefully clarify things for me," she states confidently.

I say nothing, hoping she'll understand that I mean for her to continue her inquisition.

"Was there anything preventing you two from being together? Anything that may have added extra stress to a new relationship?"

"Yes. She lives in Chicago."

"So, living in two different states ruined what you had? I mean, you travel so much because of your job. It's not like you're in one place all the time. I can't imagine a long-distance relationship would ruin things. Couldn't you just fly her to you? It's not like she's in another country. Don't you travel to Chicago or a nearby city multiple times a year? What else came between you?" She pries further, knowing we probably could have worked through the travel issue.

I smirk before I answer her. "You know how a few

months ago I introduced you to Christian from Fox Sporting? It was about a month before I signed with them for representation?" She clicks her tongue, meaning she's with me, so I continue, "Well, Samantha's full name is Samantha Fox."

She gasps loudly. "Lucas, you didn't sleep with Christian's wife, did you? I know I raised you better than that," she says sternly. She's riled up now. Thankfully, she's in another country and hours away.

"No, Mom, I didn't sleep with Christian's wife. Samantha is his sister, and she works for her family's company, so in a very roundabout way, she's kind of my boss." I cringe at that last part.

She laughs, not at all sounding angry like a moment ago. "Is that everything?"

I shake my head, even knowing she can't see me, and run my hand through my hair. How is she going to respond to this? I take a moment, forming my response, trying to make sure I don't sound like a complete asshole before delivering it. "No, Mom. You know I don't do relationships, right? So, when this started, I suggested being casual." I drop off toward the end of my admission, wondering if she'll understand what I mean.

The line goes silent. I hear her breathing, so I know she hasn't hung up on me. She seems to have paused. Probably to think about what I said. After a few moments, she shocks me when she asks, "So you suggested to her you wanted to be... what is it called these days... oh, that's right, you wanted to be fuck buddies?"

I almost swallow my tongue. I don't think I have ever heard my mom swear, and then she dropped that on me. Once I'm able to speak, I shamefully admit, "Yes."

She scoffs at me and says, "No wonder she ended things."

"Wait! What?"

She laughs like I've told her a joke. "Lucas, remind me again. You're male, right?"

I nod to myself, unable to figure out where our conversation is headed. "You know I am, Mom," I tell her, my annoyance building.

"One last question and I think I'll have it all figured out," she says haughtily.

"Sure, go for it," I sarcastically say, knowing she hasn't figured out shit. There is no fucking way.

"Did you tell Samantha how you felt about her? At any time, while you were involved, did you share your thoughts or feelings with her?"

"First off, Mom, that is two questions. And second, no, I didn't."

She laughs and laughs, only driving my frustration higher. *Why the fuck is she laughing like the Joker as my world is imploding around me? This isn't funny at all!*

"Mom," I whine like a petulant child.

She hiccup-laughs like she's had too much to drink or she's gone certifiable.

"What is wrong with you, Mom?"

The laughing abruptly stops and she clears her throat. "Sorry, Lucas, but although you are quick to throw Samantha under the bus here, *you* did this. You set it up to fail before you even gave it a fair chance."

"What? How the hell did I do that? I didn't make her break up with me. She did that all on her own. So, see, she's to blame for it all. If she wasn't cool with being casual, she never should have told me she was. After all, she's the one with the relationship experience. She knew how this worked," I shout angrily.

My mom goes silent. I shiver because that's never a good sign. Actually, it's terrifying. She only does that when she's trying to teach me a lesson and I'm taking too long to learn it. But she's stubborn and determined for me to figure it out without her having to say too much. Going mute, I wait for what seems like forever before she finally speaks up.

"Lucas, I understand it hurt you, and I'm sorry for that, but I don't believe Samantha is solely responsible for all of it. I think if you thought about that, you would agree with me. I think you should ask yourself whether you think she had any other choice."

She gives me a minute to let that question marinate.

"If she wanted to be with you, she would have to agree to be casual, so you'd be with her, right? So then, what if she, too, was falling for you? Would she have known that you were open to more if you never told her? What was her option? She likely ended things before she got in any deeper. You told her at the beginning you were unavailable for more, so again, what choice did she have?" Her questions stun me. *Holy shit.*

"What else is holding you back, Lucas? Why aren't you ever in a relationship?" she asks.

"Relationships don't last," I growl out.

"Lucas. Is this about your father?"

Flippantly, I respond, "Who else would it be about? You never remarried or even dated after we got away from that asshole. Why not?"

A chuckle fills the line. "You are right about one of those things. I never remarried. But I dated and still do, occasionally. There aren't as many great choices at my age. And you won't see me signing up to swipe left or whatever those dating sites have you doing nowadays."

Amused, but mildly disgusted, I ask, "You dated? How did I not know?"

"Oh, Lucas. You didn't know because I didn't need to flaunt strange men in your face. I wasn't willing to introduce my son to just anyone. So, on nights that I had a date, Patty would watch you for me."

Then, as if puzzle pieces sliding into place, a picture floods my memory. Every Friday night, religiously, Patty watched me. We'd always watched movies and ate pizza. Patty, the director of the shelter we escaped to, and my mom's best friend for over twenty years, who's still like a second mom to me. Baffled, I clear my throat. "Uhhh... you dated... and often?" *What? When? Who?*

"Yes, and no. At first, it was all about getting out and socializing. Your father had done a number on me and I had to learn to trust again. For me, learning how to be around people my age in a social setting without being fearful was a challenge. Over time, I met some great people. A few of the guys I even went on dates with, but not one of them was 'the one.'"

"But how do you know? Obviously, my dad wasn't it, but what if I am not 'it' for Samantha? What if I'm just like him?"

"Listen here, Lucas. You... you are nothing like that man. The only part of him you got was your eye color. Everything, and I mean everything else, about you is his opposite. I don't know if you're it for Samantha, only she can decide that. But I believe that when you find each other, you feel it deep within yourself. You recognize something within that person no one else has been able to."

The whole idea of "the one" was intimidating. Did you really just have one perfect match out there? If so, without a doubt, I know mine is Samantha. She stirred up thoughts and feelings I'd never had before. She made me want something more than I'd ever considered. With her by my side, my future looked complete. The only problem is that I don't have her anymore. If she is my one, I need to get her back.

Everything my mom shared with me makes sense as to why I'd avoided relationships. I'd seen her do it, and she still seemed perfectly happy. I assumed I'd follow the same path. Plus, over the years, I'd seen so many relationships crash and burn. Honestly, they'd never seemed worth it. It wasn't something I wanted. That is until Samantha.

During our conversation, my mom's questions resonated with me the most, making me think I might share some of the responsibility of what happened between us. What if she was right and Samantha ended things because she didn't think there was a possibility for more between us? What if she was falling for me like I was for her? Even if there's only a slight chance it could be true, I need to know. Maybe things don't have to be over with us.

"I've got to go, Mom," I rush out.

"Are you okay, Lucas?" she asks with love in her voice.

Feeling more balanced and clearer than I have in days, I answer, "I am, Mom. Thank you for listening. Right now, I need to find out how Samantha feels about me."

Chapter 33

Samantha

When I arrive at my parents' estate, I'm feeling mildly better. At least I don't actively feel nauseous. True to my mom's word, Jacque is working in the kitchen, and after I drag myself upstairs, I see my old room is ready for me. I close myself within its familiar walls, crawl into my bed, and fall asleep.

Hours later, I wake up to a soft knock at my door. It's my dad, and he's home from work and checking in on me. He walks to the edge of the bed and sits down. "Samantha, is this about a boy?"

I nod at him while I rub the sleep out of my eyes. I never imagined surviving a heartbreak required so much sleep to heal. But if that's what it takes, I plan to sleep through the next few days, so when I have to head back to Chicago, I'm feeling much better.

"Want to talk about it?" he hesitantly asks. My

parents are great, but communication is not one of their strong suits. In fact, it's probably why Christian and I are so close. We've always talked about everything. Well, everything but sex, and since that's all Lucas wanted from me, Christian knows nothing about us. I need to figure this out on my own. Shaking my head at him, like when I was younger, he grabs my hand and squeezes it twice to tell me he understands but won't pry any further.

"Your mom asked me to come tell you that dinner is ready if you're interested in joining us. If not, I can have Jacque prepare a tray that I can bring up," he offers.

"Can I eat up here?" He nods and heads toward the door.

"You know we love you and we're here to help you any way we can?" I nod and he leaves. He returns later with a plate filled with food that smells absolutely divine. He hands over one of Jacque's most prized meals, Coq Au Vin. My mouth waters and my stomach growls, reminding me how hungry I am. In no time, I inhale the delicious meal.

I set the empty plate on my desk and head into the bathroom to shower. In the bathroom lies a clean pair of yoga pants, a tank top, a bra, and panties. *My mom must have been here.* After I shower, I pull on the new clothes and melt into the buttery-soft fabric of them.

Headed back toward my bed, I notice that my dinner plate has been removed and a peach and raspberry clafoutis sits in its place. "Yum." I hum to myself. It's still warm, and it melts on my tongue. The raspberries are slightly tangy and a perfect match for the sweetness of the peaches. It is completely decadent, and I enjoy all of it. Once I'm done, I grab my phone off the nightstand and see that I have about a million missed calls and texts. Still not interested in talking to anyone, I am, however, curious about who tried to reach me. Most of the missed messages are from Mom, Dad, and Christian from over the weekend. Monica has left several as well, but I'm not ready for that conversation either. Honestly, I haven't told her about breaking up with Lucas, because I wasn't sure how to. Knowing I can't avoid everyone forever, I tell myself I'll reach out soon. After all, based on Christian's shifty phone conversation at the hotel, I'm aware she knows something major went down. Tomorrow I'll call her and tell her everything. That way, she'll know the entire story when I head back to Chicago this weekend.

The next day flies by and I'm still not any more ready to confess my feelings for Lucas to Monica. But I'm not so lucky. As I sit on my childhood bed, rationalizing how I'll call her tomorrow, my phone rings. I look down and see it's her. "Ugh!" I groan and then hesitantly answer. "Hi, Monica."

"Sam, I have been calling you for days. Why haven't you answered? Christian called me, absolutely panicked, on Monday afternoon. He was grilling me to see if I knew why you were curled into the fetal position for the second time in less than two weeks. And I, your best friend, couldn't tell him anything. It wasn't even because I didn't want to but because you haven't told me what's going on," Monica hollers in an aggravated voice that still sounds sweet.

Feeling embarrassed, I bury my head in my hands. "I know, and I am sorry. Things progressed and then failed so quickly that I'm still trying to wrap my head around it. I wanted more clarity before I tried to explain it all to you. Can you forgive me? Please? I need my best friend right now more than I can say."

Monica lets out an audible breath that sounds like a tire deflating. "I feel like I've missed so much. I'm assuming this is about Lucas, right? Last time we talked about it, the two of you had agreed to a casual relationship."

I laugh sarcastically and ask, "How much time do you have?"

Sweetly, she answers, "I have all the time in the world for you, Sam. In fact, Christian and I are flying to New York after work on Friday so I can see you and get you back to Chicago this weekend. That's if you're ready to go home."

"Oh, you and Christian?" I say in a teasing tone. Maybe I can distract her from having to explain what happened with Lucas?

Slipping into her teacher tone, she cautions me, "Oh no, you don't. We aren't talking about me and

Christian. We're talking about you and Lucas. So, spill." For a petite thing, she can be intimidating. I hear the warning in her voice and decide it's time. *Here goes.*

"Honestly, Monica. There is no Lucas and me. It died before it even started," I tell her, noticing the tightness in my chest increase. Silence fills the line, making me feel ashamed I've been keeping secrets. Especially from my best friend.

"What do you mean?"

I explain to her how we'd struggled to connect once he was back in New York and how being long-distance was too difficult.

Monica clears her throat. "Aren't you in New York?"

"Yes."

"So, what happened in the few weeks between planning to visit and now?"

Taking a moment before answering her question, I consider multiple things. How much did I want to confess? *She's your best friend. If you can't tell her, who can you tell?* "The morning he left, we planned our future visits. However, between then and last week we had some miscommunication, and I was not only disappointed, but I also got my feelings hurt. Lucas tried to clear the air between us, even sending me gorgeous flowers. But the separation and my insecurities got in my head. I questioned whether or not our arrangement was even worth it. When we finally talked, I thought we'd worked it out. But then my fears came roaring back, and I decided it was best to end things before they progressed any further."

Monica's silent for a moment, then interjects, "You were concerned you were falling for him?"

"Yes," I admit in a whisper.

"Oh, sweetie, what are you going to do now?"

Letting out a sigh, I say, "I don't know. He acted like everything was normal when I saw him at the bar with my brother on Friday night."

"He was with your brother?" Monica questions defensively.

"Christian doesn't know about Lucas and me. And obviously, Lucas isn't as distraught as I am if he could go out and hit clubs with my brother and a bunch of random women." Silence again fills the line.

"Monica, I... I just need to get over him," I confess sadly.

Monica tries to sound upbeat as she reminds me, "I'll be there Friday night. We will talk, laugh, scream, whatever. And then we'll head back to Chicago on Sunday, okay?"

I sniffle. "Okay. I'm feeling pretty tired and I'd like to go to bed. Can we talk tomorrow, maybe?"

"Yeah. Totally. Call me tomorrow when you're free. I love you, Sam."

"Love you too," I respond before hanging up. Exhausted, I fall asleep in no time.

Chapter 34

Lucas

Another shitty day is followed by an even shittier night. Basically, my life is crappy right now. My hockey game is shit. My love life is craptastic. And my mind feels like it's buried in a steaming pile of excrement. Nothing I do makes any difference. I can't eat or sleep. Even though I still make it to my practices and meetings, it only takes minutes for everyone to figure out my mood is, as my Irish teammate Sean says, shite.

Following my conversation with my mom, I know I need to figure out how I feel. Then I need to find out how Samantha feels. With each day that passes, I'm losing more hope. I can't call her because she won't answer. Nor would she tell me how she feels about me. So, I'm stuck sitting on my couch, wearing my holiest sweats, trying to figure out how to ask Christian without him becoming suspicious. My phone rings, and just as I'm ready to silence it, I notice it's Christian. Thanking my lucky stars, I quickly answer, hoping to mask my sad, pathetic mood.

"Hey," I say in a weak voice.

"Hey, man. How the hell are you?" he asks, sounding my complete opposite. He's light and happy, where I'm weighed down and depressed. And, like everything lately, it grates on my fucking nerves. What can I say? Heartbreak has turned me into a moody bastard.

"What's up?" I mumble. Not really feeling up for a lengthy conversation, but knowing it's my best option to find out about Samantha.

"Not much. Will you be in New York this weekend?" he asks.

"Yeah, I've got two home games this weekend. Do you want tickets?" I offer.

"Wish I could come see you play, but I'm dealing with a family matter. But I'm sure I'll need an escape at some point. Are you down with grabbing a beer or something?"

"Family matter? Is everything okay?" I inquire, trying to hide the amount of concern in my voice.

He lets out a growl before he answers. "Yeah, everyone is mostly fine, but some dick did something to Samantha and she's been a mess for the last few weeks. I'm actually bringing Monica with me on Friday to see if she can't get her to come back to Chicago. She's been at my parents' estate since I found her trashed in a hotel Monday afternoon." My heart pounds in my chest and my worry for Samantha feels like a thousand-pound weight draped across my shoulders. I'm speechless.

"Shit! I shouldn't have said anything to you. I forget you're a client, not just my friend, and you probably shouldn't know our family's drama."

Fuck! Now I feel even worse. It sounds like Samantha isn't doing any better than I am, but why? I'll pull the trigger and ask. What's the harm? He wouldn't be talking to me if he knew I was the dick he's referring to. And he's right, I am a dick. King of the dicks. Captain Dickface. Dickhole. But this may be my only opportunity to get any information, so I'm taking it.

"Do you need me to help you kill someone?" I offer, knowing full well he doesn't know he's talking about me. Because once he finds out, I'm as good as dead. He'll finish me, and not only will I have lost Samantha, but Christian as well. It's a chance I have to take. I want her back, and if this is what I have to do. So be it.

"No, man. Not yet. Monica won't give me much information, but I know it's because of a guy. I'm hoping to get more details this weekend. So, about that beer? You down?"

Ashamed, I hang my head. Grateful he can't see me, I finally answer him. "Yeah. We can grab one after my early game Sunday. It'll be before you head back to

Chicago. Does that work?" He agrees and tells me he'll call me when he gets into the city in a few days.

The next day drags by. I feel like a robot moving through the motions of my pathetic life. Each step is painful. When I attend practices, weight room sessions, team meetings, and promotional spots for my new Gatorade sponsorship, I'm there, but I feel nothing. I've become a hollow vessel. Hearing that Samantha is doing horribly is agony, and I wish I could fix it. Even though her breaking up with me is still so raw, I don't want her to hurt. I wish I knew what I could do to make things better, but the circumstances haven't changed. All the reasons we can't together remain. If I'm honest, I was so hurt and angry when she broke up with me; I hadn't given any thought to the reasons she'd listed. Now they seem incredibly important and something I really need to consider. As painful as it is to admit, in order for me to understand her actions, and to move on with my life, I need to accept her reasoning.

The next day, it seems the proverbial fog has lifted and I realize all the reasons Samantha gave me for us not working were flimsy at best. All except one, and even I can agree it's definitely major. Living in two different cities will destroy our relationship even before it begins. We've already had a taste of that and it ended terribly. With me traveling so much for hockey, we wouldn't want to be apart even more. Racking my brain, I question, is there any way around that?

After doing my best to avoid Jack and Miles for the past week, I decide to join them today for lunch following our standard practice. It's good for the team, right? Or that's what I tell myself. Since we have a game tomorrow, positive chemistry between teammates is key, or that's what the team's sports psychologist is always saying. *I wonder how this will go.*

When I enter the cafeteria, they're already seated, eating lunch and joking around. When they see me, they stop what they're doing and stare. As I grab my lunch, I feel their gazes follow me. I'm not hungry, but I know I need to eat. *Fuel the body.* Grabbing two grilled chicken breasts, a sea salt baked potato, and broccoli, I turn back toward the team tables. When I do, I notice the silence of the cafeteria. Looking out, I notice the entire team staring at me, waiting to see what I do. Feeling uncomfortable, I give them a small smile and wave before I walk toward Jack and Miles. Approaching slowly, I am trying to gauge whether I'm welcome. Jack and Miles look at each other, then at me, and smile, giving me the all-clear. I set my lunch down and pull out my chair before saying anything. They stare at me, waiting. Even though it's uncomfortable, I agree their hesitancy is justified. I admit I've been an asshole the last week or two, and I understand they might be uncertain about how I may behave.

"Hey, guys," I start slowly.

They both grunt "Hi" as they dig back into their lunches. *Shit.* They're going to make me earn their forgiveness. This is going to suck ass. I wonder what they're going to make me do to get back in their good graces. As I'm imagining having to cover the tab every time we go out or some other hair-brained idea they'll come up with, Miles pelts a roll at me. I flinch, grabbing it just before it hits me in the head. *Thank you, peripheral vision. I may not be a goalie like him, but I've got great eye-hand coordination and spatial awareness.*

"What?" I growl at him.

Miles just laughs. I wish my life were as easy as his is. I'm not sure he really has it as good as I think, but he lets everyone believe that. He embodies the "no worries" lifestyle. Standing there, I wonder if my coming over was a mistake. I make to leave, ready to move over to another table to eat my lunch in peace, when Jack stops me. He grabs my wrist and growls, "Sit your ass down, Lucas. Do you think you're done pouting yet?"

He glares at me until I sit back in my chair with my arms crossed against my chest, and sternly answer, "I'm not pouting."

Again, Miles laughs, and that pisses me off. Moving my focused glare to him, he stops immediately. I rein in my anger for the moment, knowing it won't help me mend fences. Jack says just two words to me. "Spill it." When he levels me with a menacing look, one that says *go on, try me. I dare you,* I do just that.

I blow out a big breath and start in, trying to catch

them up on the past few days. Once I've filled them in about my conversation with Christian, I chance a look at them, trying to gauge their reaction. Nothing but shock stares back at me. Meanwhile, my heart is pleading with them for the answers to solve this dilemma with Samantha.

"Is she worth it?" Jack asks.

Without even missing a beat, I nod my head, answering him confidently, "Definitely. I can see forever with her. And you know me, I've never considered that. Ever."

Miles sits back in his chair, then says something that shocks me. "Lucas, the only thing that will even come close to fixing this is by making a grand gesture to show her exactly how you feel and what you want."

"Grand gesture?" I question, sounding confused.

Jack nods his agreement but doesn't offer any suggestions. *Helpful!*

"What should I do?" I whine. Great, I sound like an irritable child now. Perhaps that's a step up from my grumpy-asshole demeanor? Apparently, over the past few weeks, I've regressed from acting like an adult to doing whatever the hell I want. Everyone would agree, I'm certainly winning at this thing called life. *Fuck me.*

"Okay, I can do that. I can come up with something exceptional that will win her back." I'm not even sure I believe the words I'm saying.

"It's got to be epic, Lucas," Jack warns, and Miles nods his approval, mouthing *"Epic"* at me.

"So... what you are saying is no flowers, chocolate, or offers for fancy dinners?" Unamused, they both roll their eyes at me, which makes me laugh. "You guys, suck! You're no help at all," I scoff as I push back from the table. There're only hours for me to come up with something monumental to show Samantha how I feel. To tell her I need her in my life. I only hope that afterward, she still wants me. Thinking she'll walk away again is terrifying. But I keep reminding myself that she's worth it and if I don't figure this out, I'm not even worth a second chance.

"Where are you going?" Jack asks as I clean up my lunch remnants that remain mostly untouched. *I'll eat when I've got this all figured out.*

"I'm going to come up with a plan to win my woman back. I need to do it before any more time passes and she realizes she doesn't need me."

Chapter 35

Samantha

I think I'm all cried out. I'm not saying I'm over Lucas—not even close—but I'm sick to death of my childhood bedroom. What hasn't helped is reliving what happened between Lucas and me, wishing things were different. But nothing has changed. If we only lived in the same city, we could have made it work. I know it. Unfortunately, I don't plan to move back to New York until they have deemed the Chicago office a success. That's if I decide to move back at all. When it comes down to it, I really like Chicago, and it's feeling more and more like home every day. Maybe I'll stay and convince Christian to do the same. After all, my dad has skilled agents working with him daily. He doesn't need us permanently. New York is only a flight away and so much can be accomplished via technology. Plus, Christian's destined to marry Monica and she will never leave Chicago. So there, the decision is made. I guess we are staying in Chicago indefinitely.

I return my thoughts to my current predicament. I've decided that from now on, there will be no more crying. First, I need to get a good night's rest and then I want to eat something other than ice cream or rich, decadent meals. No offense to Ben & Jerry's or Jacque, but my yoga pants are feeling snugger. I need some greens and water to help balance out all the sugars and carbs I've gorged in my attempt to rid Lucas from my brain. Unfortunately, no matter what I've done, it hasn't worked. He's still taking up quite a substantial amount of real estate in my head. A fact that I find incredibly annoying.

Christian and Monica are coming tomorrow night to check on me and whisk me back to Chicago to heal. Whatever that means. In reality, I just need time. Alone. Thank goodness I have my place in Chicago, because even though I adore my mom, her hovering over the past few days is driving me insane. I'm not ready to tell her what happened. And I might never be. Unfortunately, I had a weak moment yesterday and confessed to her I had been falling for a guy and that I ended things between us. When she asked why, I explained we had some hurdles that we couldn't overcome. I know she wants to be supportive and helpful, but she's smothering me, and I need to get some space.

Honestly, I appreciate having been able to hide out for the last few days, but it's time for me to pull up my big girl panties, take the bull by the horns, and make life happen.

Friday afternoon arrives and the calm I'd been experiencing this last day as I spent much of my day alone, shifts. Suddenly, I'm a ball of anxiety and nerves. I'm ready to see Monica and get home, but I'm not ready to see my brother and face his inevitable inquisition and his mopey expression. He reminds me of Eeyore and that only makes me feel worse. I haven't talked to him since he and my mom whisked me out of my hotel room Monday after finding me a complete mess. I'm not ready for his protective-big-brother routine.

Waiting for the arrival of my escorts, I pace around the kitchen. Jacque putters around me. She's finishing up things for dinner, and I try my best to stay out of her way. When she notices I'm worked up, fiddling with my hands, she asks for my help to make a loaf of bread. As I busy myself with measuring ingredients and mixing them, I don't notice the time pass by.

Just as I'm returning the bread to an oiled bowl to let it rise, I hear familiar voices enter the front door. Silently, I listen to the banter between Christian and Monica. It's comfortable and flirty. I hear my best friend laugh at something Christian says, and it feels so good to hear her happy.

They walk toward the kitchen as I'm pulling the moist towel over the bowl of dough. Looking up just as they enter the kitchen, I can't help but notice how close they are. Unaware I'm watching, I see Monica lay her hand on Christian's arm as she says something. I can't hear what she's said, but I see his eyes widen as if he's surprised. The smile he's wearing grows larger. I'm mesmerized as I watch him shift his focus to her, taking in her eyes and then her lips. *Interesting*. I feel like a voyeur watching a secret mating ritual, but I can't look away. After all these years, they're still dancing around each other, pretending their attraction isn't real. But I can see it, plain as day. Almost like it's screaming out to be acknowledged. I wish they'd just figure it out. They'd be so good together. And win for them, they're even in the same city.

At the thought of that, pain races through my chest, tightening it and robbing me of breath. I used to have that same chemistry with Lucas, but being in different cities convinced me things couldn't work out. Not wanting to think about him anymore and needing some distraction, I clear my throat, letting Monica and Christian know they aren't alone. In a split second, the privacy bubble surrounding them pops. They step away from each other and focus their attention on me.

Suddenly, I feel incredibly exposed, and I wish I had just slipped out of the kitchen undetected and their moment could have continued. But that didn't happen, and now I'm staring into two faces filled with pity and sympathy. I hate it. I don't need anyone's pity or sympathy because it only makes me feel worse. I know I'll get through this. Honestly, I really don't have any choice in the matter. I remind myself of what I decided earlier. There will be no more crying. Even though it still hurts so badly, I need to return to my life.

Chapter 36

Lucas

I'm trying to get myself pumped up for my game tonight. I skated this morning, and I took a small nap earlier. Overall, I feel pretty good. The constant ache that has refused to leave my chest these last two weeks isn't as intense today as it's been. I wonder if it's because I know Christian is in town and I plan to pump him for information about Samantha. Or maybe I'm finally accepting her rejection of me and that hurts at a cellular level, which registers deeper and feels different. I don't really know about it. But it's still uncomfortable and annoying.

Talking to my mom about all this again has provided some much-needed clarification. Her suggesting that Samantha maybe hadn't wanted to call us quits was tough to swallow. *Is it true?* Even now, I wonder if we could have made it work. Hashing it all out with myself over the last few days, I better understand Samantha's concerns and fears. If my mom's theory is correct, I too would hate to spend more time together, fall for her, realize it's too hard, and break up. That would hurt so much worse than what I'm going through now. Considering all of that, I can't help but wonder if breaking up was the only outcome we could have had. If we'd talked it out, could we have come out with a better option, one that worked for both of us and kept us together?

As a professional hockey player, before each game, I always try to get myself in the zone. Clearing my head, dressing in my gear, and lacing my skates are ritualistic. I've done this since I was a kid and it's become second nature. On my way out to the ice for warm-ups, I grab my favorite stick and hit it off either side of the door before taking the ice.

Ever since I can remember, I've loved everything about hockey. I feel beyond lucky that I can play at the level I do; living out the dream I've had since I was eight. I crave the feel of the puck at the end of my stick, the slice of my expertly sharpened skates, and the wind I create as I lap around the rink. It's all energizing, but the thing that always centers me is the smell of the ice when I first step out onto it. The cool bite tickles my nose and reminds me I'm alive. And over the last few weeks, I've questioned if I am.

Like always, I skate around the rink a few times before stopping to do my stretches in front of our team bench. Dropping onto the ice, I start with my groin.

Then I move to my hamstrings and glutes. Today, as I'm stretching, I notice a song come over the sound system. It's "Warrior" by Imagine Dragons. It pumps me up and readies me for what's ahead. As I refocus on my stretches, everything clicks into place. I stand up and do some back and oblique stretches with my stick. And as I do, my eyes wander to the stands. The fans are already filling the arena. I'm optimistically looking for Samantha, wishing she were here, wearing my jersey, and cheering me on. But she isn't.

According to Christian, she's hunkered down at their parents' estate outside the city, completely destroyed. At the reminder of that, my heart drops and the pain that's plagued me for weeks comes roaring back with such intensity it takes my breath away. Swallowing hard, I lean down, forcing my lungs to suck in a breath.

All I ever wanted was to play in the NHL and to have someone cheering just for me. Sure, I have plenty of fans screaming my name, wearing my jersey. It's great, actually. And I'm not complaining one bit, but I desperately want someone who knows and loves me for me, cheering me on, and wearing my name because she believes in my dreams as much as I do. I know, without a doubt, Samantha would have done that. The reminder that I don't have her hits hard, like a Mack truck slamming into me. And that force... it takes more than a second to recover from.

Jack passes me and taps his stick to my shins,

checking in, and I remember what I need to do. Nodding, I take my stick and warm up my wrists. Then a thought strikes me. *Could I have her if I lived in Chicago?* I'd definitely have a better chance of seeing her since we'd be living in the same city. Other questions flood my brain. *Could I trade to play for Chicago?* I've been playing in the NHL for the past seven years and I know retirement is imminent, but I'm not ready to hang up my skates yet. *Maybe New York would willingly trade me?*

As the music continues to pump around the arena, I wonder if asking Christian to approach Chicago with that proposal is foolish. Will he laugh at me and tell me it's career suicide? I'll have to tell him why I want to force a trade. That conversation needs to happen, but I'm dreading it. Jack and Miles said something about making an epic grand gesture. Changing teams and moving to her city would certainly be that, right? I need to think more about it before I approach Christian. The idea of it excites me and gives me hope, which has been nonexistent in my life over the past few weeks. I feel a gigantic smile on my face for the first time since Samantha's and my night together in Chicago.

As I debate both sides of the issue, Jack again slaps his stick into my shins, forcing me to shift focus back to the ice. I look up and realize that my teammates are skating toward the exit leading to our locker room. I skate after them and follow them down the hallway. Jack stands there as I exit the ice. "You good?"

Smiling, all I can say is, "Yes."

After we enter the locker room, Coach jumps into his pep talk about what he expects against Philly. While listening to him talk about swift feet, puck handling, maximizing power plays, and scoring, I look around at the faces of my teammates. Surrounding me is an elite group of men. Some are wild and rowdy, others are quiet and reserved. Being on this team has afforded me so much, and I've found my two best friends. Leaving this team means leaving them as well. Even though I'd miss them, I remind myself that Chicago plays New York often throughout the year. Plus, there's the off-season and the cities are only a quick plane ride apart. If I left, I'd miss playing together, hanging out, and relying on them, but if I had another chance with Samantha, wouldn't I be moronic not to jump at it?

Jack, who's sitting next to me, smacks my chest and smirks. "Hooker, you're distracted. What are you concentrating so hard on?"

Shaking my head, I answer, "Just figuring some options out, man."

His eyes go wide and he questions, "Options? Sounds ominous. Want to share?"

I laugh and say, "You said an epic grand gesture, right? Just trying to figure it all out." He nods, accepting what I've said, and goes silent. I wonder if he's guessed what I'm thinking about. I worry about what he'll say. Will he talk me out of it? Maybe I should ask for his advice before I talk to Christian. After all, he knows everything that has happened with me and Samantha. Christian just knows I was having some minor woman problems because that's all he got from me last weekend. He doesn't know it involves his sister or that we broke up because I live in New York and she's in Chicago. I wonder how much I'll have to explain to him to justify this trade. Will he push until he gets the entire story? If I tell him all of it, what will he do? My stomach fills with dread and I have a sudden urge to puke.

Jack clears his throat and whispers over Coach's speech, "Grab a beer with me after the game. It looks like you have a lot going on, and I can be a good sounding board." Swallowing hard, I nod.

The game proves a great distraction. I managed a goal and an assist. And I barely got away with a hooking penalty at the end of the second period while on a penalty kill. Skyler Johnson, a forward for Philly, got a breakaway, and as he headed toward my side of the ice, I hooked my stick around him, tipping his balance, and he lost control of the puck just in time for Dylan and Scott, two of our defenseman, to sweep in and slow him down. Just as I thought the referee was going to call me, he didn't, shaking his head as if he wasn't sure what he saw. And that's what earned me my nickname. I'm a sneaky shit.

We win the game 3-1. There are so many hosers on their team and all they did the entire game is chirp. I'm proud of my teammates. More than once, I wanted to lay a few of their guys out. Surprisingly, we didn't accrue more penalty minutes. Tomorrow's game will probably be a cluster and likely be extra chippy. Hopefully, no one gets too badly banged up.

Thinking about tomorrow, I need to be in the right mental space for the conversation I'm debating having with Christian before he heads back to Chicago with Samantha and Monica. Our conversation could make or break me. Get the girl or lose her forever. Speaking of girls... Monica is here too, and I remember Samantha mentioning the intense chemistry between her and Christian. If my conversation with Christian goes well, I may have to explore that further.

Regarding Christian, I still haven't decided if I want to tell him all about Samantha and me. Not telling him prevents me from potentially ruining a friendship and business arrangement. Plus, it saves me from getting my ass kicked. I'd at least give him a free punch because of my part in contributing to Samantha's pain, but I won't just stand there and take the anger I've seen he's got brewing. By not telling him, it only delays the inevitable. Eventually, he'd find out, especially if Samantha gives me a second chance. And finding out I withheld it from him, I'm not sure we'd recover from that. Even though I'm dreading it, I know I have to tell him. I wish I could talk to Samantha about it because I don't want to blindside her. I'm not sure if it will cause trouble in their relationship, but I can't ask her. I only hope that Christian won't talk me out of pursuing the trade. After all, if it goes through and Samantha doesn't want me, I only have a few more years left in the NHL and Chicago wouldn't be a horrible city to live in. If I'm being honest, I don't care where I play, as long as I get to play. So if there's even the slightest possibility I can convince Samantha to give me another chance, I'm taking it.

Chapter 37

Samantha

My brother has been pretty nonexistent since he and Monica arrived Friday evening, and we're supposed to be going home on Sunday. Today my mom turned the living room into a personal spa because she figured I wouldn't be up for heading into the city. She was right, and we spent the entire day being pampered with manicures, pedicures, facials, and massage treatments. It was heavenly. When I go to bed, I feel better than I have in days. I'm still heartbroken, but I don't feel like I'm drowning in despair.

Sunday morning is a treat, a family breakfast with all of my favorites. Belgian waffles, strawberries, whipped cream, bacon, orange juice, and coffee. Everything looks amazing. It's the first time in weeks I have actually had an appetite. The food looks perfect, smells incredible, and tastes superb.

At breakfast, Christian informs us he will meet us at the plane this evening because he's planning to attend the early afternoon Chargers game and then grab a beer with Lucas.

He still doesn't know about what happened between us and I try to school my reaction so he doesn't notice me wince when he says Lucas's name. Despite my pain, I know they're good friends. I don't want to cause any trouble between them. I'll just avoid him if he's ever around. Simple as that.

But at the mention of Lucas, my parents suddenly have questions about him. I can't escape it. Running from the table with tears spilling from my eyes would be a dead giveaway. So, I screw on a smile and ignore the conversation only inches away. Sensing my discomfort, Monica squeezes my thigh, showing her support. She knows this is difficult for me. I mean, I know he is an important client of Fox Sporting, and in our industry, you need to be invested in your clients. But right now, I wish they were a little less invested. Unfortunately, they don't know why. But hearing about how fantastic Lucas is doing is absolute torture. Monica even tries to change the conversation repeatedly, but my dad won't seem to let go.

"You're going to the game and then to get a beer?" Dad asks, his tone suggesting he's mildly jealous he wasn't invited.

"Yep. Lucas mentioned needing to talk about some

business decisions he's been thinking about," Christian discloses.

My dad looks at him, worried. "Does he still seem happy with us? I'd hate to lose him. He seems like both a super-talented hockey player and a great man." I look at Monica and roll my tear-heavy eyes. She winces.

Christian nods his head, agreeing with Dad. "He is. I don't sense that he's unhappy with Fox at all, but he mentioned some changes he's been entertaining and wonders whether they're plausible. I'll know more after I meet him tonight."

Sitting at the large maple table, I feel like a ping-pong ball, trying to keep up with their conversation. I shouldn't care what Lucas is planning, but I do. What changes is he looking to make? Maybe Christian will tell me about it on the flight home to Chicago tonight. Well, that's if I can figure out how to ask him on the sly. He can't know about us. I'm not ready for that. I thought he was bad with Mitch. But just thinking about how he'd react to one of his good friends not only getting involved with his sister but breaking her heart makes me queasy. The fallout of that won't be pretty and I don't want to bear witness.

The afternoon is a perfect combination of slow and relaxing. Monica and I wrap ourselves in oversized blankets and watch a few chick flicks while munching on popcorn. When we head into the city, we grab a few slices of Joey's pizza on our way to the private airfield.

We get there before Christian and stay busy devouring our delicious dinner.

"This is so good. Why didn't we grab extra to take home?" Monica mumbles to me over her bite. Grease lines her smiling lips. With my mouth full, I just nod.

Half an hour after we finish our greasy dinner, Christian arrives. Stopping at the top of the staircase, he looks lost in thought. He's off, for sure, looking quite frazzled. I find it unnerving. Wasn't he just with Lucas? What did they talk about? From Christian's current state, I'm guessing it wasn't good. But instead of my trying to finagle it out of him, Monica homes in on his state and approaches.

"Christian, are you okay?" She pulls him to a couch and sits next to him. He focuses all his attention on her, looking at her as if he's seeing her for the first time. They intently stare deeply into each other's eyes before he rasps out, "Yeah. Just processing what Lucas and I discussed."

Monica smiles at him. "Can I do anything to help?"

He mirrors her smile and answers, "No, I got it, but thanks for offering." He grabs her hand and squeezes it before saying, "I appreciate the offer. I just need to get back to Chicago to take care of some things for him. Not sure I can do what he's asking."

Sitting back, I watch their conversation, absorbing everything. It's like they're both completely unaware of my presence, even though I'm sitting only a few feet away. They are completely absorbed by each other. And he thinks there is nothing going on?

"Christian, you are a skilled agent, and I know you'll do everything you can to represent Lucas in whatever he wants to pursue," Monica gushes. I really wish my brother could see the way Monica looks at him. It's as if there isn't anything better in the entire world to her. I imagine I used to look at Lucas that same way. Monica's confidence and faith in Christian is unshakeable, and I hope he'll see that. Maybe this weekend and the exchanges they've had will move things forward for them. They deserve to be together.

Chapter 38

Lucas

Last night when I grabbed a beer with Jack, I confessed all the thoughts rushing through my head at warp speed. He listened intently, asked questions, and gave some great thought-inducing feedback. I returned to my penthouse late and fell asleep easily. It was the first time in weeks that I didn't toss and turn.

When I woke up on Sunday, it was actually before my alarm went off. I fixed myself a smoothie and sat on my patio and stared out at the city skyline. I pondered what I wanted to do. Thankfully, both my mom and best friends weren't afraid to call me on my shit, and because of that, they helped me work through my issues and fears about not only asking for a trade to Chicago, but asking Samantha for a second chance. Honestly, both were enormous life-altering changes that were terrifying. But I know Samantha is worth the risk. If I don't try, I would always regret it, wondering what would or could have happened.

Sunday's game was just what I thought—a cluster of penalties. Some of the Philly players were pissed at our win from the previous night. We kept our record against them unbeaten, though. I ended up in the penalty box twice: a two-minute minor for roughing and a five-minute major for checking. They both were justified, but it didn't stop me from having to serve my time. It gave Philly a couple of opportunities with a man advantage, but thankfully, they didn't score either time. Jack and Sean seamlessly worked together to get the only point of the game. And man was it was a beaut!

After handling a few questions from reporters, I shower, dress, and head to my meet up with Christian. He'd suggested a bar closer to the airfield so he'd be close for his flight. Plus, we'd be less likely to be interrupted by a fan who had been at the game. What I want to discuss with Christian is serious, and I need his full attention. I don't need him to be distracted, trying to score with some random puck bunny.

I spot him in a booth as I enter Scythe, a dark and obscure bar that I'd never been to before. Before I head over to him, I order a Samuel Adams from the bartender. When I slide into the booth, I immediately notice his dark mood. Something's up.

"Why do you look like someone stole your puppy?" I ask him.

He takes a drink of his beer. When he rests the bottle back on the table, he finally speaks. "It's my sister. I'm really worried about her."

My stomach bottoms out. My palms sweat and my button-up strangles me. How am I going to have this conversation now? I rethink my plan. Maybe asking Christian to initiate a trade with Chicago isn't the greatest idea. Especially since it involves his sister.

Swallowing past the large boulder cemented in my throat, I roll my beer bottle in my hands. I remain quiet while trying to still my thoughts and get my unsteady breathing under control. How do I tell him about how I'm to blame for what Samantha's going through? Will he understand? Will our friendship and business relationship be over? My fears boil up within me. *It's time to sink or swim.*

"Is she worth it?" Jack had asked me that a couple of times during the last few days. *Yes, she definitely is.* Not allowing myself any more excuses, I leap, hoping the fallout of what I'm about to confess to this man, who is not only my agent but one of my best friends, isn't catastrophic.

I look over at Christian and suck in a breath. "Christian, I have a confession."

He just stares at me, waiting.

"I'm the reason Samantha is so upset. But I think I have a way to fix things. And I'm going to need your help." I grimace. Waiting to gauge his reaction is agony.

A few seconds later, once it all registers, his face

transforms. Instead of his eyes being dark and sad, they are bright, filled with hostility and anger. I think I even hear the crunch of him grinding his back teeth together. My fight-or-flight response is on high alert, but every time I want to run, I fight back the urge and remain in my seat. I know Samantha is worth the fight I just invited upon myself. I will do anything to make things right between us, but I need her brother's help. That's if he'll give it to me.

Before I can further panic, he growls out, "You have five minutes to explain yourself, Lucas, before I walk out that door." I look down at the table, as if it will give me the words I need to convince him not only to stay but to support my fight for his sister. I only need one more chance with Samantha. There is no way I'll screw it up with her again. I won't let myself. I'd rather cut off my own arm than hurt her again.

"You know Samantha and I met at my signing with Fox Sporting," I state. He begrudgingly gives me a grunt as he acknowledges me.

"I won't give you all the details of that night because you're her brother, but I majorly fucked up and hurt her feelings. Then when I came to Chicago for a series a few weeks later, I convinced you to bring her to one of my games and out to dinner after, remember?" He nods, and the anger in his eyes tempers a bit. *Keep going.*

"That night was the best night of my entire life. After you left us at dinner—thank you, by the way—we talked about what had happened and I apologized for the miscommunication on my part that led to her feelings being hurt. We realized that the attraction we'd felt for each other during the previous meeting was still very active and real. Long and short of that, we spent more time together and decided to date casually." I look to make sure he's following me. He is. Aggressively picking at his beer label as he listens to me. He doesn't look as murderous as he did earlier. *That's a good sign.*

"So, if you're dating, why is she acting heartbroken?" Christian sneers.

"She's heartbroken?" I ask him, still thoroughly confused.

He nods and says, "Yeah, she is. Why?" I don't miss the well-guided accusation lobbed at me.

I shake my head, trying to understand. Throughout everything, Samantha being sad is still something I haven't been able to wrap my mind around. Why would she be heartbroken if she's the one who ended things? It doesn't make sense.

"Man, I wish I could tell you. When we first started things, we both were really busy, and we didn't understand the importance of connecting. I thought we talked it through and agreed that we'd each make more effort regarding that. But then she ended things between us two weeks ago, telling me that the distance made it so things wouldn't work for us."

He looked at me, confused. "I was just here two

weeks ago, hitting clubs with you. You're telling me you were heartbroken? No. That's bullshit!"

I'm embarrassed to have to explain my behavior to him. We went to a club that night. But I'd been furious with Samantha for ending things between us. When I'd seen her at the bar, I'd reacted without considering the consequences.

That night, as Samantha watched the woman at the bar trying to get close to me, I'd enjoyed making her squirm in discomfort. I wanted her to suffer as much as I was. I wanted to prove to myself that she would be jealous of me giving attention to another woman. And it had worked. Yes, it had been childish, but it was what it was. I hadn't taken any of the women home. Other than talking to some of them occasionally, I did nothing with them. Honestly, I haven't been able to even think of any other women since I met Samantha. In my eyes, no woman could ever compare.

"Yes, I went out with you because I was hoping to get your sister out of my head. I wanted to prove to myself I didn't need her like she didn't need me. However, all I proved to myself that night was I was completely wrong. I need her in my life. She is all I want, and I have fallen hopelessly for her. I am suffering as much as she is, and I want it to stop. For both of us," I confess.

Christian sits quietly in the booth. My mind races with all the fears and thoughts I've had over the past few weeks. My heart thunders in my chest, my leg bounces uncontrollably under the table, my hands sweat, and my mouth is dry like I've sucked on several cotton balls. Christian's staring at his beer bottle, and the more time that passes, the further my hope of getting his help falls.

He starts slowly when he finally speaks. "So... you hurt my sister and you want my help to fix things?" He pins me with a glare again.

I nod. "Yes, I'm asking for your help. I care for her so much, and I want to make things right. Multiple people, including my mom, have told me I need to make an epic grand gesture, so I need your help to do that. I know I'm probably the last person you want to help, and I understand that I've most likely ruined our friendship, but I need to at least try to fix things. Please help me," I plead.

He looks like he's about to leave, so I reach over and touch his arm. "Please, Christian. She's it for me." His eyes widen and the seriousness of what I've admitted hits him. He knows me well enough to know settling down is not something I've ever considered, so his surprised reaction doesn't shock me. He and I are a lot alike. But just like it happened with Jack, it only takes one incredible woman for you to want something different. Samantha is that woman for me.

He swallows hard as he processes the truth in my words. "Holy shit," he mutters to himself. "What do you need from me? You're still here and she's there. How will it work?"

I clear my throat, not believing I'm about to ask my agent to trade me to another team so I can win the heart of the only woman I will ever want. "I need you to initiate a trade with Chicago."

His face falls and he stutters, "W-what?"

"If I'm in Chicago, there is no reason for us not to be together. I have never felt the way I do when I'm with her. She makes me laugh, challenges me, and makes me want to be a better man. I love so many things about her. She's strong, determined, kind, loving, funny, smart, and selfless. I miss her so much. It feels like when she walked away, she took a piece of me with her and now I'm incomplete." I haven't ever told anyone the depths of how I feel about Samantha, but if that's what it takes to convince Christian to help me, then I'll do it. I'm pretty sure at this point I'd do anything he asked of me.

He smirks at me, which confuses me. "You're telling me you... *love* her?"

I'm flabbergasted. Thinking for a minute, I realize he's correct. I hadn't given my feelings for her a label yet, but he's right. I've never said it to anyone before, and I wish the first time I admitted it, it was to her, but that's not possible. So, I answer Christian. "I do. I love her."

He smiles and runs his hands through his hair like he's stressed out. I just sit there, waiting for his response. A few minutes later, he leans in and calmly says, "Yes, I will help you as much as I can. I'm not making any promises, because that's a big ask, but it doesn't seem impossible. I will caution you that if I make this happen, you have to do everything to make her happy. If you cause her any pain, you'll have to deal with me. Do you understand?" His threat is crystal clear and I nod my understanding.

"If this works, I will do whatever it takes to win Samantha's heart back."

"Okay. I'll make some calls tomorrow when I get back into the office."

"Can I ask one more favor? If it's possible, can we keep this quiet? I want to surprise Samantha," I admit sheepishly.

"I'll try my best. Once it's official, it'll be tough to keep it under wraps, but Samantha doesn't pay attention to sports news. And that might be your saving grace."

I let out a breath, relieved our conversation went the way it did. I was fearing the worst and, thankfully, we avoided it. Feeling much lighter than I have in days, I decide to press my luck and rib my friend a bit. "So... you traveled here with Monica, Samantha's best friend? What's going on there?" I wiggle my eyebrows as I ask, wondering if Samantha's suspicion about them is accurate.

Christian laughs and sits back, relaxed in the booth like he has all the time in the world. I side-eye him.

"Yes, she's Samantha's best friend, and that's it. She's gorgeous, kind, and smart, but fuck, man, she's too good for me. She needs a guy who wants to settle down and start a family, and that's not me. Honestly, she has been great about helping me with Sam. On the way out here, she had me laughing the entire flight. We actually have been talking a lot recently. I guess that's thanks to you. But like I said, she is completely out of my league and my sister's best friend, so she's off-limits." He doesn't realize he sounds just like I do when I talk about Samantha. I decide not to continue pushing my luck since he still has to work some magic with Chicago.

In fact, I'm already looking forward to moving to Chicago and all that I'll experience as I try to win Samantha back. I know that in doing so I'm bound to see Christian and Monica interact, and I can't wait to see how that unfolds. I highly suspect, like Samantha said, they are perfect for each other. Hopefully, they'll figure it out sooner rather than later. *Why waste time when you know?*

"I need to go or else I'm going to miss my flight," Christian says as he stands up. We exchange a bro hug and he promises to call me in a few days once he's talked to the Chicago team.

I watch him walk away from the bar, hopeful of what's coming.

Chapter 39

Samantha

Flying back home is entertaining and the perfect distraction from my heartache. I'm captivated by watching Christian and Monica. The sexual tension surrounding them is unmistakable. But by the time I get back to my home, I'm completely wiped, even after napping in Christian's car.

My mom kept me outfitted in yoga pants and tank tops the entire time I was hiding out at their house, so I actually need to check and see if I have some clean work clothes for the upcoming week. Seeing that this work week is only hours away, I need to get myself organized before I can sleep. Thankfully, I didn't leave my closet in complete chaos before I headed to New York. That's amazing considering the emotional wreck I was and still kind of am.

Scanning my closet, my eyes land on my red

Banana Republic power suit. I grab it and a black silk tank top. It'll help me look like a boss bitch. All the while embracing the "fake it till I make it" mantra. As I unpack my suitcase and am about to throw all the clothes in the hamper, I realize my mom did my laundry and repacked my bag. *Outstanding*. It's one less thing I need to worry about getting done this week. Just forcing myself to show up to work is going to be enough of a battle. Too much and this ship is going down.

Thinking ahead to the coming week, meal prep is the only major hurdle I have. Tomorrow, I'll order some of those already-prepared meals. I've never tried them before, but I've heard Susan, the marketing genius in our office, mention them. By doing that, if things go sideways, I'll at least have something nutritious in my fridge. I'm thinking a hiatus from Ben & Jerry's might also be a smart decision, or my next move will be to consult a nutritionist for a pre-diabetes test and diet assistance.

After I do all my remaining chores for the evening, I take a hot shower. I'm trying to work out some of the residual stress from my body. I fall into my bed at eight. How amazing is that? Ha! I'm probably competing for bedtimes with my eighty-five-year-old neighbor, Neville. But at this point, I don't care. I'm exhausted, mentally and physically, and I can't keep my eyes open any longer. Apparently, my body knows what it needs to heal and move on, and sleep is a major part of that.

The next week of work is a blur of hiding out in my office and crunching numbers. I'm trying to get prepared so I can present to the Fox Sporting board of directors about the Chicago office and it being a success. Spoiler alert, it is. I don't mean to pat myself on the back, but Christian and I have done a fantastic job setting up this new satellite office. We've not only made smart decisions on locations and office design, but we have also hired exceptional employees and forged great business relationships with the city of Chicago, too. I'd pored over our budget and kept it under control, which wasn't always easy. Our success so far will not only please our dad but the entire board when they fly in next week to see what we've accomplished.

Tackling my to do list regarding their upcoming visit, I decide I need to speak with Christian. He's been so busy this week, I haven't even seen him. I want to make sure he's aware of all the things I have booked and planned for the board's visit.

Dialing his office line proves pointless. He's always on the move, but I know he'll at least answer his cell. I try that next, and he picks up on the first ring. "Hey, Sam!" he says in a playful tone.

"You're in a good mood. Want to share why, or maybe just share some of your good vibes with me?" I ask seriously. I would love to celebrate something good and happy. I'm sick of feeling sad. Although work has been very busy and kept those feelings of Lucas mostly at bay. However, when my days slow down, they still creep in, reminding me of the firm grip they still have on me.

Christian laughs. "Although I would love to make you smile, this needs to stay on lockdown for a little longer until all the i's are dotted and t's are crossed. You understand, right?"

I huff at him. "Yes, I get it. It's something big and you don't want to be the one who spills it prematurely."

"Yep. That's it exactly. Promise. Now, why are you calling?" He sounds like he's hiding something, but the sarcastic tone of his voice makes his statements sound accusatory, even though he's not.

I match his sarcasm with my own. "Is now a bad time, big brother? Got a hot hookup waiting for you? Or would you like to do your job and talk through the board's visit next week?"

"Harsh! No hookup is waiting for me. You want to grab dinner tonight and talk it over?" he suggests.

"Sure. Meet at my place in an hour. I'll have Thai delivered. Sound good?"

"Tasty Thai?" he requests.

"Of course. See you in an hour."

Placing my order of spring rolls, cucumber salad, pad Thai, panang curry, fried rice, and fried bananas on Tasty Thai's app is a must before leaving the office. I quickly clean up my office, making sure it's ready for the next day, then I head home. The food arrives shortly after I do, and Christian shows up soon after.

We have a great night, eating, talking, and laughing, which feels refreshing after all the heartache of late. It feels like a new beginning for me. And one that I desperately need.

The board of directors' visit goes well. They're pleased with the setup in Chicago, and that's evident in the pride stretched across our dad's face. There's even talk of further expansion within our offices, but that has been postponed until we've been operating for a full year. Christian and I celebrate with a champagne toast after Dad and the board leave to head back to New York. In Christian's office, my brother pulls a 2010 bottle of Dom Pérignon Brut champagne from the fridge hidden in the sideboard. He tells me he's been saving it for something worthwhile; something like tonight. After a good ribbing from me about him being fancy, he tells me it was a gift from one of the NBA players he represents and not normally a luxury he'd buy. He pops the cork and pours me a glass. After I've had a sip of the bubbly nectar, I say, "I'm proud of us."

He looks at me, smiles, and answers, "Me too." Nothing more needs to be said. In fact, the moment is perfect. After I finish my glass, I set it down on his desk, give him a hug, and leave the office.

Slowly, I feel like I'm getting back to myself. I'm

not plagued by all the sadness I was only a month ago. I'm shaking off the chains that were wrapped tightly around my heart. My steps are lighter and my breathing easier. Once again, I'm discovering who I am. It's been years since I've done this. After everything that happened with the Mitch scandal and then the Lucas situation, I needed to forge a fresh path for myself and my life. I needed to discover fresh turns, twists, and nooks I've yet to encounter so far and embrace the journey fully to realize who I really am.

The next month flies by as I keep myself busy with work, yoga, and time with Monica. Self-discovery is a full-time job. I constantly question myself in my attempt to figure out the real me. I played so many games, trying to be what I thought people wanted me to be, but I discovered that doesn't make me happy. In order to do that, I need to find out what I want and go for it. And I do.

The only time I allow myself to think about Lucas is when I'm alone. The pain over him is still so real and raw, but I'm hopeful eventually it'll pass. Feeling that strongly, despite being new, takes a long time to get over. I'll never understand how I could feel so intensely about someone I knew so little about.

At the beginning of this healing journey, Monica removed all filters regarding Lucas from all my devices. She didn't want me to be bombarded or surprised by what he'd been doing with his life. I'm tempted to look him up from time to time, but I haven't. This pretending that I'm okay and no longer affected is harder than I thought it'd be. I say nothing to anyone because I don't want people worried about me. My coping mechanism is to always appear fine. That way, if I run into him, I'll seem unaffected. Even if that's complete bullshit, he'll never know either way. It's not like he'd care, anyway. As far as the world is concerned, I am doing fine.

Chapter 40

Lucas

We just completed the trade from New York to Chicago and I have movers scheduled for tomorrow. I'm set to report to my new team next week and Coach Tristan has already told me he's excited to get me on the ice. I'll probably skate the weekend after next. Christian flew to New York last week to complete paperwork so I wouldn't run into Samantha at their Chicago offices. She can't know what I'm doing. We've tried to keep it all quiet.

Later today, Fox Sporting's marketing team will release an announcement to the press acknowledging the trade. And that makes me nervous. Will she find out before I even have the chance to surprise her? I mentioned it to Coach Tristan when we met. I wanted to make my first appearance special. He seemed to support it, so hopefully, I can pull it all off. From his response, I suspect he's a closet romantic, even though I don't think he's married. Either way, I appreciate his willingness to help me.

Christian told me he and Monica have locked down Samantha's exposure to media. Shortly after I asked for Christian to work on the trade, he asked if he could tell Monica so she could run interference if necessary. I agreed that was probably smart, but told him he couldn't tell anyone else, not even his dad.

Christian also put me in contact with his real estate agent friend, who found me an amazing house in Burr Ridge, a suburb of Chicago. Christian toured it for me while I was on FaceTime, and it's perfect. It'll be more of a commute, but I want Samantha to understand I'm ready to settle down with her in Chicago. I want to support her fully as she continues being a badass for Fox Sporting. With her, I am all in. I only hope that she will be too.

It's been a month since I saw her in that hotel bar, and I know my behavior hurt her deeply. I'm embarrassed by my actions. In fact, if I'm completely honest, I'm dreading how she may respond to me. It wouldn't be surprising if she snubbed me. She deserved so much better than what I offered. I'm terrified it's really and truly over between us and that I'll never be able to convince her to give me another chance. I probably don't deserve one. But I have to have hope. From conversations with Christian, he tells me that Samantha seems to be doing better. Has she forgotten about me and moved on? Guess I'll find out soon. At least with me moving to Chicago, we will be in the same town.

I'm flying my mom into Chicago a day before my debut. She should be with me. I want to introduce the woman I've loved my whole life to the woman I am completely in love with and will love for the rest of my life. I told my mom about my plans and she has been a significant support, as always. In fact, everyone, from my mom to Jack, Miles, and Christian, has been supportive of what I've done and what's coming.

Jack and Miles admitted they were going to miss me, but they understand I need to do this. Plus, I made sure the house I bought was big enough for them to visit. Epic guys' weekends are in our future, for sure.

The day before my debut, I have early practice with the team, the closing on my house, and picking Mom up from the airport. She's never been to Chicago, and she's excited to do some exploring.

The moving company will arrive at the new house the next morning, and my mom is planning to be there to facilitate it all. I rented a hotel room for that night in case I win Samantha over at the rink. The Ritz Carlton has agreed to make some special accommodations for me. I know it's cliché, but I asked for them to scatter red rose petals on the floor and bed. They're also placing a chilled bottle of La Marca Prosecco and some strawberries in the room. When we check-in, a concierge will rush up to the room to run a hot bath.

Hopefully, Samantha will be with me, or check-in might be awkward.

I'm still finalizing the details of my debut at the rink, as it's my first official night as part of the Chicago Steel. Christian has confirmed that he and Monica will get Samantha to the game, but I'm not about to ask how.

I've asked Steel management to have the announcers play a specific skate-out song as they introduce me to the arena. I selected "Sugar" by Maroon 5. It's certainly not a traditional song intended to get the crowd pumped up, but it's an anthem to Samantha. I only hope she figures out it's for her. I've asked management for specific seats in the arena for Samantha, Christian, and Monica. My mom will also be near them, but she'd only briefly met Christian when he came to Canada.

There are a lot of moving parts to my plan, and I want it to be perfect. Just thinking about it all makes me incredibly edgy. I have never put myself out there like this and it's terrifying. All I want is for her to say yes and that she loves me, too. I guess I have to wait to see. Until then, I'm trying to keep it all together.

Chapter 41

Samantha

It has been an incredible week but also very draining. All I want to do is go home, take a bath, order takeout, and watch a movie on Netflix, but I've been informed that isn't going to happen. My brother asked me earlier in the week to go with him to the Chicago Steel game to check on a new guy he's trying to secure a representation deal with. I tried to convince him to take one of his various buddies, but that must not have worked because he stormed into my office about lunchtime and demanded that I attend. He was desperate and slightly crazed. He even called Monica and convinced her that a night out was just what I needed. When she called me after he stormed back out of my office, she informed me that Christian invited her too. I'm feeling completely bullied into attending this hockey game, but I can't say no to them. He better at least feed me.

The things I do for him. Ugh! Brothers are so annoying.

Honestly, attending the game is the last thing I want to do. It's hockey, after all, and all that reminds me of is Lucas, and he's not something I need to be thinking about. Even though I've tried, I can't seem to push him from my head or heart. He moved in and refuses to leave. It's maddening, really. It's tough to rebuild yourself when you're being held captive by something you can't control.

Of course, I didn't share with Christian the real reason I didn't want to go. I just told him I don't have the energy for it after the crazy week I've had. He promised to buy me a mocha with extra shots at the arena before vacating my office.

Hours later, before he's set to return, I look down at my wardrobe and let out a breath. At least I'm wearing something cute and semi-comfortable. This morning I chose my favorite pants that make my ass look stellar, a benefit to all the yoga I have been doing to take care of myself. In addition, I have on my Kristin Cavallari Leopard Copertina heels because I was feeling sassy. One last check in the mirror in my en suite bathroom and I'm ready to go. I hadn't needed much, just a slight touch-up on my makeup and hair. *Not like I'm trying to impress anyone.*

At five o'clock on the dot, Christian stops by my office with Monica in tow. *They look chummy.* I'm thankful my best friend will be with me, so this night won't be completely ruined. We all ride to the arena together. Christian promises us dinner during intermission. On the menu: the dangerous Giffords' sliders. Fist pump! Looks like I'm winning tonight. I guess this isn't so bad after all.

After we arrive at the arena, Christian begins acting strange. Looking around, I notice that the teams have just started warming up. Christian drags us over to a section of seats next to where the players come out. His focus shifts rapidly. I look over to Monica to see if she notices his atypical behavior, and she seems unaffected. Maybe I'm just being sensitive?

The players on the ice do their pregame warm-ups. While standing there not paying attention to the ice, I launch into a conversation with Monica.

At one point, I notice Christian leave and walk up to the railing that blocks the fans from the players. He looks to be talking to someone, but I can't see who. I shrug my shoulders. It's probably the player he's trying to sign. Whatever. I turn back to Monica, feeling slightly impatient. All I'm thinking is *let's get on with this game so I can go home and take a relaxing bath.*

Time passes quickly, and before too long, Christian rejoins us and lowers himself into his aisle seat. I can't help but notice his incessantly bouncing leg. Why is he nervous? It's weird. Never in my life have I ever seen Christian get nervous. But that's what's happening, right? I wonder what it's about, but when I turn to ask, Maroon 5's song "Sugar" starts playing and instantly

I'm confused. This isn't typical hype-up-the-crowd music. Why would they be playing this song? Then I catch the announcer speaking over it, introducing a new player to the line-up. Hearing him say, Lucas Bouchard, I wonder if I'm imagining things.

Out of the corner of my eye, I focus on the last name on the jersey of the player who has removed his helmet and is waving to the crowd. The crowd is giving him a standing ovation. It's Lucas. *My Lucas.* He's here. And it appears he's now playing for the Chicago Steel. After rubbing my eyes, I look harder at the player. Are my eyes playing tricks on me? Maybe I've made a mistake. But when his eyes connect with mine, he gives me a wink and I know I haven't. How is this happening? Then the announcer speaks again.

"Chicago Steel fans... Tonight is a special night. We have signed a new player to our roster, and he's quite a legend. He hails from Canada originally and then played for the New York Chargers since he was drafted by them seven years ago. Tonight, it thrills us to welcome him to the Steel family. Let's give a warm Steel welcome to Lucas Bouchard."

When I hear his name again, my stomach drops. It's confirmation I'm not imagining things. I guess knowing that is a relief. But why is he here? In my city? And did he really wink at me? Did he know it was me?

I watch as Lucas does several laps around the ice, waving to the cheering fans. Wait! My brain struggles to grasp what is happening. Lucas is actually here.

Why didn't Christian tell me? Did he know? He had to know. He's Lucas's agent. Monica and Christian sit silently next to me, monitoring my reaction. They knew about this. Their faces confirm it.

Suddenly, I realize I can't be here, and as I go to stand up to leave, Lucas notices me. I turn toward the stairs, looking to make a swift escape, but I'm stopped by him calling my name. "Samantha." His deep, rich, sexy voice makes my knees go weak and my heart skips a beat. I slowly turn back toward him and notice not only has he left the ice, but he's standing by the railing across from our seats. He's almost close enough to touch, and he's saying my name. He's also holding a dozen red roses, and my heart stutters. Then soars. *Is this really happening?*

"Samantha," he says again, and I realize he's waiting for my reply. I look around and realize that he's not the only one. The whole arena is focused on us, and I'm front and center on the Jumbotron. I bite my lip nervously as I step toward him. I'm not sure what's happening or what to say.

"Hi," he tries again, with a hopeful but hesitant smile plastered across his handsome face. He's nervous. I can tell by the shake of his hand holding the beautiful roses, which he's extending to me.

"Hi, Lucas. What are you doing here?" I ask, trying to sound neutral. I move closer but am weary of being too close.

Knowing he's short on time, he launches into a

speech he's prepared. "Samantha, I know our primary problem was the distance between us, but now that's no longer an issue. I asked to be traded to the Chicago Steel so I could be with you. If you'll have me." His words come straight from the heart. I move over to the bars, take the roses, and tenderly kiss him. He takes his gloved hand and puts it behind my head, pulling me closer, deeper, and the arena explodes with cheers, catcalls, whistles, and clapping. I laugh against his lips and pull back. He nips my bottom lip and says, "Babe, I have to go play a hockey game now. Can we talk after? The roses have a letter in them. I hope it will explain what I've been going through the past few weeks without you."

I give him another chaste kiss and agree to meet him in the players' tunnel after the game. He backs away, winks again, and goes into the locker room to join his new team for their pre-game talk.

He traded teams and moved just to be with me. *Swoon.* The Jumbotron makes me the focus of the entire arena. Giggling nervously, I wave. Moving back to my seat, I sit at the end, seeing that Christian has moved to sit next to Monica. My heart flutters. *Those two.* When will they ever figure it out?

The game flies by, and since it's a new team for Lucas, it's obvious his line hasn't developed their chemistry yet. The score at the start of the third period is still 0-0. Thankfully, another Steel line is successful and they score, winning the game 1-0. During the first period, I read the letter Lucas gave me with the roses and it was so full of honesty and love.

Samantha-These past few weeks without you have been my worst ever. At first, when you broke up with me, I was angry with you. My behavior at the hotel bar was to hurt you as much as you hurt me. Childish, I know. But I needed to know that you were hurting, too. I realized early on that I wanted more with you, but I couldn't figure out how to make that work or even how to tell you. When I finally realized I wanted you in my life more than casually, you ended things between us. You said you couldn't do casual, and I was too scared to believe that what we already had was true. Over the years, I heard all these awful stories and forgot to consider us and how we were together.

Since we've been apart, I've asked myself so many questions, and the only things that remained constant was that I wanted to play hockey and figure out where things could go with us. My boys, Jack and Miles, told me that in order to show you how serious I was, I needed a grand gesture. So, my transfer, my move, is for you. I want to be with you. I want to see what happens between us. I've missed you so much. Your smile, laugh, quick wit, sexy body, determination, and fight. All of it makes me want to get to know you better. I'm falling for you and I only hope you feel the same way. If you do, please meet me after the game in the players' tunnel so we can talk and see where things stand.

~Lucas

He's poured his heart out to me, and I realize we both struggled so much separately. I figured when I'd ended things between us, it would be better than prolonging the inevitable. However, I've learned that being away from him is so much worse than the possibility of us failing. I hadn't realized how much I already felt for him until it was too late. It's reassuring to hear he's feeling similarly. His whole gesture is beyond romantic and has blown me away. I will definitely be in that tunnel tonight to see what's next for us.

Chapter 42

Lucas

I'm trying my best to stay focused on the game, but I'm desperate for it to be over. The periods are dragging on. I badly need to see Samantha in that tunnel. Then I'll know for sure everything will be okay. I know we can work this out. Even though it's new, we clicked in a way I never have with anyone else, and I would be an imbecile not to fight for it. People say finding your soulmate only happens once. So, I'm jumping at it.

When the time on the clock finally runs out, I have to remind myself to shake hands with the other team before leaving the ice. All the while, I have my eyes glued to the stands. I notice Samantha, Christian, and Monica waiting near the bleachers for me.

Finally, I step off the ice and my gaze lands upon the most breathtaking woman I've ever seen. I suck in a breath and take a moment to appreciate her. She smiles at me, and I feel a sense of calm wash over me. It's confirmation I've made the right decision to pursue her. A giant smile stretches across my face and I'm sure I look absolutely ridiculous, but I don't care. This is the happiest I've ever been. I step out of line and toward them. Our eyes lock and everything else disappears.

"Hi, babe," I croon at her.

"Hey," she responds, with a flirty tone that I love. My heart gallops in my chest. Instantly, I feel antsy. I want to get to the locker room so I can shower, change, and get back to her immediately. I need to have my hands on her. It's been too long, and being this close is torture. My hands itch in my gloves, but there's no way I'm not showering before I pull her into my arms again.

"Meet me in the tunnel in fifteen?" I ask.

She nods and looks over to her brother, who's standing close to a petite blond who looks a little like Blake Lively. He gives her a nod.

"I'll show you how to get there and then I'll take Monica home," Christian informs her. Monica beams next to him. So, this is Monica? I notice she has stars in her eyes. Samantha was spot on when she said they were perfect together. Maybe now that I'm in Chicago, I can help Christian figure that out. Samantha leans over the bars and pulls me closer before she places a tender kiss on my lips. I have never been so grateful that I don't wear a full-face mask because I can taste her sweet lips. And it's amazing. Like coming home. It's heaven on earth and something I want to savor for the rest of my life.

"You're stinky," she mumbles across my lips, causing me to laugh.

"I am, but I'll go clean up," I say cheerily before I give her another quick kiss. I turn to the locker room, but in my peripheral vision, I see my mom move toward Samantha to introduce herself.

Yesterday, she caught up with Christian, and I'm good with him facilitating the introduction of the two most important women in my life. I'm confident they will get along well. Actually, if I'm completely honest, they will probably get along so well they'll actually team up on me if I get out of line. As I move down the hallway, I laugh to myself about the likelihood of that.

Coach Tristan gives us his commentary on the game as I'm stripping off my gear. I know I played decently in my first game for Chicago. My line and I will need to spend some extra time working on drills and developing chemistry so we can anticipate each other. Walking onto a new team is never easy and requires work. I'm sure it'll be tough, but I'll make the best of it. The guys on my line—Mika, Rocco, and Ace—seem decent so far, and I look forward to getting to know them better in the coming weeks and months.

Right now, however, my girl is waiting for me. Stepping into the shower after Coach's talk is revitalizing. After all, I've endured in the last few days and weeks, it feels like I have shaken off fifty pounds of worry and stress. Finally, I can move forward in my life. I'm free and hopeful about the future.

Before I leave the locker room, I dress in my suit. There, standing in the hallway, is my mom with a giant smile plastered across her face. She's deep in a conversation with Christian, Monica, and Samantha. I'm quiet as I take my time crossing over to them, watching the interactions between them. They all look comfortable.

Suddenly, I hear the best noise I've ever heard. It's melodious and cheerful. Samantha's laughter fills the space and my knees go weak. I walk up behind her and place a chaste kiss on her neck, right below her ear. She sighs and melts into me. This was something I missed. *Her*. I nuzzle my nose into her neck, taking in her soft skin and mouth-watering scent. I place my hands on her hips, pulling her closer. In seconds, I am lost in her, forgetting everyone and everything entirely. Christian clears his throat. I open my eyes and focus on him. I groan my annoyance at being interrupted. Samantha giggles. Christian rolls his eyes. Monica and my mom both sigh. And I know it. I've got it bad. All I can do is smile and shrug. I'm okay with everyone knowing I am completely gone for Samantha. She is my everything.

"Lucas, I introduced your mom and Samantha. I hope that's okay." Christian smirks while telling me. I look between my mom and Samantha and am grateful to see they're both smiling widely. Relief washes over me and edges out some of the anxiety I've had the past few days.

"Thanks, man. I appreciate it." I look over to Monica, whom I've never officially met, and extend my hand to her. "I'm Lucas. You must be Monica. I've heard a lot about you from both Samantha and Christian. It's great to finally meet you." I can't miss the shocked look on her face when I disclose that Christian talks about her, too. Her cheeks go rosy, like she's embarrassed. She shakes my hand, but before she speaks, she narrows her eyes and, in a warning tone, says, "I've heard a lot about you, too."

I nod and answer, "Understood."

She smiles happily, and I'm positive I've just survived my first threat from my love's bestie. I bet she can be scary if she wants to be. She doesn't have me fooled, even if she's a kindergarten teacher. I heard she was raised on a farm. I bet she can throw down if she has to.

Christian also senses Monica's warning and pulls her into his side before he tells everyone, "I'm about to head out. Monica, I'm giving you a ride home, right? Mom Bouchard, can I get you anywhere?" He knows about the hotel suite, which was awkward as fuck to tell him about. But he's trying to give us some space and time, and I appreciate it. My mom understands too and takes Christian up on his offer of a ride. After a quick hug from Mom, a handshake from Christian, and a goodbye wave to Monica, they leave Samantha and me in the hallway, alone.

Without hesitation, I spin Samantha around and gather her in my arms. I hug her tightly, never wanting to let her go. I feel complete for the first time in months. With her in my arms, I finally feel peace. Our cocoon of bliss is interrupted when I hear people heading down the hallway toward us. I kiss her forehead and ask, "Do you have any other plans tonight, or can I take you somewhere?"

She nods, and I can't help myself when I pull her in close for another kiss. Sparks fly around us and the insane attraction and chemistry we've always had comes rushing back. Even though it's tough, I pull myself back before I take things too far. I know we should have a conversation before anything too physical happens between us.

I realize that my plan of taking her to the hotel suite is a risk, but I want to have a conversation in private while pampering her. Once we talk, if things progress and move to more, we can stay there together. But if she wants to go home, I'll take her. Although I want her completely, I'm not forcing her into anything. I truly respect her and I trust she'll tell me what she thinks and wants. I completely understand that the past few weeks have possibly changed her opinion of me and she may need more time and answers to figure out what she feels.

Samantha takes our hands and intertwines our fingers. In a husky voice, she asks, "Where do you want to go?"

I look deep into her eyes, wanting her to hear exactly what I say next. "Full confession. I rented a suite at the Ritz Carlton and I may have asked them to add some special romantic touches, but it has a living room where we can talk. I have no expectations for tonight, but I wanted you to know how I feel." My confession is full of my nerves and hope.

She squeezes my hand and gives me a smile that lights up my entire body. "Let's go, Lucas."

I take a moment to see if I detect any hesitation in her response, and I see none. My body rejoices as I playfully tug her down the now abandoned hallway and head out into the players' parking lot. My Audi shipped with my household belongings and I got it this morning. I drive us over to the Ritz and leave the keys with the valet.

We walk hand in hand to the front desk, and my heart pounds in my chest. I feel like I'm on the precipice of something life-changing. I'm sweating and my stomach churns. When I check in, Samantha doesn't seem to notice as the desk clerk radios to someone on his staff, asking them to prepare our suite. I know what that means, but Samantha is none the wiser. When she walks into our room, I can't wait to see her reaction.

Samantha is instantly drawn to the windows and

the stunning view of the Chicago Skyline when we enter the suite. "It's amazing," she gushes.

Coming up behind her, I kiss the side of her head, whispering against her ear, "You are too." When she turns to me, I catch her against my chest. Having her this close is a dream come true. One I wasn't sure would ever be possible again. Thanking my lucky stars, I reach for her hand and cradle it in mine. "Want to see the rest of the suite?" She nods and I pull her away from the view.

We enter the bedroom and I see dark-red rose petals sprinkled over the king-sized bed. "Oh, Lucas," Samantha squeaks out beside me. My heart picks up the pace, as I know the next surprise is the biggest and kind of presumptuous. My gaze shifts to the partially opened door of the bathroom. Her eyes follow mine and I nudge her gently in that direction. Stepping forward, she walks through the door. "Is this for me?" Inside the large space is a massive soaker tub. If my planning worked out, they filled it with bubbles and rose petals. The faint scent of lavender tickles my nose. Samantha's beautiful brown eyes widen as if she's surprised by it all. Tracing her fingers along the edge of the tub, she catches a bubble and sighs.

"Babe, I thought we could talk while you take a bath."

"Really? That sounds amazing." Her excitement is palpable, and I give myself a mental fist bump.

"I'll just step out and let you get in. When you're

covered up, let me know, and I'll come back and sit by the side of the tub while you relax. Would that be, okay?"

Samantha nods. "You can stay the entire time. You've seen me naked before, and after we talk, I hope you'll still want to."

Chapter 43

Lucas

Did she really just invite me to stay? *Holy shit, I haven't lost her.* After she floors me with her sexy invitation, she walks over to me, pushes up on her toes, and kisses me tenderly.

Instead of reacting like a caveman and dragging her out to the bed, I lift my fingers and slowly unbutton her shirt. Before I know it, she's standing before me in a dusty-pink silk and lace bra. Her nipples strain against the fabric, as if they're reaching for me, and I lick my lips. Her creamy, soft skin calls to me, begging to be touched. My fingers twitch, desperately wanting to do so, but I'm nervous. Does she want this too?

Not wanting to lose another moment, I trace my hand up her arm, across her collarbone, and up her slender neck. Once I reach her hairline, I curl my hand around her head, pulling her mouth to mine. And I kiss her with more passion than ever before. She melts into me, and our tongues swirl and twist around each other. She bites my tongue, and I'm both slightly startled and intrigued. Never did I imagine that she'd like a firmer touch, but I'm here for it. I growl my response and she answers with a throaty moan. Every time I'm with her, I feel like I'm unveiling a new treasure, opening her up, revealing a new side of her she's kept locked away until now. Like she's saved it only for me. I revel in that thought. It turns me on even more. What we are experiencing here together is something only for me. It's a gift she's giving me and I can't help but feel rather possessive about it, and her. She's mine, now and forever.

While still holding her head in my hand, I tighten my grip a bit, restraining her a little more, and she sucks in a tight breath. Her eyes roll back into her head and I feel her heart rate climb. She seems to be even more excited. Taking my free hand, I run it down to her waist and to the top of her sexy as fuck black pants. I don't know shit about fashion, but I love these pants because they are positively sinful. She needs them in every color. They highlight her firm, squeezable ass. They're also short, showcasing her seductive ankles.

Her entire outfit, while semi casual, screams temptress. I'm already fantasizing about how I can get her in nothing but those magnificently dirty leopard heels. I trace the lines of her pants. When I reach the hook at her waist, I slip my fingers behind it, causing a mind-blowing reaction. She simultaneously sucks in a deep breath and shivers. It's extremely hot to have her so incredibly responsive to me. I tug at the hook, lean into her, and bite her plump, pink lower lip. The gasp deep in her throat sets my blood on fire. I want her so badly.

After I unhook her pants, I slide down the zipper, revealing matching panties. Releasing my hold of the pants, they fall to her ankles. I step back and take her in. She is radiant, and I am completely in awe of her. She is beyond beautiful.

Releasing her head from my grip, she whines momentarily. Then she sees me lower to my haunches. I place a kiss at her panty line, right below where a tiny bow sits. Samantha sighs. I chance a look up, and the lust swirling in her eyes makes me feel like I'm ten feet tall. She raises her hand and runs it through my hair. With Samantha, I crave intimacy. The way she looks at me, the way she makes me feel. I'm hers and hers alone. Looking back at her center, I remind myself to take my time. This isn't a quick hookup. It's something more. Not the time for fast and dirty. Next time, maybe?

I meant for tonight to be an apology, and I need to do that before anything else. Placing her hands on my shoulders, I carefully remove her pants and heels. Once she's standing in front of me in nothing but her matching lingerie, I take her left hand and kiss her ring finger. I don't know if she understands my subtle suggestion, but after tonight, I plan to make her mine forever. Right now, though, I'm not ready to tell her. I don't want to scare her. Knowing I need to be a gentleman, no matter what, is what that kiss is about. It's a promise to her. Standing back up in front of her, I lock my eyes with hers. She looks confused, possibly hurt. Taking her hands in mine, I tell her, "Babe, I want you so badly, but I think we need to clear the air first. Once we've talked, we can do whatever you want. From this point on, you call all the shots. The power is yours. I only ask that you listen to what I have to say and that you tell me what you're feeling."

Samantha nods and then asks in a quiet tone, "Can I still take a bath? It'd be a mistake to let this go to waste." She smiles, and I can't help but fall deeper.

I totally agree, but having her naked and wet in front of me is going to make it incredibly difficult for me to concentrate. But for her, I'll manage. Dipping my hand in the bath to make sure it's still hot, I look at her and ask, "Do you need me to step out so you can get in?" Again, I'm trying to be a gentleman, but I'm hoping she'll say no.

Samantha looks at me and lets out a laugh. "I'm practically naked now, and you've seen me before. You can totally stay if you promise not to mount me." She laughs again, making me smirk. If only she knew the things going through my head. The things I can't wait to do with her, to her. My list is growing increasingly long, kind of like something beneath my pants.

I hold up my hands in defense, smile, and mutter, "I'll try my best."

Chapter 44

Samantha

Removing my panties and bra before stepping into the bath feels like I'm shedding the last wall of protection. It's both exhilarating and frightening. As I lower myself into the hot water, letting the bubbles, petals, and oils cover me, I feel my trepidation wane. In just moments, my racing heart and mind have calmed dramatically.

When I turn to Lucas, letting him know I'm ready for our conversation, his smile melts me. He loosens his tie, removes it, and unbuttons the first two buttons of his dress shirt. Rolling up the sleeves, he reveals his muscled forearms. *Holy hell, those are incredible.* Then he grabs another towel from the rack and sets it on the tiled floor like a pillow before he lowers himself. Once he's settled, he reaches over to grab my hand, which is resting on the edge of the tub. He tenderly caresses it. His touch comforts and excites me. I lean back farther into the hot water and rest my head against the edge of the tub. Closing my eyes, I feel all the tension of the past few weeks melt away. The light scent of lavender wafting in the air helps to calm and relax both my mind and body. For the first time in weeks, I am at peace.

"Lucas, this is heavenly. Thank you," I whisper, with my eyes still closed. It's quiet as I wait for him to start the conversation. I hear him let out a deep breath before his deep, deliciously sexy voice permeates the air.

"Babe, like I said in my letter, being without you was unbearable. I realized after I got over the initial sting of the breakup that you were what I wanted. Unfortunately, shortly after that, I understood that the reasons you'd given me for splitting up still applied and didn't change our situation. And I became heartbroken for a completely different reason. Anger didn't motivate it anymore. My hopelessness did. I knew if I didn't get you back, I wouldn't ever find anyone else who compared." He squeezes my hand again, making my heart gallop in my chest.

"I know I was extremely childish when I saw you in the bar. I was angry and wanted to hurt you. Although, when I saw what my behavior was doing to you, it didn't make me feel better. Only worse. Regrettably, my ego and some liquid encouragement kept me from righting it. I should have walked away from that woman at the bar and apologized to you for being a dick. But that didn't happen. Days later, when I hashed through it all with my mom, I finally realized I'd been trying to make you jealous. Except doing that just made things worse, didn't it?"

As I listen with my eyes still closed, I feel tears fall down my cheeks. Then I feel Lucas's fingertips trying to wipe them away. Opening my eyes, I look up at him, and my heart aches. His eyes are filled with tears, too. But they're also filled with remorse and regret. I lean forward and tug his face to mine and kiss him. Tasting the tears from our lips, I offer forgiveness and love to his kiss, which feels tender but needy. He cradles my head, stroking his fingertips across my jaw. His light touches speak volumes about how much he cares for me.

Suddenly, I need to tell him exactly how I feel. I pull out of the kiss and place my forehead to his. Once I catch my breath, I share my heart. "Lucas, I need to confess a few things to you before we go any further. Yes, I was jealous, hurt, and angry with your behavior in that bar, but those feelings made me realize something. If I wasn't willing to be with you, then I had no say as to what you did. I had no right to be jealous at all. I had told you we weren't together, so it shouldn't have mattered what you did or who you did it with. But it did. To me, it felt like I was being betrayed, and that hurt so much worse than our parting. I was angry too, but not just at you. I was so much angrier with myself for ending things." I breathe out a shaky breath before I continue my confession.

"When I look back at it all now, I know my choices and reactions were because I was scared. You, Lucas, scare the shit out of me. I have never felt with anyone the way I feel with you. I have never allowed myself to want something extraordinary when something practical existed. Before now, I've never wanted something more than what was expected of me." Squeezing his hand back, I know the scariest part of my confession is next.

"Because of you, I allowed myself to dream, to imagine a future that not only excited me but made me want. It wasn't one that just checked the standard boxes. With you, the thing that scared me the most was that I could finally be me. I was unashamedly me and you seemed to still care about me. Because of our arrangement, when I fell for you, I thought I was more invested than you were. I felt I needed to protect myself from what I was sure would be tragic for me later on."

Instead of saying anything, he stands up. A wave of panic washes over me. *I've said too much.* My heart pounds nervously in my chest. I quickly glance around the bathroom, looking for a robe or something I can toss on in a hurry when I scramble out of this tub to escape. Why did I say all that? He didn't want to hear my confession, and when he did, it all became too real and now he wants out.

Just as I'm about to get out of the water, I notice he is stripping out of his clothes. I watch as item after item drops to the tiled floor. Before I know it, his perfectly muscled body, with all its heavenly dips and peaks, is on full display, and I'm gawking. I force my mouth shut but run my eyes up his body, appreciating it all. When my eyes finally reach his, I know they are filled with desire. I lick my lips and watch his eyes widen in surprise.

He breaks the silence and sexual tension drifting between us by dropping his voice and asking, "Can I join you? I need to be closer to you."

I can't answer with words. My mind has turned to mush, so I just nod. I scoot forward and he climbs into the tub behind me, pulling me into his well-defined chest. I can't help the giggle that falls from my lips. He laughs, which only ramps up my heart, mind, and lust for him. He places gentle kisses on my right shoulder, up my neck, and under my ear, before he whispers, "I have a confession to make. I have completely fallen for you. I love you, Samantha Fox." His words make my heart soar and I feel like the luckiest woman ever. In an instant, my worries are eviscerated, and I want to confess that I feel the same.

I turn my head sideways and look into his dreamy eyes that have never seemed so clear. Words rushing through my mind tumble from my lips. "I love you too, Lucas. I think I fell during our first conversation at your signing, and despite the road this relationship has taken, I can't seem to do anything but fall harder for you." He smiles, tugs my chin toward him, dips his head, and seals our confessions with a kiss. We fill the kiss with force and passion. I reach up and wrap my hand around his neck, pulling him even closer.

Soon, his hands are on my hips and he's turning me around. His quick movement of my completely relaxed body breaks our kiss, and before I can blink, he has me straddling him. The water in the tub, which has gotten colder, sloshes around us like an ocean during a devastating storm. I know we're making a mess, but who cares? My legs tuck neatly around his waist and I can't help but enjoy the feel of his very hard erection settled between us. I grind against it and my clit screams in ecstasy. He lowers his head and takes one of my nipples in his mouth. He sucks, swirls, and bites me into submission. On the other breast, he uses his fingers to twist, tug, and pinch my nipple.

Even though we've only been intimate a handful of times, it's always explosive between us. When he takes his other hand and slides it over my clit, my body trembles. He makes circular motions, pushing my building orgasm over the cliff. I feel my legs quiver and I tip my head back, close my eyes, and fully embrace the combustion encompassing my entire body. "Lucas!" I scream out his name and grind even harder into him. He growls around my well-used nipple.

When I finally come down from the high, I lower my head. Opening my eyes, I look at this insanely gorgeous man in front of me, feeling thankful for where we are. When our eyes connect, he drops my nipple, and it continues to throb in amazing ways. I can still feel my clit trembling from the quake that just rocketed through it.

"Watching you just now was mind-blowing. You weren't just beautiful and sexy, you were magical." Lucas kisses me, and I have never felt like this in my life. Not only do I feel beautiful, I feel sexy and craved by the man I am completely in love with.

"I need you inside of me right now," I tell him.

Chapter 45

Lucas

Watching Samantha orgasm is so far beyond thrilling; it's spectacular. It's almost like experiencing a miracle. It is truly a gift. And one that I'm grateful for. I wasn't sure I'd ever bear witness to it again. Samantha is more beautiful and sexier than she's ever been. She is ethereal. Watching her is like getting a taste of heaven. As if it couldn't get any better, she tells me she needs me now. Even though I haven't explored her body fully, I know I won't deny her.

After all, being inside her is one of my favorite things. I've only had her a handful of times, but I'm already an addict. Being with her is so much more than sex. It's also about connection, vulnerability, and love. I am the luckiest man alive. She wants me. All of me.

I lick my lips in anticipation and look outside the tub, trying to find my pants and a condom. She's still grinding herself against me and it's making it difficult to hold focus as my eyes run over the bathroom, desperate for a condom. Finally locating my pants, I slide my hand out of the tub and grab them. Samantha stops me, placing her petite hand over mine, and says something that stops me in my tracks.

"Lucas, we don't need a condom. Since we were last together, I haven't been with anyone else. I'm clean and on birth control." I look into her eyes and see they're swirling with unspoken emotions.

"Me too. Are you sure?" I ask, hearing the rasp in my voice.

A shiver runs across her body and she smiles. "I'm beyond sure." Her words stun me and reaffirm her feelings for me.

This is a dream come true. If everything works out the way I hope, Samantha will be the last woman I kiss, make love to, and love. I want everything with her. I want to be her husband, partner, and the father of her children. Flashes of her round with my child bring a lightness to my chest and a smile to my face. I know I shouldn't get too far ahead, but for me, she's it.

Instead of getting lost in the daydream, I embrace the now and lift her up so she can line us up before she slides down my unbearably hard shaft. When she bottoms out, I hold her steady, relishing the feeling of completeness. Our eyes meet and I know we feel the same.

"I love you," I tell her, and she smiles before she

kisses me again, stealing my breath. She is stunning and all mine. Samantha moves her hips and my hands drop to them, stabilizing her. Every time she lifts, it feels just like the anticipation of a roller coaster climbing. When she nears the tip of me, the pending thrill and rush of her coming back down electrifies my body. When she crashes down, a heady explosion of lust rips through me. Nothing else matters at this moment except the joining of our bodies. I am lost completely in this goddess before me and the ride we're on.

Chapter 46

Samantha

Desperation claws through me as I ride Lucas. I feel wild and out of control as I chase the divine pleasure building within me. My orgasm starts and he must feel it because he tightens his hand on my hip, digging into my skin and pulling me into him harder. He also moves from stroking my breast to draw figure eights on my clit.

In moments, the most intense orgasm tears through my body. I ride it out, moving up and down him faster, becoming almost spastic. My body doesn't feel like I'm in control of it anymore. Lucas pinches my clit, setting off another mini orgasm, and my inner muscles grip him tightly. That pushes him over the edge. He pumps ferociously inside me. "Samantha. Babe." He groans loudly and then releases a deep grunt. I feel him swell within me and then a forceful pressure releases—the spray of his cum. I did that to him. Knowing that makes me feel powerful.

Collapsing against his chest, I'm completely exhausted. He wraps his arms tightly around me, and I experience a rush of emotions. I feel so many things: safe, loved, satisfied, and complete. His heart is pounding in his chest and it matches the crazy beat of my own. Scents of lavender, sweat, and sex swirl in the air, and it's intoxicating. We sit there, allowing our bodies to regulate, our breathing to slow, and our hearts to settle. Then Lucas kisses my forehead with tenderness. "Babe, the water has gotten cold. Why don't we dry off?"

I push myself off his chest and look him in the eyes. He looks happy, which makes me smile. Lifting my hips, he slides out of me, breaking our connection. Trying to make my satiated body move proves to be a challenge, and I fumble, trying to get my legs and arms to work accordingly. I can't do anything but laugh, so that's what I do. "My body doesn't want to cooperate," I say with a giggle. He laughs and lifts his hands to my hips to help me stabilize. I grab the side of the tub with both hands and carefully crawl out. I'm careful with my footing because my legs feel like Jell-O and I'm not confident my knees or ankles will work. Plus, the floor is slippery from the water splashing out.

Once I'm out, I grab a towel and begin drying off while Lucas exits the tub easily. How does that happen? I feel like I've channeled Gumby, and he seems to be no worse for the wear. I snag another towel and hand it to him, all while muttering to myself "showoff." He wraps the towel around his waist, tucking it right at his treasure trail. I'm mesmerized by his moves, and I can't help but watch and fantasize about what he's just covered up. My eyes won't release him, and I lick my lips. I want him again.

My attention doesn't go unnoticed, and his body responds. My eyes widen as the towel tents. He just laughs. I break my focus from the thunder down under —wait, he isn't Australian—and look up into his eyes. They dance in delight. My cheeks get hot, embarrassed that he's caught me. His response and my reaction to him do not embarrass him at all. Nope. He just stands there confidently, knowing his body is incredible. Smiling widely, as if he can read the dirty thoughts floating in my mind, I bite my lip and his smile melts away. Instantly, he looks serious.

"What?" I ask apprehensively, not sure why his demeanor changed so rapidly. My stomach flutters with nerves. He stalks toward me, never losing eye contact. The temperature of the room seems to drop rapidly and I feel goose bumps crawl all over my body. When he reaches me, he lifts my chin up, strokes my bottom lip with his thumb, pulling it from my teeth, and releases a low growl from his throat. Damn, could he be any sexier?

Chapter 47

Lucas

This woman is going to kill me. I'm still young enough that I don't need too much recovery time after I come, but my uncontrolled response to Samantha is new for me. We literally just got out of the tub and, as I watch her watch me, I'm already responding again. She hungrily watches as I wrap my towel, securing it low on my waist. Her stare appears focused, and it makes my blood boil. My dick knows he's the object of her fixed stare and makes himself known. She reacts to it immediately. Seeing her cheeks redden feels like scoring a breakaway on the ice. It's both electrifying and demanding. It's the best high and makes me greedy for her and her attention.

On the ice, when I have this feeling, it's a goal I'm after. But here and now, it's her. My focus is solely on her, and I'm confident nothing could break it. I walk over to her, lift her chin up toward me, and stroke her bottom lip with my thumb. She releases the hold she has on it, and I recognize the hunger that flashes in her eyes. It's enrapturing. I hear myself growl and I feel my heart thud hard in my chest. My dick grows harder and heavier. I pull her flush against me and I know she feels how aroused I am. I walk her backward from the bathroom to the king-sized bed.

When we reach it, she scoots back onto it. I settle between her legs and push her towel open, exposing all her nakedness to me, then I revel in her beauty. Her skin is soft and dewy. I stroke my hands up and down her thighs as I stare into her eyes. Her hands trace the tuck of my towel. Before she can release it, I stop her and instead lower myself to my knees, making me perfectly lined up to love her center. I lick my lips, anticipating her taste.

Our first time, I had a brief taste, but it wasn't enough. I haven't gone down on many women, because I've never wanted to. But Samantha, I crave. Tugging her to the end of the bed, I tuck her knees over my shoulders, kissing each thigh. She lets out a breath and then a moan, and it amps me up. I slowly lick up toward her clit a few times and her hips thrust into the air. She wriggles when I suck her nub into my mouth. I steady her hips with my hands and give her clit a nibble. She thrusts her hands down into my hair and tugs. I repeat the process, and she runs her fingers through my hair, sending shivers down my spine.

When I move from sucking to nibbling, she

tightens her grasp, letting me know she likes what I'm doing. I slide two fingers into her and begin moving them in and out slowly. When they become soaked in her juices, I curve them toward me, rubbing against her G-spot. "Ahh." A loud moan falls from Samantha's mouth, followed by her begging. "Yes! Lucas, more of that."

I respond without words, doing exactly as she asks. Giving her pleasure is mind-blowing. I never imagined it could be like this. I increase the speed of my fingers, increase the suction on her clit, and reach up with my other hand to pluck at a nipple. Isn't there a saying about good things coming in threes? Well, it's true!

An orgasm overtakes Samantha's body, and it's breathtaking. Before she comes down from it, I stand up and thrust into her. When I pull her tight to me, I feel the rapid pulse of her clit against me. I pound into her, chasing the high I know will come quickly. I was fighting my impending orgasm the entire time I was eating her out.

The pressure building up within me is indescribable. My balls tighten, and I know I only have moments left. Quickly, I reach one hand to her clit to stroke it, then lower my lips to a breast. I've discovered that Samantha likes a little pain with her pleasure, and I am more than happy to oblige. As I thrust into her, I bite her nipple and pinch her clit. Moments later, she's meeting me thrust for thrust. She's got both hands on my ass, pulling me tighter to her. She trembles around me and I let myself go. I come with such force it rips my breath from me. After I come, I continue to thrust my hips because she is still grinding against me. I can't help but think she's chasing another orgasm. I stopped sucking her breast and rubbing her clit when my orgasm hit, so I start both up again, hoping that will push her over the edge once more. Her hips roll, crushing my fingers and her clit to me. She's creating more friction. I look up and see her eyes are closed tight and she looks to be holding her breath. I continue to pinch her clit and bite her nipple, and again she reacts, exploding around me. "Lucas!" Her throaty scream of my name makes me smile against her nipple. Softly, I suckle until I feel her body stop quaking.

I pull out of her and step into the bathroom to clean up. Returning with a warm cloth to clean her, she sighs and whispers, "Thank you." Her eyes remain partially closed the entire time and her breathing has slowed. I toss the washcloth back into the bathroom and crawl into the bed, bringing her with me. I tuck her into my side and stroke down her side as I watch her drift off to sleep. Hoping she's still awake enough to hear me, I whisper, "Babe, thank you for giving me another chance. I love you." The excitement I feel thinking about building our life together is indescribable. I kiss the side of her head and she makes the most adorable noise, a soft contented hum. And I'm gone.

Epilogue

Samantha

The morning after our reunion, waking up in each other's arms, was magical. The intimacy of having breakfast in bed, getting ready for our day together, it all made me wish for those small beautiful moments together, every day. During breakfast, we talked about what happened between us, our feelings, and what we were hoping for in our future. Thankfully, we were on the same page. Just like our first conversation at his signing, we easily slid back into fun, flirty, and familiar dialogue.

That afternoon, after we checked out, Lucas took me over to his house to show me what he'd purchased. The house he'd chosen was incredible, and I loved it. I moved in six months later when the lease on my penthouse expired, and it's been like a fairytale ever since. Okay, not every day is perfect. He likes to leave his dirty clothes scattered over the bedroom floor, and I never get all my dirty dishes into the dishwasher the first time around. But the point is, we're working on it. Living together is something new for both of us. An adjustment. Other than college, I've never had a roommate, so there's a learning curve.

Having Lucas on the road is tough and I miss him like crazy, but I maximize those times by seeing Monica or occasionally visiting my parents in New York.

Today is a monumental day. The Chicago Steel is playing in the finals for the Stanley Cup against the Ontario Thunder. They lead the series 3-0, and if they win tonight, the cup is theirs.

When Lucas moved to the Steel, talk of a cup followed him. Fans hoped that he'd be the secret sauce. Usually, when a player moves to a new team, it takes a while to establish chemistry, but with Lucas, it seemed immediate. Commentators were ready to rip him apart if the Steel had a tough year. To say they were totally unprepared for the magic that occurred on the ice this season was an understatement. A lot of the credit for the success of the season goes to Lucas, as well as the Steel's captain, Josh Logan, and assistant captain, Mika Popov-Stevenson.

At the beginning of this season, Lucas worked extra hard to establish relationships with all the guys on the team, both on and off the ice. At first, many of them were resistant. But because of his determination, and with the help of Josh and Mika, the team became more cohesive and united. Coming together on their own time was a big ask of the guys. They were also busy with normal practices, workouts, games, and travel. But they figured out quickly that if they used some of their free time to work on cohesiveness between teammates, they'd benefit on the ice. The team morphed into an over-energized frat. Thankfully, unlike a standard frat, they did it without all the booze and women.

During the first months of this season, Lucas often had the guys over to the house for fun activities like movie nights, life-sized foosball, and when the snow finally fell, sledding and epic snowball fights. These grown men had an absolute blast acting like kids. They fully relaxed and had fun together. Thankfully, during all these escapades, no one was hurt, or Coach Tristan would have chewed their asses.

Lucas's suspicions were right. These team-building activities worked wonders for their level of play and their sportsmanship. The team became a formidable unit. The league took notice of the precedent they were setting and often mentioned it in commentary. These guys showed time and time again they could maintain incredible focus and concentration. They became more like brothers than teammates. They trained, played, and won together. And, of course, they celebrated together too.

So, to say tonight is groundbreaking is no exaggeration. Not only was it the first time this team, the

Chicago Steel, has made it this far in the finals, but this year's team's ability to operate on a different level than ever before spoke loudly to the hockey community. Their attitudes, work ethic, focus, and determination were unique and unfamiliar to the NHL community. Sure, there had always been standout players who held up a standard that was notable, but never had an entire team embraced it.

Before what could be the final game, I am out running errands and solidifying plans for a giant July 4th barbeque Lucas and I are hosting for the team in a few weeks. It'll be a big send off before everyone takes some much-needed R & R before the next season begins. We're hoping to celebrate not only a fantastic season but a Stanley Cup win too. It would be a first for Lucas, as well as for most of the other players.

Just as I'm finishing up with the caterer, my phone rings. It's Lucas. My heart flutters and a smile spreads across my face. When I left this morning, he'd still been sleeping and, as tough as it was to drag myself out of our bed, I knew I needed to get everything organized before the game tonight.

If the Steel wins tonight, Lucas plans to leave tomorrow to take his mom back home to Ontario. He's also staying for another week to help host a non-profit hockey camp for kids that his old teammate from New York, Miles, started a year ago. It's a great camp that rotates cities every summer, and this year it's in Lucas's hometown.

I, too, am busy. I have some crazy weeks ahead at work, so everything planning-wise has to be done now. No rest for the weary, right?

"Hey. Good morning, sleepyhead," I answer as I touch the screen in my new white Audi Q5. Since I moved out of the city, I decided I needed a vehicle and I fell in love with this. She handles like a dream and is as silent as a ninja.

"Babe, where are you and when are you coming home?" he asks, sounding groggy. He must have just woken up.

"Headed your way now. I had to meet with the caterer and grab a few things for the barbeque," I remind him again. Being in the middle of the finals, his attention is definitely waning, so I've been repeating myself a lot lately.

He laughs. "That's right. Sorry. I really do listen to you. I'm just preoccupied with the cup and everything."

"No worries at all. I understand. So, are you ready for the game? When are you heading out?" I ask as I make my way through downtown Burr Ridge.

"Soon. I have one more thing to do before I head to the arena. You're bringing my mom with you, right?" he asks.

I nod my head like he can see me and then realize he can't. "Yes, I have your mom covered. Need me to grab anything for you while I'm out?" I offer.

In the background, I hear sounds from the kitchen,

and I wonder if Lucas convinced his mom to make him breakfast. "You better not be eating a big breakfast," I caution, and he rewards me with a hearty laugh.

"Nope. I'm making my pre-workout smoothie, even though my mom offered to make me her famous Grand Marnier French toast. Do you know how hard it was to turn that down?" he whines. Good thing he's not with me or else he'd see the smirk plastered across my face. He's not wrong. It's really the best thing I've ever eaten. But it's definitely not what he needs to eat before a game as big as this. Thankfully, he recognizes that too.

"She can make you all your heart's desires next week when you aren't fighting for the cup." He audibly pouts and then grunts. I laugh at his toddler antics. Knowing a kiss will make things better, I tell him, "I'll be home in about fifteen minutes, okay?"

Lucas

I hang up with Samantha and spring into hyper-speed action. She thought I was asleep when she left this morning, but I was only pretending. I should get an Academy Award for my skills. Hey, if this hockey thing doesn't work out, I can always go to Hollywood. Watch out, Dave Annable, I've heard multiple times I am your doppelgänger. With my looks, acting chops, and being younger than you, you may be in trouble. Just kidding. I don't want that life.

As soon as Samantha drove off, I called in my reinforcements. All week I had pretended to be scatter-brained so she wouldn't be suspicious when I kept asking about her schedule for today. I needed to know exactly how big of a window I was being gifted while she was out running errands.

Within a half an hour of calling, Christian and Monica arrive together. I'm beyond curious about that, but don't have the time to explore it. I'll save my investigation for another time, although it intrigues me. They both climbed from his black Mercedes G Class wearing casual clothes. Both look rumpled, like they'd just hopped out of bed and pulled on whatever they could find when I called. I cock my head in question as I glance at Christian. *What is going on?* my look says. Good thing Samantha isn't here to see this, or we'd never make it anywhere today because she'd launch into the role of the inquisitor.

Instead of responding to me and giving me anything, Christian just shakes his head and walks past me. Confused, I say nothing. I know I have limited time to pull off my surprise. Turning back to the house to follow them in, I tell myself it isn't any of my business who he involves himself with. Unfortunately, this situation concerns Monica, so it might be something I'd have to make my business. Just not at this moment. I mean, Monica is an exceptional woman. I'm not totally sure how Samantha will respond to her best friend being the next plaything to her brother, but I'm guessing it won't end well.

Over the last year, I'd learned that Monica was the yin to Christian's yang. But he was a man. Yep. One hundred percent stupid when it came to love and women. I'll admit he was one of my best friends, so I knew well what he was like with women. I didn't want him to screw it up with Monica and treat her like a casual fuck. She deserves more. Christian is a fantastic guy, but he hasn't truly grown up and out of his bachelor ways.

Monica steps up to me next, and I notice the rosy cheeks and the stars in her eyes. "Morning, Lucas. What can I do to help before Sam gets here?"

I smile down at her and point toward the front door. "Let's go in. I need your help to arrange some things. We have a few hours before she gets home and I want everything perfect."

When we enter the kitchen, I watch Christian's eyes roam all over Monica. He lingers on her for too long for this thing between them to be nothing or even casual. I clear my throat and he finally breaks his focus on her and makes eye contact with me. You couldn't miss the hungry look in his eyes before he masked it. I can't help but snicker to myself. He has it bad. He's in love with this woman, and the only person he's lying to is himself. I hope he figures it out sooner rather than later. Definitely, before he really hurts Monica or loses her forever.

"Hey Lucas, what do you need me to do?" he asks.

I slap my hands together, ready to get to work. "Monica, I ordered these floating flower thingies and I need you to put them in the pool. Let me grab them." I pull a dozen white kissing ball floating pomanders from my office closet and haul them into the kitchen. I hand them to Monica and she heads off to place them in the pool.

Christian is rummaging through my fridge when I look over at him. "Dude, your sister is going to be here soon. Help a brother out, would you?" I growl and glare at him. Obviously, I'm nervous and on edge. He just laughs at me. I growl again, and he stops immediately and closes the fridge.

"Fine. What do you need me to do?" He looks expectantly at me, waiting for his instructions. I shake my head and mutter, "Follow me."

We set out the rest of the decorations on the patio and then wait for Monica's approval of our decorating ideas. Once she gives us a thumbs up, we get started. On the wooden patio table, I place a gigantic bouquet of blush pink peonies, a mini cake that looks like the Stanley Cup, champagne on ice, and glasses.

It all looks perfect, but I have one more favor to ask of them.

"Christian, do you have your phone with you?" He nods. I walk toward a hidden nook in the backyard that

I discovered the week before and motion for him to join me. He saunters over and mocks, "What's with the looky-loo corner? This gives me creeper vibes." He laughs at his seemingly witty comments and I just roll my eyes like a preteen girl.

"Shut it. I want you and Monica to stand here, quietly, in the corner and record the proposal," I tell him.

Monica sighs, clasps her hands together, and says, "She'll definitely want to see it. This is all so romantic, Lucas."

I smile, proud that I came up with it all on my own. Of course, I ran the ideas past my mom—my loyal forever confidant—before I put them in motion. She has always been the most important woman in my life, and I know she's happy to step aside for Samantha to take that place. She loves her almost as much as I do. Thankfully, Samantha's parents like me too. In fact, they are part of this too. I had to lie to her a few weeks ago when it looked like we had an excellent shot at the finals. While she was at work on a normal Tuesday, I flew to New York to ask her parents for their permission for her hand. After some nervous moments and some ribbing, they gave me their blessing.

While I was there, I bought a ring. Monica was very helpful when I asked for her input. I selected a two-carat round-cut solitaire from Tiffany's. It's currently tucked in my pocket, waiting for just the right moment. And since this is that moment, I dressed in a nice pair of designer jeans and an untucked button-up shirt, going for casual, not sloppy.

As I look around the patio, making sure everything's in place, I get lost in my thoughts of how I'll finally get to call Samantha my fiancée. And then after that, my wife. How lucky am I?

Christian tears me from my thoughts by not so subtly clearing his throat. "So, we hide here in the corner and record the big moment and then sneak out the side yard?"

I nod emphatically. "Exactly. Please make sure you record it."

Monica smiles at me. "We will both record it to ensure we're covered. Right, Christian?" He nods his agreement while focusing his eyes on her. I smirk at them and then I hear the garage door open. Breaking into a sprint, I'm hoping to get to Samantha before she gets too far into the house. I arrive at the door to the garage just as she's pushing through. Her arms are loaded with her iPad, party store bags, and an iced coffee. She gives me a smile that immediately melts my nerves. Again, I'm reminded she is the only woman for me. I can't wait to officially make her mine.

"Hey," she whispers as she sets down her purse and toes off her flats. I take the iPad and bags from her hands and set them on the kitchen counter. I turn back to her and pull her into my arms, picking her up and holding her tight to my chest—right where she belongs. She squeals and laughs. I laugh too and then kiss her passionately, as if it's been months we've been apart, not hours. When I finally pull away, I cheerfully say, "Hey, babe."

"That was quite a greeting!" she says as she lays a hand on my chest. I set her down and she steps back and looks at me closely, squinting her eyes as if she's trying to solve a complex problem. "Did I see my brother's car?" I can feel my eyes go wide. *Crap!* I forgot to have him move his car. How am I going to explain that? I pull her back into me and nuzzle my head into her neck, kissing her tenderly, desperately trying to come up with a believable excuse. I draw a blank, so I'm hoping the distraction will work.

"Babe." Pulling her to me and nuzzling her neck, I ask, "Can I show you something?" This isn't how I expected this moment to go, but I'm rolling with it.

She sighs and answers, "Sure, I just need to go to the bathroom, then I'm all yours." When she steps away, I grab my phone and quickly text Christian.

Samantha saw your car, and I didn't want to lie to her, so get ready. You and Monica hide. It's go time.

He texts back a thumbs up and I drop my phone back in my pocket before heading to our half bath to gather Samantha. Just as I make it down the hallway, she steps from the bathroom and gives me a smile that could easily bring me to my knees. She looks completely gorgeous as always and I couldn't feel any luckier. Samantha Fox is the perfect woman for me and I can't wait to make her my wife.

When she gets to me, I grab her hand and thread our fingers together. "What do you want to show me?" she asks with rapt curiosity.

"Something out by the pool," I try to say in a calm, confident voice. I tug her toward the back patio door. One thing I love about our backyard is that our pool sits off to the left of the patio, so it isn't entirely visible from the back door.

After a few steps outside, the edge of the pool comes into view and she gasps when she sees the large floating flowers. I squeeze her hand, letting her know it's okay. We step out farther. The patio table comes into view next and she can see the flower arrangement, champagne, and mini cake I ordered. She looks at me and I say nothing as I watch her take it all in. She turns to me.

"Lucas, babe, what is going on?" I look at her, and before I answer, I drop to one knee. The hand I'm not holding flies up to cover her mouth, showing her surprise. Her eyes glisten and plead with me to say something.

I speak slowly, making sure I say everything I'd planned. "Samantha, from the moment I met you, I was blown away. Before you, the whole idea of being with someone in a serious relationship wasn't something I'd ever considered, but you changed all that. The more time I spent with you, the more I wanted. I craved you. Your laughter, your smile, your fight, your determination, your kindness, your beauty, your kisses, and your love." I let a breath out.

"When you walked away from me, it not only destroyed me, but it showed me what I truly wanted. *You*. You are all I ever want. Since I was small, I wanted nothing more than to win a Stanley Cup, but now that dream seems trivial. On this day, the day a cup is finally within reach, I want to ask you the most important question I will ever ask. Today, I can fully admit that I am completely, hopelessly, and forever in love with you. Will you marry me?"

A single tear falls down her cheek, causing me a moment of panic. I lower my head in a moment of defeat, wondering what I'll do if she says no. I never ever considered that. Samantha runs her hand down my face and to my chin before she tugs it up. She looks down at me with tears in her eyes and softly says, "Yes. Yes, I will marry you, Lucas. I love you so much!"

The shock of it stuns me for a second before I stand up and pull her into my arms. I lower my forehead to hers and clarify, "You said yes, right?" She nods, and I don't waste any time kissing her desperately. She has made me the happiest man on the planet.

The icing on the cake is that hours after the woman of my dreams agreed to marry me, we won the Stanley Cup. I certainly don't deserve this life, but I'm determined to enjoy every bit of it. As long as Samantha is by my side, it will be perfect. This man has officially been hooked.

Thank you for reading, **Hooked By You**, my debut book. I'd love to hear your review of the first book in the Chicago Steel series.

If you'd like another peek into the Chicago Steel world, visit my website at www.jessicabuss.com or scan the QR code below and sign up for my newsletter. While there, check out the extended epilogue for **Hooked By You** and get your first taste of Mika Stevenson-Popov, the co-captain of the Steel.

Happy Reading.

Scan to sign up for my newsletter!

World of Chicago Steel

Have you read any of the Chicago Steel Series? If not, you can click on the link to start reading. The entire series is available with your Kindle Unlimited subscription. Here's a small taste of each to wet your palate.

Owned By You-Chicago Steel Novella Prequel

A journal changes everything.
Words written by a father to his son, explaining an ultimatum
that forever colors the course of their family's history.
Love.
Abandonment.
Hatred.
Ownership.
Death.
Reconciliation.

Hooked By You–Chicago Steel Series Book One

Lucas

She's a goddess in heels. Absolute perfection. Well, almost. Samantha Fox is the heiress of Fox Sporting, my new management team. As one of the best wings in the NHL, I have never shied away from a challenge, and she is definitely a challenge. But if her company representing me doesn't stop me from wanting her, the fact she's engaged should, right? But the noticeably absent sparkle from her left ring finger makes me question. I vow to myself that I'll find out what that's all about. And if she's single, I plan to make her mine. Or at least, mine for the night. I just need one taste of the divine.

Samantha

Off-limits. That's what he is. Lucas Bouchard is the prestigious new client acquired by my family's company. From what I know, not only is he an amazing hockey player, he's a humble and generous philanthropist too. Also, he's a walking aphrodisiac. It doesn't matter that I've just broken off my engagement to a cheating, using loser. Every time our eyes lock, I find myself captivated. But he's not for me. No matter how many times I remind myself of this, though, it doesn't compute. Plain and simple, I want him. And keeping my distance might prove impossible.

Checked By You–Chicago Steel Series Book Two

Mika

She's the uber-sexy, single mother living next door. Everyone tells me to keep my distance. But there's something about her. Specifically, her eyes. They speak to me. Drawing me in like a siren. I want to know her, but she's more guarded than Buckingham Palace. However, after one afternoon in her presence, I find myself addicted and wanting more. Willing to do whatever I have to just to make it past her defenses.

Shiloh

My next-door neighbor is an insanely hot, single professional hockey player. As if that isn't bad enough, he's a nice guy too. After spending an afternoon where he showed my son how to skate and took us out to ice cream, I want to let him in. My past cautions me to put on the brakes, but I find myself going full steam ahead, ignoring all the red flags waving at me.

Clipped By You–Chicago Steel Series Book Three

Monica

She's his. Or she has been since her freshman year of college. According to Monica Fields, no man will ever hold a candle to Christian Fox. Too bad he's completely unaware. Or is he?

Christian

Since meeting her, a sweet dairy farm girl has captivated Christian entirely. But he's a guy. And he's the one who isn't quite ready to be done sowing his wild oats. Will he ever be? In this game called love, sometimes chasing after a woman is just the wake-up call you need. But what if chasing her to her family's farm and following her through a field scattered with cow patties in limited-edition white Nike Air Force 1s is the only way to catch her? And, when you finally do catch her, will she want you? Forever?

Speared By You-Chicago Steel Series Book Four

Tristan

Since he was little, Tristan's dream has been to play in the NHL. Then he falls in love with his soul mate in high school. A few years after being drafted, an injury cuts his professional career short. Devastated, he questions what is next for him. Instead of seeking solace from the woman who's remained faithfully by his side, he pushes her away.

Stephanie

Since high school, Stephanie's known she is going to do two things: marry Tristan Murphy and get a degree in business. Her plan is to work for a non-profit that focuses on breast cancer. Several years later, though, she finds herself recently divorced and in a new city with a new job. And she's learned a couple of major life lessons. 1. Life can be tricky. 2. We don't always get what we want.

What happens when their paths cross again?

Slashed By You-Chicago Steel Series Book Five

Josh

As the captain of the Steel, Josh is always in control and confident as hell. In relationships, not so much, especially after being majorly burned. Then a gorgeous baker enters his life and changes everything. Her confections are pure magic, and now she's all he craves.

Kenzie

Kenzie's always dreamed of owning her own bakery. With a heart of gold, everything she does is filled with love. Busy running her shop, she doesn't have time for relationships. However, priorities shift when she catches the eye of a kind and sexy professional hockey player who has developed a major sweet tooth.

Delayed By You-Chicago Steel Series Book Six

She's always been his. He's always been hers. Best friends since they were kids, everyone always assumed they'd end up together. But Rocco and Jasmine forge their own life paths. Despite remaining close, she discovers she needs a break from the life she's been living in Chicago. When she moves to New York, things change for him. And he panics, thinking he's lost her forever.

Rocco

Since the day she moved in across the street when we were kids, Jasmine has held my attention with her sparkling green eyes and spunky spirit. She's independent and headstrong, and I've always admired that about her. Hiding behind my bachelor status, no one is the wiser about the secret feelings I harbor for her.

Jasmine

Rocco has always been by my side. Whether it's making me laugh, teaching me something new, or sharing confidences, he's been steadfast. When he morphs into a man seemingly overnight, I find it tough to temper my attraction to him. But he doesn't see me as anything more than a friend.

Tripped By You - Chicago Steel Series Book Seven

Janica

Befriending a professional hockey player, especially one like Ace, is not something I ever expected to happen to me. We hit it off right away, and though I might have not-so-friendly thoughts about him sometimes, our friendship is strictly platonic. I have a boyfriend, and besides, Ace is way out of my league.

Stuck in a broken relationship, I question whether I deserve anything better. And when I catch my cheating boyfriend in the act, my life collapses. Not only have I lost my boyfriend, I've lost my home.

When Ace finds out I need somewhere to stay, he offers to open his home to me. But can I handle living in the same house with the gorgeous man who has haunted my thoughts since the day we met?

Ace

Trapped in a broken body, I need a distraction to help pass the time while I'm away from my one true love: hockey. It appears in the form of a curvy brunette who works at the library I've chosen to study at. Our friendship begins when Janica promises to show me her secret study spot. And I'm instantly captivated. But then I find out she has a boyfriend.

When I learn Janica needs help, I have to ask myself an important question that just might change my future forever. Now that she's single, will I do whatever it takes to show her I'm the man she needs and deserves?

Blocked By You - Chicago Steel Book Eight

For years, we've been like two ships passing in the night, bound to collide eventually. When it finally happens, will we both survive unscathed?

Jersey

From the first moment we meet, I hate her. She is the epitome of what's wrong in the world. She's a yoga instructor. Can you imagine anything worse? Unfortunately, I need her help to deal with a possible career-ending injury. Will I be able to swallow my distaste for her for the sake of the game I love? And what happens when I realize she's nothing like I assumed?

Emily

He intrigues me from the moment I first hear about him. Then we meet. And the fantasy I've entertained about us shatters. Instead of Mr. Amazing, I discover he's a class-A jerk. When an injury threatens his hockey career, he's sent to me for help. What am I to do? Is he really as bad as I think he is? How will I handle it if he's not?

Happy Ho, Ho, Holidays-Chicago Steel Novella

Trey

As soon as I see her, I'm bewitched by the bohemian beauty. One look from her and I'm done. Too bad after spending most of the evening together, I forget to get her number or her last name. As the owner of the Chicago Steel, the city's professional hockey team, you'd think nothing is out of reach for me, but finding her has proved challenging. Months pass, and as my hope of ever finding her fades, she walks through my office door, hired to be my temporary PA.

Nicole

He can't be real. The summer heat must be getting to me, because everything about this man seems too good to be true. We spend most of the night together, talking and laughing. And guess what... he is the complete package. The one worthy of a trip home to meet the parents. If you ever visited home and hadn't written it off years ago. But as soon as he appears, he's gone without a way to contact him. Do I write it off as bad luck, or do I storm their headquarters demanding to be seen? But what if it's all one-sided and he isn't longing for me like I do him?

Stick By You - Chicago Steel Finale

With most of the guys now retired from hockey and their families growing, it's the perfect time to take a group trip to Alaska. Come with them as they explore a small snippet of what the majestic forty-ninth state has to offer.

The Finger Lake Chalet promises that adventure awaits its guests. With the amazing Thatcher family, Francisco the chef, and Monty the mischievous raven, memorable moments are in store. And because it's the Steel men and their ladies, it's bound to be funny and hot.

***Keep reading for the sneak peek of Hooked By You, book one of the Chicago Steel series**

Acknowledgments

This journey to becoming an author has been full of emotion. But the one that I cherish the most is thankfulness. I am beyond humbled by the road that I find myself on. Never would I have guessed that I'd ever be a published author. But here you hold the fruits of my labor.

When I originally released the first books of the Chicago Steel series, I did so with a sense of trepidation. I was not confident in my storytelling ability. Because of those I have met along the way, I have dug deep and worked on bettering not only myself but my craft. I hope that you enjoy the words I have cried and rejoiced over. Thank you to those who have come alongside me during this season and gifted me with their time, encouragement, support, and love. It is truly invaluable and I am so grateful. Any success is not mine alone. In all things, be blessed.

To my husband, Darren, even though romance or reading books, in general, may not be your jam, you always support me in all things and I cannot thank you enough for that. I love you, babe.

Karen Hulseman at Feed Your Dreams Designs—You wear so many hats and I am grateful for each one you've chosen. To the woman who makes absolutely incredibly drool-worthy covers to the one who formats my words perfectly. You are the BEST cheerleader and encourager ever. Not afraid to speak your truth, your guidance and friendship have given me multiple boosts in the chaotic world of self-publishing.

Shauna at Ink Machine Editing—Your editing has been a lifesaver. Your encouragement, suggestions, attention to detail, and support have allowed me to stretch my wings and have more confidence than I ever thought possible. Thank you for sticking with me through the good, bad, and ugly.

Nicole at Emerald Edits—Our paths crossed at just the right time. Thank you for giving me the push to strive for more. I would like to thank you for not just believing in me, but also in the story I was trying to bring forward. Thank you for asking the questions and making me dig deep. Your guidance and speedy feedback have made an enormous difference in my writing. Your friendship has as well.

To my reader friends—WOW. Thank you for your support. Whether you found this series when I originally published it in 2022, are rereading the revisions, or you're discovering it now, I appreciate the time you dedicated to me. Hopefully, you feel it was time well spent and you'll continue to enjoy the Chicago Steel series books as they become available. I cannot wait to see what you all think of the Steel men. They've stolen my heart, and I hope they steal yours too.

Also by Jessica Buss

Chicago Steel Series

Chicago Steel Series

Hooked By You (Lucas & Samantha)

Checked By You (Mika & Shiloh)

Clipped By You (Christian & Monica)

Speared By You (Tristan & Stephanie)

Slashed By You (Josh & Kenzie)

Delayed By You (Rocco & Jasmine)

Tripped By You (Ace & Janica)

Blocked By You (Jersey & Emily)

Chicago Steel Series Novella

Happy Ho, Ho, Holidays (Trey & Nicole)

Stick By You (Finale)

Owned By You (Prequel) Add to Goodreads

About the Author

Jessica Buss was born and raised in Anchorage, Alaska. She is married to her high school sweetheart and has two sons. Although she has both her bachelor's and master's degrees in Psychology, she stepped away from that field to be a stay-at-home mom. Now that her kids are growing up and she's getting more time to herself, she's giving this writing thing a chance.

Jessica Buss

jessicabuss.com

Sign Up for my newsletter

Made in the USA
Las Vegas, NV
28 December 2025

38025702R00212